Erased
A Dark Romantic Thriller

Sansa Rayne

Sasha Rich Books

PROLOGUE
MARLA

After what I've been through, I shouldn't still be this scared. The visceral, bodily reaction I'm having — rapid heartbeat, sweating, dry mouth — is purely a byproduct of the last several weeks of my life, not current circumstances. In my head, I know I'm safe.

I hope I'm not becoming permanently claustrophobic. I can tell it's the room freaking me out. It feels too much like a high-security prison cell; it's actually a police interrogation room, so the similarity is unsurprising.

I'm not even being interrogated. This is just the best place in the building to give a preliminary deposition. The door isn't locked; I could walk out. I'm not handcuffed. Steam rises from a foam cup of coffee. It could be the worst coffee ever made by man, but right now it smells like a dream.

The real danger is gone, I remind myself. The men who hurt me? Those monsters will never touch me again. They left scars. Some are worse than others, but they'll fade in time. What I did to them... There's no coming back from that.

No, there's no need to be scared. I've been to Hell — I've met the devil. He tried to take my soul, tried to extinguish every part of me. It nearly worked.

I wasn't the only lost soul there, trapped in the pit. If it wasn't for my love... Some would say his suffering was worse than mine. He was imprisoned too, in a way.

We gave each other what we needed to survive: I lent him my strength, he inspired the reason. And now we're the ones left standing.

There is still one danger ahead of me. When the police step through that door, not everything I tell them will be the truth. You don't escape from Hell without learning some of the devil's tricks.

But the lies I tell won't hurt anyone. They will help me get what I want: my love and my revenge. I will have both.

And then I will hunt. So many monsters are still out there, but they don't know I'm coming.

A month ago I was nobody. They've awoken a terror, and now they're going to pay.

CHAPTER 1
MARLA
SEVERAL WEEKS PRIOR

This is a mistake, I think as two drunks staggering by stare at me for a little too long. Tonight is my last night in town; tomorrow I say good riddance. I'd like my last memory of Hunter's Valley to be a good one. Something handsome and a little funny — low-key and surprisingly honest.

No, I'm serious. Just looking for a nice night, I'll say. *Tomorrow I'm leaving, you probably won't ever see me again. No pressure, for real.*

Tommy's Place barely counts as part of the valley. It's a big bar, but it has a woodsy, log cabin motif, with canoe oars and fishing nets hanging from the high walls. Nestled amongst the forests covering the nearby hills, Tommy's lies outside the town line. Some nights this place is full of bikers passing through, while on others students from the three nearby state colleges come to slum. Tonight Tommy's is host to townies like me, and it's not especially busy. There's no crush of bodies circling the bar, cash or card in hand, waiting to be served. Without the din of countless people yelling over one another, the handful of conversations fail to drown each other out.

Sometimes I like to close my eyes and focus on one of the threads of speech, to see if I can follow it. It's better than stewing in my regrets for the night.

I take another sip of my martini and pretend I can't smell someone's perfume from across the bar. Laughing at every word someone says is a floozy with a low-cut, extra tight miniskirt.

Floozy. God, I sound like my mom.

I shouldn't be so judgmental, but I'm jealous. All the hot guys are drawn to her and I'm worried I'll be taking a cab home alone. My dress is not as tight as her's, and my boobs aren't hanging out, but I look good. I'm in decent shape. My long, chestnut hair is silky. My subtle scent costs $200 a bottle. Yet, I'm on my third drink and no one has looked my way.

This is stupid, I think, berating myself some more. Striking out at the bar was depressing, but making matters worse was how little I even truly wanted to have a fling. I've done it before, each time I broke up with somebody, and the face looking back at me was never a kind one. More often than not, it was just me. *So why am I even doing this? Hunter's Valley won't mind if your last night here is spent in a cleaned-out apartment lying on a bare mattress feeling sorry for yourself.*

I tell myself it's not my fault that Fred left. We both agreed the long-distance thing wouldn't work. I tell myself it's not my fault I got fired, though it's only half-true. Considering the local notoriety I'd gained a week ago, I'm surprised no one has recognized me yet. Maybe the lighting in the bar is too low. Maybe nobody really watches the news anymore.

It's the anchors that get all the play. Nobody pays attention to the field reporters, I lament.

Giving up, I drop two twenties on the bar and throw back the last of my drink.

"Got somewhere else to be?"

I turn to the voice, expecting the worst. Smiling modestly is a not totally unattractive man in jeans and a black, leather jacket. I place him in his late thirties, making him a decade my senior, but I don't mind a sprinkle of salt and pepper in his short, dark hair. The white t-shirt below his jacket is tight around his chest, and I can tell he's got a respectable build for his age.

"Not at all," I reply, setting my purse back down. "I was about to give up."

He smirks. "Maybe you should. I don't see a lot of potential in a place like this."

I laugh for the first time in days. "So then what brings you here?"

He shrugs. "Got the night off for once. I wanted to relax. You know how it is." He motions to the bartender and gets a beer. "And another of whatever she's drinking."

"Thanks," I say. "I'm Marla, by the way."

"Jack Vaughn."

We watch the bartender work until our drinks are poured, then clink glasses. "To having the night off," I say.

He grins and we drink. "What about you?" he asks.

I sigh, a buzz in my head. "Where to begin? How about getting the fuck out of Hunter's Valley?"

Vaughn acts hurt. "What, you don't like it here?"

Shaking my head I glance at the TV above the bar. It's on mute but tuned to my old station. "There's nothing for me here. Nobody in this town's going to hire me."

Setting down his beer, Vaughn turns on his bar stool. "Why's that?"

Rather than try to explain, I get out my phone and load up the video from the Internet. It's up to 48,276 views — about 1,200 more than the last time I checked. I hand him my phone and listen to the exchange I've long since memorized.

"That's the news for tonight," says Lisa King. "Before we go, we'd like to say goodbye to reporter Marla Angel, who is moving on. Marla, it's been a great two years."

"Thanks, Lisa," I say, genuinely. I liked her; she was fun, with a keen eye for digging through the bullshit of local politics. "I appreciate the opportunity to get to know Hunter's Valley. I just wish our boss, Gerald, wasn't such a spineless, dickless bureaucrat."

"Whoa!" laughs Vaughn as he watches the video.

I grin, thinking about the expression on Lisa's face, trying to suppress her own amusement and stay professional.

"Thanks, Marla," she says as the producer cuts my mic and switches back to Camera 1. I can still feel Buck the security guard's iron grip on my upper arm as he escorted me from the building.

"It was worth it," I say after downing the rest of my martini. "But I'm not going to work again in this town. Maybe even the state."

Vaughn hands back my phone. "I guess not. But hey, you told it like it is. People appreciate that these days."

"Thanks," I mutter. I'd told myself the same thing, but it doesn't change the fact that I'm unemployed and most likely unemployable.

"It's too bad you have to move, though," adds Vaughn. I hear what is meant to be concern in his voice, but really it sounds like something else. I'm not sure what. "Your family must not be happy."

I shake my head. "I'm not from here. And they probably don't even know. I'm not close with my parents."

"Really?" Vaughn is about to finish his beer but instead sets it down. "What about your friends? They're going to miss you."

"The ones from around here haven't known me very long. They'll move on." I'm surprised at myself for admitting this, but it feels good. I often wonder if I'm broken somehow, unable to make close bonds. Fred left because... I don't know. He gave no specific reason for leaving, which was like throwing a bolt into the gears of my head. Everything ground to a halt, trying to break through the obstruction, but ultimately falling apart instead.

Vaughn nods. "Where you moving to?"

"Buffalo."

"Wow. Why there?"

I take a deep breath, looking for the bartender. "I like winter, and it's pretty far away. That's what I do. I get away."

Vaughn frowns. "You don't have anyone there?"

"Nope. That's the point."

"I get it," he says, darkening. "It's just kinda sad."

At the other side of the bar, the floozy snorts a laugh as a bearded man picks her up and sets her down on a pool table that's seen better days.

"What about you?" I ask. "You said you got the night off. From what?"

"It's a private security gig," he mumbles, turning to the bar. "Keeps me pretty busy."

I'm not surprised. He looks built for it, and there's an edge to him that suggests he's quite capable. "I'm sure. Been at it a while?"

"Yeah, going on eight years now. It's challenging work, but... there's perks. Really good ones."

An alarm bell goes off in my head. I don't like the way he said that, but I don't have any reason to feel that way, so I dismiss it. I ask, "So, you're like a supervisor or something?"

He nods. "Yeah, I'm in charge of a few people."

"Cool. How did you get into that?"

Nostrils flaring, he sneers at some offense I don't understand. "Private recruiter. It's one of those things. I was available. They had an opening."

"Sure." I nod, not wanting to press the matter.

For a minute neither of us speaks and I wonder if I should say goodnight and go home. Snaking through my gut is a thread of fear. I felt it when I first got to Tommy's and wrote it off as pre-move jitters. The concern has grown, though, since I met Vaughn.

I'm about to get up when he laughs, shaking his head.

"What?"

"Dickless bureaucrat," he says. "I can't believe you said that on TV."

"It was stupid of me," I reply, though I'm grinning now too. "But it felt good."

"I'll bet it did," Vaughn says. "I've had some bosses in my time I wish I could tell off."

"Oh yeah?"

He sighs. "Yeah. I used to be a cop, actually."

"No kidding. Well, maybe there should be a law that lets

you tell off your boss without getting fired," I suggest, lips loosening as my last martini starts to hit. "Maybe just once though."

"I'd drink to that," laughs Vaughn, signaling the bartender.

I hold up my hands. "Hey, no. Thanks, but I think I've had enough. I gotta travel tomorrow, I don't wanna be too hungover."

"Sure. One for me then." He points to his empty glass and the bartender snatches it away. "But I have to ask…"

"Uh huh," I say. "What's that?"

He looks at me now not like a friendly stranger at a bar, but as somebody who works security, sizing me up and assessing. It's unnerving, but I try to match his intensity, rather than shy away.

"When you told that guy off, was it planned?" Vaughn asks at last. "Or did it just come out?"

My lips bunch together in self-satisfaction, thinking about the moments before I said what I did. "It's sorta both," I answer cryptically.

"Go on." He's curious now. I knew when it happened that this would be a story I'd relish in the telling.

"Before it happened, I was going to tell him off in private. I'd planned what I was going to say, I'd rehearsed it and I was ready."

"Okay…"

"But then he didn't show up at the station that day."

Vaughn snorts. "No!"

"Yup. Dickless, like I said. I was so pissed off, I couldn't even. It was all I could think about during my send-off, and so then… well, you saw."

"Oh man." Vaughn swallows half the beer in his glass and chuckles. "Sounds like you have problems with impulse control."

I wink devilishly. "Not really. But I'm bad news for people who piss me off."

Vaughn snickers into his drink, bubbles effervescing from his open lips. "Is that a fact?"

"It is."

He finishes his beer. "Sounds like the sort of thing that can get a girl like you into trouble."

"Like getting fired?"

"Bigger trouble," he says, eyes roaming over my body. "I bet if Gerald was here right now he'd like to teach you a lesson."

Okay, time to go, I realize. Vaughn's shifting tone has my hairs standing on end. The snake in my bowels is squeezing hard, and I'm done ignoring it.

"Maybe another time." Getting up, I grab my purse and clutch it tightly. I dig my hand inside and feel for my bottle of pepper spray. "It's been nice chatting."

Vaughn snags my wrist and holds tight. "Stay, Marla. I promise, when you drive out to Buffalo tomorrow, you won't miss this place."

I yank my hand out of his grasp. "I'm leaving."

"Nah," he says, shooting off his stool. "That wouldn't be nice. We're having a good time."

As he speaks I get out the spray and point it at his face. "Take a seat, Jack Vaughn," I say, shouting his name.

His face contorts with rage, but it quickly evaporates into the nastiest smile I've ever seen. "Relax, sweetheart. I'm messing with you." He sits back down, looking at me like I'm crazy. "Didn't mean to scare you."

My heart racing, I step back. "You have a good night," I say, walking backward to the exit. He winks at me and grins the whole time.

The frigid wind hits me like a brick when I get outside. Still ready with the pepper spray, I fumble through my purse, my hands shaking, an after-effect of the adrenaline surge. I find my phone and dial the last number in my call list, the cab company that brought me out to Tommy's in the first place. When I rode out here I'd hoped a gentleman would be the one taking me back to my apartment, and now I'm going to have to wait for a cab to show. If I'm lucky, it will only be twenty minutes.

Shivering, I wrap my arms around my body. I could go

back in and wait, but Vaughn will be there, so I dismiss that notion. I'd rather get hypothermia. The spray bottle is getting warm and sweaty in my grip, but I don't put it away.

I nearly shriek when the door to Tommy's opens, letting loose a blast of the music and noise from inside. The woman in the extra tight mini-skirt — the floozy — is leaving with a man who beams like he won the lottery. He's holding her wrist and pulling her toward his SUV, eager to get her home. She jumps in the passenger side with equal enthusiasm. I only look away when his headlights come on, shining straight into my eyes.

"Shit," I murmur, trying to clear my vision in the darkness. I blink away the glimmers, but they shine like neon in my head. I'm still blinking them away when I hear the tussle of feet on gravel.

I lose grip of the pepper spray as the cloth covers my face. Trying to shriek, I swing my purse back at the force gripping me, but it's not heavy enough to hurt. The chemical smell is overpowering and I can't breathe anything else. The hand holding the cloth is too strong.

Is that... how chloro... form... smells? I wonder as the world ceases to exist.

CHAPTER 2
MARLA

I know right away that something is not right. My head is pounding from I'm not sure what, and my mouth is bone dry. My tongue feels twice its normal size, and I can't move it in my mouth. Is my face numb? I don't know.

I'm totally disoriented: I can't remember where I am or what I was doing. Darkness greets me when I open my eyes. Why can't I see? I blink a few times, but it doesn't help.

Shit, Vaughn! My last memory before blacking out comes back to me. I was waiting for a cab and somebody jumped me. It had to be Vaughn. But where is he? Where did he take me?

As the wooziness wears off, I start to see the bigger picture. The aching in my head is coming from the unending rush of wind, and the constant clatter of something moving, and after a minute I realize that it's me. I'm moving, only not. I'm sitting down, but everything is moving. The walls and floor are moving.

Is this… a truck?

It makes sense. I can't see yet, but if this was some kind of moving van, it wouldn't have any lights on in the back, would it? Either way, I think we're going pretty fast. A little bump in the road sets off a chorus of metal on metal, and I wonder if the vehicle isn't on the verge of falling apart.

I inhale through my nose, and a musty, earthy scent clogs my lungs. Making out a whiff of motor oil, I worry that exhaust might be leaking in, but if that were the case, would I have even woken up?

Just drift away into a peaceful sleep… Wouldn't that be nice?

I shake my head, and it's then that I feel there's something around my neck. In fact, it's going all the way around the back of my head and to the front, and it's… it's in my mouth. No wonder my tongue feels weird. I gag, trying to spit out whatever it is — some kind of wadded up cloth, yet I can't get it to budge. I shake my head and feel the shifting of something solid and adhesive.

Tape?

Yes, there's tape running around the lower half of my face, and it won't come free.

I try to raise my hand to peel away the tape and find I can't move it. For a second, terror chills my spine and I wonder if I have lost sensation in my extremities, but I can feel my hands. I wiggle my fingers and they're fine. Wherever I am, it's not excessively cold. I can even feel the long sleeves of my winter coat stuck to the bare skin of my arms, slicked with sweat.

No, the reason I can't raise my hands is because they're bound to the armrests of the chair. I pull at them, but a strong ring of some kind keeps them firmly in place. More tape, I surmise.

The world slows down as I start to breathe heavily. I'm screaming at the top of my lungs but hardly a whine comes out. I try to bang my feet against the ground but they are also tied down, probably to the legs of the chair. I wonder how I haven't fallen over, being in a truck, but then I feel a curve in the road and the chair doesn't budge, so I feel confident it's bolted down.

What the fuck?

It's every worst fear I never imagined for myself. I've spent sleepless nights worrying if I would ever find a partner, some man in sync to my needs; I've tossed and turned afraid that years of short stints and moving back and forth will make it impossible for me to really grow into a meaningful career. I can go on at length about anxieties and phobias that I tell myself make no sense, but refuse to die. Yet, I've never seriously believed I'd be abducted.

From the pepper spray in my purse to the safety seminars I've attended, I've always felt prepared. I considered myself careful. One moment of distraction and somebody snuck up from behind. It pisses me off.

No one's going to mess with me now, I'd told myself. *What a crock.*

Still, despite my rising fury, I try to stay calm. *Pay attention to the vehicle's movements*, I remember. *Isn't that what people say?*

I listen to the truck and focus on our direction, but it's worthless. Maybe if we were stopping and turning, the information might be of use, but the truck has been steadily in motion since I regained consciousness.

It must be a freeway, I reason. Okay, that's something. Or not. I don't know how long I was out, or in which direction we are going. At freeway speeds, we could be hundreds of miles from Tommy's Place, and in nearly any direction.

Be patient, I tell myself at last. There's nothing else I can do but stay calm.

Of course, keeping my mind clear is not so easy, and unconsciously I begin to struggle against my bonds. Can I slip out of the sleeves of my coat? No, the restraints around my wrists are way too tight. Can I loosen them? I attempt to generate some slack, wresting my arm back and forth, but what movement I can create is so negligible I know I'm not having any real effect.

I should give up the fruitless effort — I'm wasting my energy — but I keep going. I can't explain why, but soon I've discovered that I am enjoying the specific act of fighting against my restraints. I am even smiling underneath the gag, or trying to, at least. It feels good, and not just because I am standing strong and not giving in. There's another reason: Between my legs I feel an electric ache that can't be ignored.

Struggling to get free is... turning me on.

No, I realize, repulsed by the truth: *It's not the struggle. It's the failure.*

Had I managed to break out of the chair, my relief would have been understandable. Not being able to, however, hasn't robbed me of hope, but filled me with... desire. I can't comprehend it. I keep fighting, lost in the experience. My insides should have been burning with rage and terror, but instead I feel only warmth and need. I know all the horror will return as soon as I give up, so I don't let myself.

If I'm about to die, I may as well go out on my own terms.

I'm not one for morbidity, but it's appropriate now.

With time impossible to tell when one is alone with her thoughts, I don't know how many hours it's been when finally there's a significant change in the truck's speed and direction. We're veering to the right and decelerating pretty rapidly. *He's pulling over.*

I abruptly cease to move, lower my head and shut my eyes. My heart pounds as I both dread and anticipate the vehicle coming to a stop. My head spins: *Where could he have taken me, driving for such a long time?*

When the truck stops, I can still hear other cars going by, but it's not as loud as before. I suspect he's found a rest stop and wonder if he's taking a bathroom break. But then, sure enough, I hear the screech of rusted metal passing through gears and the back door to the truck lifts up. I'm glad I've got my eyes closed, as the light of day sizzles brilliantly.

"Wakey wakey."

I open one eye just enough to see a dark silhouette. The figure turns and lowers the door to cut down the glare. After a second, a dim light illuminates the truck's cargo compartment. Now I can see that I am far from its only contents: surrounding me are stacks of supplies. Most of it is canned food, but I also see gas canisters, cleaning supplies, toilet paper, electronic equipment and more.

"Hi, Marla," says Vaughn.

I stare at him, refusing to mumble through the tape.

"You've probably got a lot of questions, but we're not stopping here for very long. I'm starving, so I'm going to have a quick bite. Are you hungry?"

I shake my head. My last meal seems like a distant memory, but at the moment I have no appetite.

"Good, that'll save me some time. You'll be fed when we arrive anyway, don't worry."

Fed?

Vaughn leans in close. I twist my head around but he stays with me. "I want to make a little confession," he whispers in my ear. "When we get where we're going, I'm going to be in some deep shit. I wasn't supposed to do this."

Glee draws Vaughn's lips up into a devilish smirk. He'd be handsome if he wasn't such a monster.

"The boss is going to kick my ass a little, but then I think he's going to come around. He'll see in you what I saw. You're really his type."

Now I'm wishing I'd broken free from my bonds. Vaughn's crazy has gotten to me, and if I could get loose I would run until my feet fall off.

"Hey, look at me," he says, directing my gaze from my lap back to him. I hate how his fingers touch my cheeks and chin; I want to bite them off and spit them back in his face. "Are you scared right now?"

Yes, of course, but I won't let him see it, so I don't respond.

"I think you are scared. Just a little though. I think you're more angry. Isn't that right?"

It is. I nod. *You're damn right I'm angry.*

"That's what I thought." Vaughn reaches behind his back. He pulls out a black handgun and takes out the clip, showing me that it's loaded. Maybe he expects me to whimper in fear, freeze up like a deer in headlights or possibly wet myself. I don't do anything; I look at him, not at the weapon. "You really don't scare easily. This is great."

He slips the gun back into the waist of his jeans. "Keep quiet back here, Marla. If you cause me any trouble, I'll shoot you and leave your body in a ditch. That would be a shame, you know? You could be what I need to really finally get…" He pauses, stopping himself. "To get what I want. So you keep staying calm and save that anger for later. All right?"

I glare daggers at Vaughn, wishing they could punch through his skin and take his face apart with them.

"In fact, that's some good advice for you in general. Hold onto that anger as long as you can, Marla. We're going to enjoy breaking it. Breaking you."

Vaughn pats my head, stroking my disheveled hair. Every instinct in me begs to shake off his touch, but I resist the urge. He'd enjoy it, I'm sure.

Nice try, asshole.

"Oof, you're like a pilot light, you know that? Always burning, ready to really ignite. I can see it, and so will everyone else. I can't wait."

Vaughn climbs out, giving me one last look, and shuts the truck's back door. Less than a minute later, the engine of the truck roars back, and then we're moving.

Once we return to the freeway, and I'm sure Vaughn can't hear me, I finally break down, sobbing and trembling until I can't stop.

CHAPTER 3
MARLA

My imagination can only draw time out for so long before I stop doubting that it truly has been hours since we stopped. I dredge up memories of the various survival stories I've read: cases where people have found their way home after plane crashes or getting lost on a hike. Recalling methods for building shelters, or following rivers and streams, I comfort myself that once I get free, I can trek my way back to the world. As long as we're still on a road, we can't be too far from a town — can we?

Of course, we don't stay on the freeway forever. When I feel him slow down again, for a moment I'm not sure if he's pulling over or turning, but then he hits the brakes hard, and we turn sharply, presumptively for a very tight off-ramp. When he accelerates again, he doesn't reach anywhere near the same speed.

Knowing I'll want to find the freeway again, whichever one it is, I begin counting the seconds and minutes. I pay attention to when he stops, goes or turns. He mainly stays on the same road, but it's a twisty one, and I can distinctly feel that we're frequently going up hill. The engine roars as we hit an incline, and from all the turning and changes in speed, I can tell we've climbed several switchbacks.

Swallowing to pop my ears, I lose count of how long we've been traveling since the freeway, but it's been at least an hour. *How many days would that take to walk? Maybe there will be a car I can steal. Or this truck*, I think, wondering if I have the competence to hot-wire a vehicle if need be. If the area is really that mountainous, going on foot might be too dangerous.

Eventually I feel the truck slowing down and coming to a stop. Though the engine still rumbles, I hear the driver door open and slam shut. I wish I could see what's going on. After a few minutes, the door opens and shuts again, and we start moving. I'm not sure why he stopped for just a minute, but he does the same thing again after only driving a few yards.

What was that about?

A gate, most likely.

Before I can debate the theory, we've stopped again, and this time the engine shuts off fully. With nothing to listen to or keep track of, I resort to struggling again, trying to free myself, but it's still hopeless. All the tugging and grinding in the world won't dislodge my bonds, and I should be conserving my strength. Yet, I can't make myself stop.

Then I hear voices — more than one. They're getting closer, and soon I make out Vaughn from right outside.

"All right, you guys ready for the surprise?"

"Yeah, yeah, let's go," comes an especially gruff, scratchy voice, like he'd been smoking two packs a day for twenty years.

"All right." Vaughn lifts the door to the back of the truck, and there I am: bound, gagged and squirming to get free. I'm sweaty and I imagine my makeup from the night before has streaked down my cheeks.

"Fucking shit, Vaughn," says another man, who I can now see. His voice is a little high, and he's clearly pissed. He's a tall, lanky man, with a mop of sandy hair on his head and spindly arms that sprout from his torso like vines. His glasses have thick frames and an orange band that circles his practically bare skull. He's wearing a white, button-down shirt and long, white pants, reminding me of an old school barber. On top he's got a thick winter coat, but it's not zipped. I turn to Gruff, and he's wearing the same outfit, minus the jacket.

"Seriously, what the fuck were you thinking?" he asks.

"Hear me out, guys. I met this one at a bar last night. She was about to move. She has no job, and no friends or family. Nobody's going to be looking for her, not for a long time. Plus, check this out." Vaughn takes out his phone and shows it to the others. After a second, I hear the video clip of my last day on the news.

The men watch, not understanding the point until they hear me call Gerald a "spineless, dickless bureaucrat." They laugh when I do; even Vaughn chuckles again.

"You see what I mean?" he asks.

"Yeah," Gruff admits, nodding. "He's gonna like this one. They called her Marla?"

"Yup."

Gruff looks at me. "Pretty name for a pretty girl."

I turn away and look at the ceiling of the truck. *Fuck you guys*, I think, blinking fast, trying not to cry again.

"Can you bring out some wheels?" Vaughn asks the others as he climbs into the truck. He fishes through his pants for a pocket knife and flicks open the blade. "Hold still, Marla."

Doing as he says, I don't even breathe. He carefully cuts through the tape, then peels it away. To my surprise, it doesn't hurt: it adheres to itself perfectly, but not to my hair or skin. When it's all gone, Vaughn pulls the wadded up cloth from my mouth. It's completely sodden with my saliva and it is a relief to have it out of my mouth, though my jaw aches and I want to scream. Remembering Vaughn's gun, I decide not to test him just yet.

Vaughn waits for Gruff to return before he removes any more of my binding. Lanky gives me a sip of water from a bottle in his jacket pocket. I nod in thanks but refuse to acknowledge him any more than that.

It takes Gruff a few minutes to come back, and when he does I hear not his footsteps, but the rattling of something moving over asphalt. It's a wheelchair, I find out, when he approaches. Apparently I'm going from one seat to another.

This one has thick, leather cuffs on the armrests, and Vaughn wastes no time in fastening them once I've been moved.

Though I'm glad to be out of the truck, I nearly teared up during the transfer knowing that I didn't have any hope of escaping. Not with the three of them there. Even if I get loose and run, they can just pile into the truck and cut me off before I get far.

Vaughn takes the handles of the chair and pushes me forward. Gruff and Lanky stride into a jog along the path ahead of us, which winds through a dense forest of towering pines.

"Where are they going?" I ask, the first words I've spoken in what feels like days.

Vaughn looks at me, amused, as if he forgot I'm no longer gagged. "To tell the doctor."

The doctor? I wonder what that means, but I have more pressing questions. "Where are we?"

He shakes his head. "Will the state and town suffice, or do you need the exact geographic coordinates?"

"The... the..." I stammer.

He stops and locks the wheels of the chair, then steps out in front of me. "Seriously? Do you think I was born yesterday? This is where I work, and where you're going to live from now on. That's all you need to know. Now shut the fuck up."

"Fuck you," I mutter, my coalescing anger overwhelming my common sense.

I expect a slap from Vaughn, but he chuckles. It scares me a lot more than if he'd hit me.

After a few mild bends in the path, it narrows to the point where it is barely wide enough for a car, let alone a truck. Time crawls by as the wheels on my chair spin, rolling me closer to whatever lies ahead. I try not to think of the two obvious possibilities. This strikes me as a lot of effort to go to for either one, but that likely means what's coming will be even worse.

Surrounding me are the sounds of the forest and the scrabble of my chair's wheels. I hear birdsong and rising winds. We're far enough from the main roads that there's no traffic noise. A thin layer of snow covers the ground, and it's unspoiled aside from some small animal tracks. What I can see of the sky is clear and bright. In any other situation, it would feel perfectly serene.

Soon the path widens again, only this time it leads to a clearing in the woods. Standing before Vaughn and I is a home of some kind, Victorian and massive — at least three stories. It looks at least 100 years old, but it's in good condition, with fresh, white paint and tasteful landscaping. Off to the side of the house is an expansive parking lot, but it's totally empty. I don't understand: why have the lot if there aren't any cars? It doesn't even look old: the asphalt is smooth, and the lines are bright and clear. It must be used for something.

At the front door, Vaughn presses a button on an intercom, and after a second we're buzzed in.

What is this place?

The foyer we enter is spare, with hardwood floors and a gray textured wallpaper. There's no reception desk, though from the layout I see a spot where one would logically go, right in front of the entrance. The area is nearly silent; all I hear is the hum of fluorescent lighting. I see a long, dark corridor ahead with rooms on each side, like a hotel, but instead of going there, Vaughn turns me to an elevator close by.

We ride down a floor, into the basement; though the space has been finished and furnished, it is noticeably colder. Vaughn wheels me to a door and plants his thumb along a black, plastic square next to the knob. It clicks open, and he brings me in.

The room before me is small but recognizable: it's a doctor's exam room. Its table has cuffs built into it, of course, but otherwise it doesn't seem out of the ordinary: it's clean and even a little inviting, with cheap but pleasant landscape paintings on the wall. There's a sink with a wall-mounted soap dispenser, a wheeled stool for the doctor and some basic medical equipment.

I'm not happy to see, however, that also in the room are Lanky and Gruff. Without a word or hesitation they uncuff me from the chair and start to drag me to the table.

"Fuck off!" I shout, trying to break free of their hold, but each grip one of my arms with both of theirs.

"Shut up," commands Gruff. "Don't be difficult."

"It would be nice if the doc's report didn't list any contusions," adds Lanky.

I spit in Lanky's face. "Fuck his report."

Vaughn laughs, watching as Lanky rears back to take a swing, but he stills his hand. "Keep it up, bitch," he says, wiping away my saliva. "It'll make watching you suffer even more satisfying."

Whether Lanky knows it or not, he's told me what I have to do: *No matter what torture they inflict, don't let them see you suffer.*

They take off my winter coat, and soon I'm down on the table, wrists and ankles securely strapped. I'm still wearing the dress from the bar, and I wish I could close my legs, but they're locked in place.

While we wait, Vaughn tells the others about meeting me at Tommy's. If I didn't know the ending, I would swear he sounded like a man who'd been on a pleasant first date. He speaks with pride and hopefulness, not like a predator who has kidnapped an innocent woman.

Fucking psychopath.

"You're lucky you didn't get pepper sprayed," says Gruff. "She would have used it."

Vaughn shrugs. "It's happened to me before. Wouldn't have slowed me much." He looks at me and winks, making me shiver with disgust.

The door opens as Vaughn is about to speak again. A man steps inside looking like a hurricane on fire. "What the fuck did you do?" he growls, his gaze drilling into Vaughn.

This man is wearing a blue, button-down shirt and brown trousers under a long, white lab coat. The layers do little to hide the built physique underneath; his broad chest rises and falls as he seethes. His gleaming white teeth are bared in fury, and he looks like he could chew through a stone. Two or three days of light scruff cover his cheeks, chin and upper lip while short, flaxen hair ripples with every turn of his head.

"What's it look like, Gabriel?" Vaughn replies. "We had a vacancy. Now it's filled."

Pushing his way past Gruff and Lanky, the man grabs Vaughn's collar, lifts him to his feet and knocks him against the wall. "You didn't have permission to do that. I was told you weren't bringing in new girls anymore."

Anymore? How many have they taken? I wonder. I stay quiet though, transfixed by this new man, Gabriel. I've never seen someone so pissed off. Even Gerald, after I insulted him on the air, displayed more calm.

"That's true," Vaughn said, brushing off Gabriel. "But I think the boss is gonna like this one. I couldn't pass her up."

Gabriel shakes his head. "The shit you'd pull for a pat on the back. You're unbelievable."

"I try," Vaughn replies, leaning against the wall. "Why don't you just do your exam and leave the rest to me?"

Gabriel's eye twitches, but he releases his fists. He points at Vaughn's face and mutters, "This isn't over. Now get the fuck out. All of you."

Vaughn sneers at Gabriel, then marches out, trailed closely by Lanky and Gruff. I'm so confused by what happened. Who is this man, and why is he so at odds with Vaughn?

Can I trust him?

He takes a clipboard out of the drawer and starts scribbling notes. "I'm going to ask you a few questions. Then I'm going to examine you. I'd appreciate it if you made this easy on both of us."

"Oh, is this hard on you?" I snarl, pulling at the cuffs binding me to the table. "Are you fucking kidding?"

He sighs, pity in his eyes. "We're not alone in here. We're being watched. If you make this difficult, you'll be punished for it. Understand?"

I believe him. I'd like to think it had nothing to do with his good looks and slow, kind tone. I hate that I even noticed how handsome he is. Still, I don't doubt his warning.

"Fine," I mumble.

Gabriel nods. "What's your name?"

They have my purse and my ID. They have practically my entire life story. There's little point in lying.

"Marla Angel."

He writes it down. "How old are you?"

"Twenty-five."

"Are you currently taking any medications?"

"No."

"Allergies?"

"Ragweed pollen."

He pauses for a moment before his next question. "Are you sexually active?"

"Fuck off, that's none of your business."

Nodding, he takes a deep breath and holds it before letting it out. "I'm aware," he says. "Please answer the question."

I roll my eyes. "In general, yes. Not lately."

"Thanks." He waits again, his lips twisting as if annoyed. "Have you ever contracted an STD?"

"No. Fuck you, goddammit, no."

If my belligerence bothers him, he doesn't let it show.

"Last question: how much do you like that dress?"

Huh?

"My dress? What the fuck are you talking about?"

The doctor opens a drawer and retrieves a set of heavy scissors.

Oh god.

"Sorry," he says. "It was inappropriate of me to joke. But I have to remove your dress."

Adrenaline shoots through me and suddenly I can hear my heart thumping through my chest. "No, please! Untie me and I'll take it off." My motions become frantic, automatic — I fight against the cuffs like I'm having a seizure.

"I can't. I'm sorry. Now hold still." He takes the bust of my dress into his hands and starts to cut with the scissors. I immediately go limp, not wanting him to nick me by accident. The blades are sharp, and I gasp as he slices the fabric apart with little effort, exposing my skin to the cool air of the exam room. He pulls the tattered garment away, prompting me to lift my bottom, rather than just lifting it himself.

For a second I fear he's going to strip away my underwear, but he puts the scissors back in the drawer. He tries not to look at my push up bra and tight, white panties, but I catch him peering — considering I wore my best, I'm sure he couldn't resist.

Gabriel opens up a small, black box and takes out a stethoscope. He holds the ice cold drum to my chest and says, "Breathe."

He listens to my respiration, adjusting the placement of the drum a few times. "Smoker?"

"Former."

"That's good." He sets aside the stethoscope and takes out a blood pressure tester. While fastening the Velcro cuff around my arm, his fingers brush my skin. "Try to relax," he says.

"Are you serious?"

"Yes." He squeezes the bulb and the cuff tightens uncomfortably.

"What does it even matter? You motherfuckers are going to kill me anyway."

For a minute he says nothing, watching the readout on the kit. "A little high, but under the circumstances... Actually, I'm surprised it's not even higher."

"Great," I mutter. "I can die healthy."

"No," he says as he removes the cuff. "They're not going to kill you." He turns away, unable to face me. "But you're going to wish they would."

CHAPTER 4
GABRIEL

If I wasn't genuinely afraid of the repercussions, I would take Vaughn out back and beat him to death with a shovel. I'd leave him a lump of pulverized flesh and bone, just waiting for a pack of wolves to come clean up the remains. I've wanted to do this for a long time, ever since...

I can't let myself think about her, or that night. I may lose it.

On the warpath, I march up the stairs from the basement all the way to the top floor, heading straight for the office of Montgomery Halloran. I don't knock on the door.

"This is fucking unacceptable," I bark, pointing at the old man, who's already watching Marla on the giant monitor fixed to the wall.

Sitting behind a redwood desk as old and ornate as he is, Halloran smiles as the girl struggles against the restraints. His jaw hangs slightly, revealing dark, coffee stained teeth. Squinting to see, his eyes narrow until they're dark slits atop deep, dark bags. I suspect he could use an adjustment to his bifocals. His pasty, pale skin matches his crisp white, button-down shirt, which he wears with a red bow tie and an olive tweed jacket, despite the stifling warmth of his office. A large, hardcover novel lies open on his desk, most likely a text on some obscure history, one of his favorite subjects. I doubt he's turned the page since Vaughn and Marla arrived.

Finally, he shuts off the screen and addresses me. "I understand you're upset," he says.

"You gave me your word, Halloran." After everything I've suffered through for this man, the least he could do is keep the promise he made me on the worst night of my life.

He cringes. "I've asked you not to call me that."

I sneer at him, disgusted.

"You gave Vaughn a direct order."

"I'm aware!" Halloran thunders, rising from his seat as if suddenly hoisted. "I know what I told him. What do you want me to do?"

"Fucking let the girl go!"

"You know I can't," Halloran sighs.

"Yes, you can. But you won't."

Halloran stops for a moment, but then nods. "Correct. I won't. Whether you like it or not, Vaughn was absolutely right about Marla. I'm going to enjoy having her here."

He matches my stare, gray eyes piercing. For a man with no soul, there's abundant life in his eyes. And why not? His golden boy brought back a shiny new toy. What I don't understand is why my hatred brings him so much pain. How is he even capable of feeling it?

"Someday I'm going to make you pay for this. For everything."

Halloran rolls his eyes. "Get over yourself, Gabriel. You're more like me than you know. Eventually you'll see it." He sits down and reclines in the black, leather executive chair. "In fact, I'll prove it to you."

This ought to be good.

"How?"

Halloran turns the monitor on again. Marla has stopped trying to break free and is crying, her eyes squeezed shut. "If you want, I'll put you in charge of her training. Vaughn's contact with her will be minor"

It's an interesting offer, I'll grant him that. Keeping Vaughn away from Marla appeals to me, mainly because he'll be outraged. He's not going to take this sitting down. "If he didn't listen to you before, what makes you think he will now? The second I turn my back he's going to be on her."

Nodding, Halloran presses a switch on a small, triangular intercom panel along the wall. "Miller, my office," he says, his voice ringing out through the building's PA system. A moment later the com buzzes and Halloran hits the speakerphone.

"Yes," comes a deep, rough voice.

"Mr. Miller, I'm designating Gabriel in charge of the new girl," says Halloran. "Vaughn is not to see her without my authorization. You and Mr. Roy will enforce this. If Vaughn objects, tell him to take it up with me. Understood?"

"Yes, sir."

"Good. Tell Mr. Roy to get the girl a bracelet. Then get Vaughn and prep Iris's... that is, the empty cell," Halloran adds.

"Uhh... yeah, okay, sir," Miller falters. "It may take a while, though."

"Understood. She's secure in the exam room for now. Do the job right, don't rush it."

"Yes, sir."

Halloran presses the button again, hanging up.

"You're really going to put her in Iris's old room?" I ask, incredulous.

"Is there a better option?" Halloran takes off his glasses and rubs the lenses against his shirt. Sighing, he says, "Gabriel, you know I still think about Iris every day. I was as mad as you when she died."

Bullshit. He'd been plenty mad, but not for the right reasons. "Keep telling yourself that, if you need to," I spit. "Her blood is on your hands, and you know it."

"It's on all of us, as I recall," Halloran says darkly.

My blood boils, because in my heart I know he's right. "Fuck you. I should have killed you then."

"Maybe. But you didn't, and you won't. We're in this

together. I made you a promise after Iris, and I'm sorry Vaughn broke it, but the damage is done. You want to ensure we never lose anyone ever again? See to Marla's training. Make her understand what will be expected of her."

"Fine," I mutter, after a beat. I still wish I could throttle Halloran where he sits, but the consequences would be more than I could handle. "But if I see Vaughn even look at her wrong, I will end him."

"I'll speak to him," Halloran says. "If I make it up to him, he'll behave."

"He'd better." I spin on my heels and march out, feeling his stare burning my back.

I'm sorry, Marla, I think, knowing what I'm going to have to do to her. *I hope you're as much of a fighter as you seem.*

I should head down to her immediately so I can be with her when Roy comes to prep her for her stay, but I tell myself she sees me as one of *them*, and my presence won't be of much comfort. Yet, I know this is my own self-reassurance. In truth, I'm afraid.

What if I can't help her?

What if I don't do enough, fast enough, and Halloran takes the reins?

What if Halloran is right about me?

Already I shiver in disgust at how excited I was when I saw her without her dress. Her slim, beautiful body could be the most attractive I've ever seen. When I close my eyes I can see her unbearably adorable face, with her big blue eyes, pouty pink lips and rosy cheeks. Mentally I wipe away the dark streaks of her mascara and stroke her hair. It's perverse, but my heart rate ratchets up at the thought of being with her... disciplining her...

No. Fucking no.

I could slap myself.

You're not like him.

To remind myself of what's at stake, I take the stairs to the first floor and head down the block. I stop at the door to Iris's room, which sits open. Retching at the smell, I cover my nose and inhale shallow breaths through my mouth.

Inside, Miller and Vaughn are kneeling on the floor. Cloths are tied around their faces and tucked into their collars, filtering the odor. I don't announce my presence, and they don't see me right away, too focused on their task: using crowbars, they are dislodging wooden panels from the ground, and the sound of snapping, cracking wood brings me back to the night it all happened. Between the two men rests a pile of boards that have already been removed, as well as several torn apart segments of leather padding; a dark, red film covers them, the blood long since dried into the material and grain.

When Vaughn finishes prying off one of the boards, he turns and sees me watching. "Hey, you going to help us, or just stand there?"

From where he's kneeling, I could kick in his face like a punter nailing a football.

"How about you do your fucking job, and I'll do mine?" I say. *Someday I'll see you in Hell, you piece of shit.*

"The fuck is that supposed to mean?" Vaughn shouts, but I'm already striding down the hall, making for my quarters. I can't go to Marla yet. I'm not ready. If I'm going to be of any use to her, I'm going to need a plan.

CHAPTER 5
MARLA

The only way I could have possibly dozed off is by surrendering to sheer exhaustion. I launch back into struggling the second I hear the door to the exam room click open. Lanky is there, and he's holding a clipboard and a tape measure. He sets the clipboard down on the stool next to me and peels the tape a few inches.

"Remember: if you make this harder than it needs to be, I will have to report it, and you will be punished," he says, his eyes locked on my breasts. "I'm just taking your measurements. This will only take a minute."

"Measurements for what?"

Lanky looks me in the eyes, a sadistic smile curling up his lips. "You'll see. And if you want to avoid getting whipped, get out of the habit of asking questions. You're here to obey."

Obey. The word echoes inside. It stirs me in a way I can't explain, even though Lanky is utterly revolting. As if his participation in my kidnapping wasn't repugnant enough, he reeks of raw onion and what's left of his greasy, stringy hair hangs down to his shoulders from his balding skull.

Sadly, I expect him or Vaughn or that doctor will make good on his threats of punishment, and there's little I can do about it right now. I spit off the side of the table and say, "What do you need me to do?"

"Be still while I get this done, okay?" he answers, voice shaky.

Is he... afraid of me?

Lanky holds the tape measure to my wrist, but can't get his hands to steady. He's trembling. Working quickly, he examines my wrists, my hips, collar and much more. Beads of sweat roll down his forehead, and more than once he writes a little, only to cross it out furiously and write it again.

He's nervous. Why? Is it me?

I know I shouldn't, but I opt to test my theory. The next time he moves in, his face close to mine, I jerk suddenly in my bonds, throwing my hands at him and rattling the chains of my cuffs. The sound and motion cause him to jump back in shock.

Cowardly little shit! I think, grinning as Lanky stares at me. My amusement grows into a full on laugh. The sound makes the room feel that much smaller and me that much bigger.

Lanky comes back and glares at me, then slaps my face. Maybe it's the strange angle he's forced to attack, as I'm lying down and he's standing, or maybe he's as weak as he is skittish; the slap is like a hard tap. I don't even stop laughing because of it.

"What was that?" I taunt, my anger taking the wheel. "Why don't you uncuff me, you limp-dicked sack of shit? I'll show you how to slap proper."

Lanky raises a fist like he's really going to punch a half-naked, defenseless woman. He only stops himself because I'm staring him down, rather than flinching.

"Oh wow, you crazy bitch," he laughs. "You're a real hellcat... for now. Give it some time. You're going to be on your knees, begging to suck my cock." He grabs the clipboard and pockets the tape measure. "I've got what I need for now. I'll be back very, very soon. See you then."

He leaves, and I'm alone again. *I have to get the fuck out of here,* I think. *But how?* I try to reason it out. These men know what they're doing. They've done it before. How do I get them to let their guard down?

Out of all the men I've encountered so far, Lanky strikes me as the weakest link in the chain. He's fearful and not physically intimidating. How can I exploit that?

Get in his head, Marla.

I've interviewed dozens of complete strangers for the news. Most were for fluffy human interest pieces, but sometimes I got to harangue a local elected official. Getting the story means pushing the right buttons: ask a smart question that shows you've done your homework, or bring up a sensitive subject for an emotional rise, or come up with an unexpected inquiry that can't be deflected with a canned answer. Warm them up with a softball that strokes the ego before launching into a more delicate issue.

So, what are Lanky's buttons?

Compared to him, the other men here look physically strong and capable — even that doctor was pretty built. Perhaps Lanky feels inferior? Maybe they give him shit, and he resents them for it? That could be used.

What would he want? Sympathy? Is he the sensitive type? Flattery? Would he like to be built up a little for once? Maybe he wants approval? Forgiveness?

I know you're just doing your job. I don't blame you...

This is assuming he's susceptible to manipulation. What if he can see right through me, making up for his less impressive stature with guile and will?

In that case, I'm fucked.

I deliberate over my strategy for what feels like hours. I nearly cry when I remember that, even if I can get out of this room, I'm going to need an extraordinary amount of luck to get past Gruff, Vaughn and Gabriel — and anyone else I haven't yet met. Then get to the truck, get it started and find help. No money, no phone — they've taken my belongings. I'll be in my underwear in frosty weather, and I shouldn't even attempt to run in my heels.

But what choice do I have?

At least, in the course of my inner discussion, I've settled on how I'm going to work Lanky. It sickens my stomach, and I'm not sure I can pull it off convincingly. Yet, it feels right. When Lanky returns, I spasm as if just woken and immediately start struggling again.

"You still think you can get out of that?" he chides. "You're insane." He holds up a small strip of plastic. "Know what this is?"

I shake my head, widening my eyes in fear, which isn't difficult: if the item he holds is what I think, it's bad news.

"I'm going to fasten this to your wrist. It will be tight, but not painful, so relax."

"Please, no," I plead, pulling extra hard on the cuffs. "You don't have to do this."

Lanky grins and grabs my wrist. He wraps the strip around it and it's barely long enough to fit. A row of hard plastic teeth link together, and then it's done. The band feels tough and tight — getting it off without scissors seems unlikely.

"Now if you behave, we don't have to keep you locked down all the time. But we can't have you wandering around the building," Lanky explains.

"I'll behave, I will," I say, nodding vigorously.

Lanky stops and gives me a long look. "What's this? Are you... scared?"

I turn away. "No," I mumble unconvincingly.

"Oh, this is good. A few hours ago you were singing a different tune. What happened, sugar plum? Did reality finally sink in?"

When I look at Lanky, he's grinning, and my skin crawls. The only consolation is that he's responding to being feared. That is what I assume he would want, especially after the way I got the better of him earlier.

"Please, I want to go home," I cry, ignoring the fact that I don't even have a home anymore.

Lanky laughs and I feel my anger burning in my chest. *Careful, Marla. Control yourself.*

He lowers himself to my eye level and says, "This is your home now, bitch. But the best thing you can do for yourself is do what you're told and don't make trouble. Don't give us extra reasons to hurt you."

"Oh god," I moan.

He reaches to my chin and holds it in place. "Do you think Vaughn is watching right now? Do you think he's seen how quickly your courage ran out? He thinks he's hit a home run with you. He's going to be so disappointed. The boss, too. But that's fine. We can still have lots of fun with you."

I could bite one of his fingers off right now if I wanted, and my racing heart eggs me on to do it, but this is working.

"Please," I beg, sniffling.

"What?"

"Please... I need the bathroom."

He nods, not doubting me. It's been hours — I really do need it.

"Okay, okay. I'll take you. But there's going to be some rules."

"Yes, of course," I say quickly, injecting urgency into my tone.

He holds up a finger, and I imagine he's given this lecture before. It belies a confidence lacking in his normal speech. "First, I'm coming into the bathroom with you. This is not negotiable. Second, when I uncuff you, you will not move a muscle unless I say so. Is that clear?"

"Yes, yes, it's clear. Please, I really have to go."

"First, tell me: what's going to happen if you disobey these rules?"

I blink a tear away and croak, "You'll hurt me."

Lanky smiles. "That's right. Now be quiet and do as I say."

To my disappointment, he doesn't uncuff me from the bed straightaway. First he takes out a set of standard, police issue handcuffs and slaps one across the wrist with my bracelet. He releases from the bed my other wrist, then locks it in the other handcuff. Finally, he opens the remaining restraints securing me to the bed. I'm still bound, hands in front, but I can get up out of bed for the first time in hours.

"Can I have something else to wear?" I ask, looking down

at my mostly exposed body.

"No. You're lucky to still have that," Lanky responds, nudging me forward.

As soon as I reach the door, I feel an overwhelming urge to bolt, but a sharp electronic buzz stops me.

"You hear that?" asks Lanky. "That's your bracelet. You get too close, the door seals. If you want out…" He steps up right behind me and presses his thumb against a smooth, black panel by the knob. After a minute, the buzz sounds again. "Only staff can open the doors. So if you need to go somewhere, you ask one of us really, really nicely. Got it?"

"Yeah," I mumble, momentarily disheartened. Getting out has become that much harder. I'll need to remove my wristband, or use his thumbprint to override it. If I can knock him out, maybe he has a knife. I'll cut through my wristband… or his thumb. Whichever's easier.

"Then let's go," he says. "Turn right. The bathroom is at the end of the hall. Walk, don't run."

I nearly laugh. *Don't run. Yeah, sure.*

Going in, I'm pleasantly surprised that the bathroom looks and smells clean. It's well lit and has a pair of stalls, a urinal and two sinks. Tiny white and green tiles run across the floor in a pattern I can't immediately see, and the walls are covered in larger gray tiles.

"Go on," he says.

I look down at my cuffed hands in disbelief. "Wait, how am I supposed to… you know… like this?"

"Stop. Just stop. I'm not taking those off, all right? Figure it out." He holds the stall door open and points to the metal toilet.

"Please," I beg, looking at my feet, cheeks burning. Acting intimidated by this man is humiliating. It can't go on much longer, I can feel it. I'll break character and this will be for nothing. "I'll go quick, and then you can cuff me again. I'll be good, I promise."

Lanky regards me for a second, unable to keep a victorious grin from his thin lips.

That's it asshole, you've won. You're in control. Prove you're the man here.

He takes the handcuff keys from his pocket and dangles them in front of me. "If you try anything, I will beat you into a fucking coma. Got it?" He likes acting tough, or what he thinks of as tough. I wonder if that line is one he parroted from Vaughn.

"Loud and clear." I hold up my arms, my eyes still trained on the floor. I hear two clicks, then the cuffs are gone.

"Hurry up," he says, watching as I hop into the stall and shut the door behind me. I take care of business, which is a relief, but I'm too focused on what comes next to really feel it. It's dawning on me that if I don't get out of here now, I may not ever.

Don't think like that, I tell myself, but sometimes the truth is impossible to ignore.

I flush the toilet and come out of the stall. I hold my hands up in front of my chest, but instead of waiting for Lanky to come cuff them, I walk toward him. He's smiling up until I rush forward, shoving him as hard as I can into the wall. He groans as he slumps to the ground, a thin trail of blood streaking down the tiles. I look at him for a second, and then he looks back at me.

Fuck! He's still conscious! In a panic, I run for the door, but it seals shut the second I get there. I slump against the wall, my terror now completely genuine.

"Oh you are fucking kidding," growls Lanky, touching his scalp. His hand comes back bloodied, and he snarls in fury. I shake the long, hooked door handle but it refuses to budge. When I turn, Lanky is charging like a bull, and his arm is swinging a tight fist toward my face.

Twisting and ducking I barely avoid the blow. My body is so charged full of adrenaline, in my mouth I taste pure cotton. Lanky's scream blasts in my ears like a klaxon, as his hay-maker flies straight into the wall, breaking loose the tiles. He's clutching his hand in obvious agony, and for a second I savor his howl.

Lanky, to his credit, sees my pause and throws out his other hand, this time flat, connecting with my face and knocking me to the ground. I taste blood and feel a wetness on my hand. I look down and see my finger's been cut by the edge of a broken tile.

"Is that what you meant by a proper slap?" Lanky asks, planting a fist in my hair and yanking me up. "You played me. Well done, Marla. But I don't care what anyone says, I'm gonna spend a whole month beating you. You're gonna look like a goddamn freight train hit you by the time I'm done."

Fuck fuck fuck! I'm crying and gasping and trying to compose myself. He hasn't let go of my hair. My hands are supporting me, but their strength is waning, especially as the pain from my cut finger fights its way through the adrenaline haze.

My finger...

Grabbing the sharp piece of tile from the floor, I raise it straight up until it hits something soft. Lanky makes a sound between a scream and a cough, and I feel hot, wet drops in my hair. His grip weakens, and I twist away. When I do, the tile in my hand dislodges, and more than a few crimson drops spray my face.

Turning, I see Lanky's holding his throat, but red is leaking out from between his fingers. In his eyes I see confusion and rage. His skin is as white as his outfit, though now scarlet stains spread downward from the collar.

Fuck me. I can hardly believe what I just did. *This is real. This is happening. I did this.*

"Hey," I say to Lanky. He blinks but is beyond replying in a substantive way. "Now who's the bitch?"

CHAPTER 6
HALLORAN

"Vaughn and Miller, to the lower level bathroom, now!" I snap into the intercom. I don't care if the whole building can hear it. Roy is dead and my new toy needs to be punished severely.

In all my years here, I have never seen anything like this. I don't know whether to throw her in a tiny, iron box for a week or parade her through the halls like an unearthed diamond. She's rough, yes: she needs to be cut and polished. She needs to be properly appraised, then worked over until she's ready to shine.

Only, I'm not sure she ever will. Judging by the way she's strained against her bonds for hours, and by the way she sliced Roy's throat, Marla may not stop fighting. Normally the idea wouldn't cross my mind, because nobody can resist forever. Fatigue sets in, or perhaps their will to fight is tied to their will to live, and with one, so goes the other. Either way, it is necessary to break a girl before she can be truly owned.

Breaking them, however, always produces the same result: a slave. An animal. They become indistinguishable from one another. As much as I enjoy that, the breaking process itself is indescribably thrilling while it lasts. With Marla, it may well last for the rest of my life, and probably her's too. If she eventually gives in, it may be disappointing, but I will have gotten a great deal of satisfaction along the way. And she can still be one of my favorites.

I almost wish I could have been there in the room with her this whole time, listening to her soft grunts as she pulls and tugs at her cuffs. Their song stokes my flame, even through the filter of the speaker system; in person, her music would fill my heart with desire. Whispering in her ear my plans for her, every filthy detail, she would struggle even harder, arousing my hunger even further, a self-perpetuating cycle.

On the TV screen I see Vaughn and Miller arrive at the bathroom. Inside, Marla is trying to cut off her security wristband with the same tile she used to kill Roy. I saw her looking at his thumb earlier, but then she lurched, her cheeks puffing wide, and focused on her wristband instead.

"Stay there," I instruct Vaughn and Miller through the speaker. They've got her trapped now, but I don't want them to force the matter. She knows they're in her way, and has given up on the wristband. She's weighing her next move, but from her pacing, she appears to understand she hasn't got one.

Maybe she's not as tough as I thought, I consider, frowning. I want her to be tough, but how can she have the instinct and will to kill Roy, and then not cut off his thumb?

I suppose I'm being unfair. It's easy for me to judge her actions from the comfort of my office. I'm not in a life-or-death situation right now. This young woman has just killed a man — presumptively for the first time. The thoughts that must be running through her mind right now... It's miraculous she's mentally collected at all.

Indeed, the act she pulled on Roy worked quite well. Appealing to his ego through fear was exactly the right decision. It's this ingenuity that has me surprisingly excited following Roy's death. The man was mostly capable but never particularly inspiring.

Vaughn would have to find a replacement, a laborious task but one he's accomplished before. Considering his stroke of luck with Marla, I'm almost glad he'll have a reason to trek back out into the world. Considering Marla will be entrusted to Gabriel, he'll certainly want to find someone for himself.

Gabriel.

My blood clots in my veins thinking about what I'm about to ask of him.

"Gabriel, to my office," I announce through the intercom.

I shouldn't have promised him Iris would be the last. My mind is not clouded anymore: when Vaughn returned with Marla, I knew he'd done me a great service. I would not break my promise to Gabriel, but Vaughn did it for me. It is a loophole he created for me, whether he meant to or not. And I had felt the stagnation of our little life here; it needed new blood. Vaughn saw it and acted. He's a lot like me in that regard.

A loud hammering on the door nearly knocks me from my chair. I growl, wishing he wouldn't do that. "Gabriel, " I sigh as he enters.

"Halloran. What is it?"

He's still angry from earlier. This isn't going to help.

"You need to see to Marla now. Her actions have earned her a punishment of the highest severity. If you won't see to it, Vaughn will."

"Fuck," he grunted. I gave him a moment to collect his thoughts. Frankly, he should have expected this. Of course Marla wasn't going to get through her first day without a serious infraction. Roy should have known this and been on his guard.

"What did she do?" Gabriel asks at last.

I can barely contain my smile. Will he even believe me? Would I have believed it if I hadn't watched it happen?

"Mr. Roy is dead. Marla killed him."

As it turns out, it is Gabriel who can't keep the smile from his lips. "Bull."

With a tap of my remote I flip the channel from the hall to the bathroom interior. His reaction is priceless. Marla is staring at the camera, shouting something, but I have it on mute. The message is clear, though: Roy's blood still coats her face, and she clutches the broken piece of tile, daring someone to try and take it from her. Behind her, Roy is slumped against the wall, his life spilled out and saturating his clothes. His jaw hangs open in shock; his lifeless eyes look straight ahead.

"Holy shit." Gabriel leans in toward the screen, wanting to see better.

"Vaughn and Mr. Miller are guarding the bathroom. You will help them get Marla under control, and then you will deal with her. You will not stop until she's begging you to kill her. Understood?"

To Gabriel's credit, he doesn't object.

"I'll do what I must, but she doesn't look like the begging type."

I nod, agreeing with his assessment. "Possibly. But let's see how she responds to her treatment."

And how Gabriel administers it. If he can't bring himself to train Marla properly, handing her off to Vaughn won't be enough. I'll have to seriously reconsider Gabriel's role here, and make some hard decisions. For Gabriel's sake, I hope it doesn't come to that.

"Fine," he says. "I expect you'll be watching."

I nod. "Oh yes. As if I'm right there with you."

Gabriel turns, unable to face me. He mutters under his breath, but I'm old, not deaf. *Sick fuck.* I heard him. I'd reply, but there's no point. If he wants to think I'm sick, he can. I'm sure most people would agree with him, and I won't convince him otherwise.

Fortunately, I don't care.

"Gabriel," I say as he goes to leave.

"What, Halloran?"

Halloran, he calls me. You want to twist the knife, Gabriel? Okay. I can too.

"When you're in there with Marla, remember what happened to Iris."

CHAPTER 7
MARLA

What are they waiting for? Vaughn and Gruff are outside; I can hear them talking softly to one another. Making out their words is impossible, but they definitely sound angry — though not as furious as their boss. I assume that's whose voice I heard over the loudspeaker telling them to get down here. He said Vaughn and Miller — I guess that's Gruff. I wonder what Lanky's name was.

I look to his corpse for the tenth time, still afraid he's about to shoot back to life like in the horror movies. He's dead, though. Not moving, aside from the occasional postmortem twitch. I remind myself that happens sometimes, and it's nothing to be worried about. Lanky is definitely gone. And I'm the reason.

Should I be horrified, or remorseful? Maybe I'm numb at the moment. Lanky wasn't in the wrong place at the wrong time — he was between me and my escape, and I don't feel my actions need any further justification. I may have tricked him into thinking I wasn't a threat but isn't it his job to see that coming?

And then there's what he said to me. The threats of what he'd do. Monstrous words to describe monstrous acts. Was I supposed to let that happen to me?

So, no: Lanky deserves to be sitting in a puddle of his own stew. I'd do it again to Miller or Vaughn, given the chance, because I know they plan to do all the things Lanky said he would. I don't doubt this, but I do wonder why they haven't come for me yet.

Should I even give them the chance? I still have the broken tile. I had to be extremely careful trying to cut the wristband. One bad slip…

I could stop them from getting what they want out of me. I kinda like the idea. Why should they get what they want? Why should I suffer?

Yet, I can't do it. *That would be letting them win*, I reason. I will not be pulled into Hell without dragging a few of them along with me.

The question is, what do I do now? They're not going to be tricked, not like Lanky. They will defend themselves.

Before I can decide, the matter is settled for me. A knock comes from the door.

"Marla, we're coming in. I don't want to see you get killed, so I urge you not to attack us."

It's Gabriel, the doctor. I hadn't heard him out there before.

"Can I count on you to cooperate when we come in?"

"How do I know you're not going to kill me for what I did to your friend?" I ask, stalling for more time.

"He wasn't my friend," Gabriel replies. "And I told you before: we don't want you dead. If so, Vaughn and Miller would have come in and shot you by now."

This rings true. They could have just done that. Not that I expect them to, though they will if I force their hand. And then they'll have won.

You found a way to kill Lanky. You'll get another chance, I tell myself, perhaps foolishly.

"All right," I say, tossing the tile into Lanky's lap.

I hear the familiar buzz, then Vaughn and Miller bust inside. Both have guns drawn, pointed right at me. "On your knees," says Vaughn. "Hands on your head."

As I follow Vaughn's commands, Gabriel steps inside. He feels Lanky's neck for a pulse, but of course there's none. He rinses the blood off his finger in the sink, taking his time to be thorough.

"How did this happen? Why did Mr. Roy uncuff you?" he asked.

"Was that his name?"

"Yes."

I look to Gruff. "And you're Miller?"

He nods.

"You're next, Miller."

He laughs, a growly grunt I'd think was a cough if I didn't see him smiling. "Thanks for the warning, toots. I'll be careful."

"Marla, I asked you why he uncuffed you," says Gabriel.

"Is that not on the video?" I respond, curious. It would be nice to know which rooms are bugged for sound and which are not.

Gabriel sees through this, however, and slaps my face with his open palm. The hit isn't hard at all, but the sound echoes off the hard tiles. Surprise gets me more than any degree of pain. My heart thumps so hard I can feel it in my skull. I grin. "Was that supposed to hurt?"

Smiling back, Gabriel slaps my face again, harder this time. "Got any more questions?"

My cheek stings, but I devour the sensation. Is this the thrill of defiance? I shouldn't enjoy getting slapped, and yet I'm tempted to see if I can get Gabriel to do it again. Through his excited expression I see some regret. Is that my imagination? Why is he not totally enjoying this? Is he not as sadistic as the rest? If so, then why is he the one hitting me and not the others?

Nothing makes sense, but asking for answers won't get me anywhere.

"No. No more questions," I say.

I can't tell if Gabriel is relieved he doesn't have to slap me again, or disappointed. Both, maybe? Or am I just projecting my own desires onto him? I hate to even think it, but with my one cheek still burning... it feels asymmetrical. Like the other could use a little evening out.

That's so fucked up, Marla.

"Strip her," Gabriel commands the other men. He clasps his hands behind his back and stands straight and firm as he watches, steely-eyed and silent. My instincts scream at me to fight as Miller and Vaughn put their hands on my bra and panties. Yet I don't flinch; I don't take my eyes off Gabriel.

With two thunderous rips, my undergarments are torn apart by Vaughn and Miller's filthy hands. I shudder as they stuff the tattered cloths into their pockets.

Gabriel retrieves from his pocket a small leather belt of some kind, with silvery, square studs and a short chain attached. Before I can guess its purpose, he fastens the belt around my neck.

Oh god, is that...?

Sure enough, Gabriel yanks the chain, testing its pull on my neck.

...A leash.

"On your knees," he says, looking not into my eyes, but at a place lower to the floor where he wants my eyes to be.

An intoxicating sensation shoots through me as I sink to the floor, but I refuse to acknowledge it.

Gabriel crouches down, drawing the leash downward, pulling my head even lower. "On all fours."

Oh god... This is not happening.

Vaughn and Miller laugh as I plant my palms on the tiles. As humiliated as I am, hearing them makes it worse still. That shouldn't be possible; I don't know why, but I didn't feel quite as mortified by Gabriel's treatment — it makes no sense.

"All right," he says. "Move."

Upon leaving the bathroom, Vaughn and Miller fall in behind us. Gabriel holds the leash but doesn't turn around to check that I'm going; he doesn't have to. If I don't keep up, he'll know. However, he walks with a deliberate pace, savoring my degradation.

My cheeks burn at the indignity of being tethered and crawling like an animal; it doesn't help that I could feel the stares of the men behind me, ogling my rear.

Worst of all, there's a growing tingle between my legs as I follow Gabriel. I try to keep ignoring it, but it's there. Every time I don't follow fast enough I feel a gentle tug on my neck; without fail I pant a little harder. *You're demented, Marla.*

How long have I really been here? I could swear it's only my first day, but clearly my brain has been rattled. Would that really be so strange? After being kidnapped and then killing somebody, I should be suffering from trauma. Could that distort time? Could it elicit a sexual hunger from humiliation?

I'm not sure which possibility is scarier: that my mind is no longer under my control, or that I'm a lot more broken inside than I ever knew.

By the time Gabriel has led our procession up one level and down a corridor, my thighs feel slick and my bare nipples are erect. I tell myself it's the cold air in the hall, but I know I'm lying.

We enter a cell through a heavy iron door, solid save for a single horizontal slot at eye level. Inside I nearly fall when the floor sinks slightly beneath my feet. I look down at the soft surface and realize it's padding, like the seat of a leather sofa. The beige material covers the floor as well as the walls. Even the inside of the cell door. More disturbing, however, are the long, metal chains hanging from the ceiling with cuffs at the end.

"What is this place?" I ask, turning to the men. "A mental home?"

"Bingo," laughs Vaughn as he checks out my chest.

Gabriel shoots him a glare. "Wait outside."

"Bullshit," Vaughn snorts. "I've been waiting for this."

"Vaughn, get the fuck out. If you want to watch with the boss, I can't stop you. But since you've identified this place as a mental home, that makes Marla a patient — my patient — and you're not a doctor. You've got your own work to do, so go."

Growling through bared teeth, Vaughn stares at Gabriel, but the doctor doesn't back down. Vaughn snarls, then gives me a look.

"I'll see you another time, sweetheart," he tells me. "You're not going anywhere. I can wait." He gives Gabriel another sneer, then leaves.

Though staring at the floor, I'm smiling from the exchange. Gabriel lifts my chin with his index finger. "And you: I told you no questions. Now get up."

So go ahead, hit me, I think, but I'm too mortified to speak. "Sorry," I mumble as I rise. I should be relieved to stand on my feet like a person, but I'm not. I wish I could explain why.

Grabbing me by the shoulders, Gabriel spins me around and slaps my backside hard. "You will address me as 'sir' from now on. Understand?"

I yelp and twist in the man's grip. "What the fuck?"

Another hand connects with my cheek in the same spot, leaving a sizzling burn on my skin.

"This is simple. Show us respect, or you'll be punished. Is that what you want?"

Is it? The idea is inconceivable, and yet my ass throbs with the same ember of exhilaration I felt after the slaps to my face.

"No, sir," I say, unconvincingly.

Gabriel nods slowly, studying me. "Miller, hold her arms. Carefully." He unties the leash from my neck as Miller grips my forearms and turns me around once more. He lifts my arms one-by-one and Gabriel locks my wrists in the cuffs hanging from the ceiling. "Go get my kit."

"Be right back," Miller says, slipping out the door.

I pull at the chains around my wrists, testing them. They don't feel the slightest bit harmed by my weak struggle. Gabriel, on the other hand, seems to enjoy watching me fight against them, so I stop. Part of me enjoyed the attempt, just as I did when I was cuffed to the exam table before.

"After killing Roy, what did you think would happen if you were caught?"

"Nothing good," I snort.

He reaches behind me to spank my cheek. "Try that again."

"Nothing good, sir," I snap, hips swiveling in place as I smart from the blow.

"You're right. Do you know what we do to people who kill our staff?"

"No, sir." *Kill me? Beat me? Imprison me? What I expected to happen anyway?*

"Neither do I. It's never happened before. My instructions on what to do with you are vague. I'm at some liberty to structure your punishment as I see fit."

"Because I'm your patient?"

Gabriel spanks my ass again, this time working the less-touched cheek. I hiss, but absorb the impact.

"No. That's not why. The only stipulation is that your punishment will be severe."

The unspoken threat has now been voiced and a chill digs through me from my fingertips down to my toes. *Severe.* The word plays and replays in my head. What does that entail? What were the hits he's delivered already — were they severe? Or merely a warm up? I'm too afraid to ask.

The cell door creaks on rusted hinges as Miller returns. He drops a large, black duffel bag on the floor. When it lands I hear the clumps and clacks of a variety of materials.

"Thank you, Miller, you're dismissed," says Gabriel.

"Call me if you need anything." It occurs to me now that Miller's outfit is one of an orderly, as was Roy's. Not Vaughn though. What is his job here?

Gabriel waits for the cell door to close before opening the bag Miller delivered. From it he retrieves a long, thin wooden cane.

"Normally I wouldn't start with this, but I'm betting you're tough enough."

I can't help scoffing. The cane is barely as wide as my pinky. It doesn't look particularly intimidating. Grinning despite myself, I say, "I'm a lot tougher than that."

Now Gabriel smiles. "Oh, are you not impressed?"

"No, sir," I reply truthfully, emboldened by Gabriel's

selection. "Don't you have a bigger one?"

He laughs loudly, tapping the tip of the cane against my backside. "No, actually, I don't. I don't *need* a bigger one." The quick succession of taps ends with one hard smack.

An inferno of agony erupts like a volcano, a surge of warmth that punches the air from my lungs and sends my body twisting back and forth.

"Hurt a lot more than you thought, didn't it?"

Sucking in my breath as tears drip down my face, I nod. "Yes, sir."

"Just a flick of the wrist. Surprised?"

"Uh huh."

I'm more surprised by the euphoria spreading through my body from the site of the hit, and the way my heart pounds with every word from Gabriel's lips.

Yet, when the tapping begins again, I whine in fear. After the pain of the first hit, I find my body tensing up for the second, preparing to take it, rather than avoiding it, which I know now is impossible.

You want this, don't you, you crazy bitch?

Does Gabriel sense it too? His tapping misses a beat, then resumes.

"The cane might not be big, but it's narrow. If it's moving fast, it hurts. Like a pin popping a balloon. Or a bullet."

I moan, fighting my bonds as my wetness churns. *God, this is wrong.*

For a moment the tapping ceases and my heart nearly stops. A second goes by so slowly it could have lasted an hour. And then the first strike whips into me, the cane swung hard, nailing my poor cheeks. Four more swings follow, leaving lines of lava crisscrossing each other along my flesh. Screaming and writhing, I try to break free of my chains but cannot.

"If you knew the punishment was going to be this severe, would you still have killed Roy?"

"Yes, sir," I mutter, sniffling and gasping.

Gabriel rests a hand on my shoulder to steady me. "No hesitation. You're sure? This isn't over yet."

"I'm sure, sir," I say, my voice regaining its balance. I straighten up, stable on my feet. The pain is intense but already pleasantly fading.

"Would you do it again?" Gabriel looks into my eyes like a bear staring down a hunter.

One of us is going to lose. It won't be me.

"Absolutely." I sneer. "Sir."

The cane swats my bottom with the same force as before, and though I grunt from the impact, I maintain my composure.

"Marla, do you feel disassociated from this experience you're having now?" he asks, sounding like the doctor he claims to be.

"No, sir," I answer, though I'm not sure exactly what he's saying.

"Are you having any difficulty accepting that what's happening to you now, and that what is going to happen to you in the future, is, in fact, real?"

Am I? How does one answer such a question? Am I doubting reality?

"I don't think so. No, sir."

"Good!" Gabriel practically shouts. He flicks the cane again, shooting sparks of electricity through my ass. "Because you're not acting like it. You're fighting me, and your punishment. I promise, this will do you no good here."

Three more jolts start to dislodge my resolve to stay stoic. Though my heart is racing and my core is quivering, my fury for Gabriel rages hotter than ever.

He leans in close and whispers, "Beg me to stop." He steps around me and I hear something click on the floor. The cane rolls across the tiles and past my feet. "Go ahead, Marla. Keep fighting me if you want to suffer. By the time I'm done training you, your instinct to resist will be broken. Your urge to escape will be erased. You will be compliant and submissive. And you're going to like it."

I should have laughed in his face at the prospect, but my racing pulse keeps me quiet. *What if he's right?*

Deep inside I feel a stirring. It's always been there, I can tell, and thanks to Gabriel, it's waking up.

He reaches into his bag and takes out a whip of some kind. It has long, black lashes that look like leather. He practices his swing a few times, letting me hear it cut through the air. "Is this what you want? Day after day of torture, until you lose your mind?"

I'm not going to give in, asshole.

He slashes the whip high, flogging my chest. I rear back in pain as my breasts burn and fresh welts rise.

"Answer me."

I remain silent. Gabriel sweeps in from behind and draws the tendrils of the flogger across my neck. He's so close, I could swing my leg back and try to hurt him, but it won't get me out of my chains. Then again, what would he do about it? Torture me?

Before I can attack, though, he whispers into my ear, "I can help you if you trust me." Then he backs away again.

Is he serious? Help me? Trust him? What reason could I possibly have to believe him?

"I'll never break, sir," I say at last. "You can torture me, or kill me, but you can't break me."

The flogger dances across my body, stinging me like a nest of angry wasps. He targets my ass and chest, painting them until they practically glow. I reach the edge of how much pain I can take without losing myself. Torment and desire battle within me, though at times I lose the sense of which is which.

"Ask me to stop," Gabriel growls into my ear.

"No," I reply, possessing only enough resolve to get the word out. If he asks again, I'm not sure what I'll say.

Sighing, Gabriel drops the flogger and thumbs open the door to the cell. After a second I hear his voice through the PA system asking for Miller. "Bring a jacket," he adds before hanging up. When he comes back he packs up his bag and chucks it out into the hall.

"You're tough, Marla. I could go harder on you with whips and canes, but I'm going to try something different. You're going to hate it. Everyone does. Maybe when it's over you'll feel more eager to obey your master."

His threat wraps around my spine like ice freezing over a lake. I'm not afraid of Gabriel, but I am genuinely concerned about what he has in mind. *Something different.* That could mean anything, and all of the horrors I've imagined are no longer adequately ominous.

"What are you going to do?"

I feel his hands massaging my shoulders and lean my head back into his chest. I shouldn't, but fatigue claws at me and his touch brings a relief I hadn't expected.

"I'm giving you some alone time."

Moaning as he works my aching muscles, I mutter, "That's it?"

He chuckles. "Excuse me. What I meant was, you're going to do some time in solitary confinement."

"Oh." I hold back a laugh.

I think I can handle being alone for a while. Better than being with any of you.

Does Gabriel really think that scares me? I'd heard stories about the cruelty of solitary, but compared to what I've already experienced, how could it be worse?

Maybe they're afraid of me. I allow myself the fantasy of being feared by these men; after what I did to Roy, why not? He may have been an idiot to uncuff me, but they don't know how far I'll go. Apparently, I don't either.

Gabriel ends the massage abruptly when Miller returns. He carries a thick, white coat of some kind. *Oh god.*

It's a straightjacket. I've only ever seen them on television and in movies. They're a lot scarier in person, an incomprehensible mess of zippers and straps and slots and locks. This one looks custom made: tighter and not designed for comfort.

My strength sapped, I fall the second Gabriel releases the cuffs holding my wrists. Miller catches me and quickly closes his arms around my chest in a bear hug, not that I could have broken free if I'd wanted to. My body aches as the punishment it endured flares up from the contact.

Limp as a rag doll, I don't fight as they work together to fit me into the jacket. I wish I could say I am lulling them into a false sense of security, but I am spent. I maintain the vitriol in my glare but don't fight.

Securing the jacket takes far longer than I could have imagined, with each pull drawing it tighter around my torso. My arms are woven across my chest, locked in tight sleeves that offer no give. A thick strap is threaded between my legs, and I try to pretend I hate the way it feels. Clutching my tenderness with an unbreakable hold, I want to squirm and experiment with its touch, but not while anyone watches.

But what if that's all the time?

I know the boss, the voice on the intercom, sees everything. Is he the only one? What about Vaughn?

"How does that feel?" Gabriel asks when they finish with the jacket.

"Screw you."

Miller laughs.

"I'll be around a few times a day to feed you, but no more," explains Gabriel. "We will not speak. You will eat and then I will leave. You will feel like you're losing your mind. You are free to scream and cry."

"Never," I spit.

"We'll see." Gabriel ushers Miller out and turns back to me before locking me in the cell. "Welcome to the Halloran Asylum, Marla."

CHAPTER 8
MARLA

I wake with a shot, trying to rise but unable to push off the ground. My arms are snagged on something. The room is dark, pitch black; my ragged breathing and the shifting of cloth produce the only sound.

Panicking, I immediately launch into battle with the jacket. Convulsing with fear I buck against its many straps and buckles, and the effort rewards me with a warm, syrupy calm. I keep fighting for no other reason than that I like it.

Completely disoriented, I have no clue how long I've slept or the time of day. Was the light out in my cell because it's night and I'm supposed to be asleep, or is it part of the deprivation designed to unravel my psyche? I wonder whether or not the lights will turn on suddenly, either because they want me to wake up or because morning has come.

Stay awake as long as you can, and maybe you'll see.

I entertain the idea but then shut my eyes. Better to keep them closed in case the lights do come back on; better to seem asleep than awake if possible; better to sleep, if I can. I'm not the type of person who hopes to wake up and find my troubles are all a bad dream; if so, I'd have been doing that for years, and in far less dire circumstances.

Calling Gerald dickless on live TV doesn't seem like as big a deal anymore.

When I wake again it's because Gabriel and Miller have entered the room. I shriek as they lift me to my feet by the straps on the jacket; I wobble for a moment before finding my balance. Pins and needles rush through my ice cold feet, but I keep the discomfort from showing on my face.

Gabriel feeds a length of rope through a metal ring on the collar of my jacket, creating a leash. He pulls it gently to let me know we're going, and then we're headed back down to the bathroom. As promised, he and Miller are silent.

In the bathroom, Roy's body is gone and the blood cleaned, as though nothing happened. They've even replaced the broken tiles on the wall, or maybe glued them back together like jigsaw puzzle pieces.

They release me from the jacket but bind my hands behind my back with rope — they aren't going to make that mistake again. They guide me to a shower area marked by a drain in the floor, but there's no spigot overhead. I find instead that Miller has retrieved a hose from a cabinet; he grins before turning on the spray.

Icy and powerful, the stream blasts my body. I instinctively step and turn, trying to avoid the worst of it, but Miller circles around me and gets me everywhere. I holler and cry out, control lost, until its over.

Shivering and on the verge of hypothermia, I don't object when Miller and Gabriel cooperatively towel me off; the fabric is rough but dry. The friction warms me some, but I only truly shake the cold when I'm put right back in the jacket.

Gabriel alone guides me upstairs, but instead of returning to the cell where I slept, he takes me to another room. Though similarly furnished with the padded walls and floor, this one has a bed and a small, barred window. Lacking sheets or a frame to lift it from the floor, the bed is just a mattress and a small pillow, but at the moment it looks so inviting I would jump onto it if not for Gabriel's tight hold on the leash.

"You'll be fed twice a day. At those times, if you need a

bathroom, ask and you will be escorted there."

Not expecting Gabriel to speak, I stare at him. He acts stern but there's a sadness to his expression. He meets my eyes only momentarily, then leaves without another word.

When I'm sure he isn't coming back I sit on the mattress, fussing with my jacket. It refuses to loosen, but I'm equally stubborn and keep trying anyway.

Halloran Asylum. That's what he called this place. It brought to mind so many questions. Is that a nickname for this compound, or is it really a mental institution? Am I the only person being held here against her will? How far would their torture go? Would they use electroshock therapy to melt my brain if I don't comply? Would there be visitors to this place that might actually believe I've been abducted?

A dark dread creeps into my mind as I wait. How long could I keep thinking in terms of escape? When do I start considering survival my goal?

All it takes is one opportune moment to break free, I tell myself, though I'm not sure I believe it. I found the right moment before, and it hadn't been enough. *You need luck, too.*

Being trapped in the cell for hours and hours didn't boost my confidence. They could have just locked the door — there's no way I could bust through it — the straight jacket adds insult to my confinement: I can't use my hands at all. The one upside, I figured, was that it prevented me from lowering my hands between my legs to seek relief.

To my dismay, fighting against the jacket continues to entice my senses and soothe my psyche. I don't grow tired of the struggle, but at times I abruptly quit, aware of the sensuality of my frustrated groans. I want to tug that strap between my legs until the bliss pours like a river, but I won't do it.

They're watching.

If I refuse to let them see me suffer, then the same goes for my satisfaction. If they want a show, they're going to have to force it out of me. I definitely don't want them to know that there's even a hint that I'm enjoying part of this.

However, without a distraction from my distraction, time

passes by interminably slowly. The most I can do is pace around the cell in endless circles, but whenever I get up or sit down I worry I'll fall. The spongy floor and lack of balance from my hands make a simple and routine act a humiliating challenge.

I try sleeping to pass the time, but my mind won't quiet long enough to drift off. When I do seem to doze, a clattering knock jolts me back. Miller and Gabriel arrive with a bowl of oatmeal so bland it tastes like wet cement. Forced by my aching stomach, I accept being spoon fed. I want to spit the tasteless goop back in their faces, but I don't. Gabriel clearly takes no pleasure in what he's doing to me.

"Have I really only been in here a day?" I ask. No response.

They depart as soon as I've finished eating. I would kill for a cigarette, a martini or a side of bacon, but mostly I wish they'd have told me what comes next. I've always been a doer, a problem solver. Waiting for a desired result always fills me with frustration, like wanting a painful cut to heal. I want it to be finished now. Whatever follows this solitary imprisonment, I'm ready for it, no matter how bad.

That's the point, though, isn't it?

It doesn't matter that I'm ready to move on. The decision isn't mine. Maybe Gabriel thinks that if he puts me in a box for a while I'll cave. I'll say or do whatever I can to break up the monotony. More than anything I've ever wanted, I want him to be wrong, but after a full three days in confinement, I'm not so sure.

Six disgusting bowls of oatmeal, three hosings and one jacket change later I'm moaning and biting back tears every few minutes.

What if they just leave me in here to rot?

There's nothing stopping them, apparently. Even if someone has noticed I've gone missing, which is unlikely, they'll have no idea where to look. Did the bar that night have cameras in the parking lot? I don't know. Could it have made out the license plate on Vaughn's truck? Maybe. But what if the truck can't be traced back here? Vaughn's an ex-cop; he would know how to circumvent detection. No doubt he's smart enough to not stop at turning off my cell phone, and either remove the battery or smash it to pieces.

Nobody's going to find me. Nobody's even looking.

I would hit myself if I could. I want to slap out my despair, but I can't even do that. The longer I waste away in the cell, the more I worry they could break me without even touching me again. For a few weeks I could probably keep it together, but if it turns into months... How patient are they? More than me, I suspect.

When Gabriel shows up alone one morning with a bowl of cereal — an honest to goodness bowl of milk and sugar — I nearly erupt in tears. I want to plant my face in the bowl and lick it all up, but I act disinterested. I hold open my mouth and wait for him to feed it to me, eyes rolled up to the ceiling.

"I'm sorry about putting you through this," says Gabriel as he sits down on the bed next to me.

Though I believe he means it, accepting his apology is out of the question. "Don't be. I'm having a ball."

He smiles thinly. "Marla, I get that you intend to fight us, but the only person that hurts is you. If you want to stay in here another week and then try this again, that's what I'll do. Or you could be honest with me now. Your call."

I sigh. He's right: I'd rather not wait. "Fine. It sucked."

Gabriel loads soggy flakes and milk into the spoon; I open my mouth and accept it. I try not to show how delicious it tastes, how rapturous it feels, to eat food with flavor, but he can see it in my expression.

"Marla, do you know what my job is here, in this place?"

I snort. "Doctor slash torturer?"

He tries to hold back a smile, but I see it.

"If somebody is sick or hurt, I help them the best I can. I don't want to see you get hurt."

"Isn't a doctor supposed to 'first, do no harm?'" I ask, thinking about the caning and whipping.

Now Gabriel can't keep from grinning. "Maybe I'm not the best doctor. But all I want is to help you in the years to come."

A sinkhole opens up underneath my feet and I fall into its darkest depths. *Years?* He says it so nonchalantly, as though describing how long it'll take to complete a new freeway or construct a dam. Hearing him speak about my stay here, assuming without a doubt that it's going to be so long, makes everything feel utterly hopeless.

Turning away from the cereal bowl, I suppress the urge to vomit. "I'm a prisoner," I mutter, tears welling up.

"This will get easier, Marla. I promise. It may become harder first, but I will help you come to terms with your new life here."

"Is that what you did? You came to terms with torturing helpless women?"

Gabriel turns and shifts his legs away from me. Sparing a glance down at his khakis, I notice a bulge at the crotch.

Fucking hell.

"I don't always like... the things that I like," he says. "If you know what I mean."

Oh really? "And what happens when you don't like them?"

"I do what I have to," he says. He turns again and offers another spoonful of cereal. I let him feed me the rest of the bowl, but now I barely taste it. Swallowing the soupy cereal mechanically, I regard Gabriel, wishing to understand him better.

How much did he enjoy caning me the other day? Has he been thinking about me, stuck in this jacket, locked in my cell, totally helpless? I put a stop to these thoughts when the strap between my legs grows damp and slick.

Stop being a freak, Marla, I scold myself.

When I've finished the meal, Gabriel stands to leave. "We'll begin the next phase of your training when you're ready, okay? But can I give you a little advice?"

He pauses to wait for my response, but I don't give him one.

"Marla, I like you. I don't want to see you end badly. You're under my protection, for now. Please, make the most of it."

Setting the empty bowl down, he pulls a roll of black tape

from his coat pocket.

"What's that?" I ask, my heart pumping faster now.

"Extra motivation," he mutters, pulling free a length of the adhesive. Before I can say another word he's planted it across my lips. Squealing furiously, I try to wrench away but Gabriel pushes me down onto the mattress and leans over me. I stare at him, sniffling, as he breaks off one piece of tape after another. Soon, the lower half of my face is entirely covered, and the rubbery, plastic smell is overwhelming.

"This is just the beginning, Marla. Remember that."

Through the tape I *hmmph* with as much venom as I can impart. *Go fuck yourself, Gabriel. Go to Hell!*

But the door to the cell closes, and he's gone.

CHAPTER 9
GABRIEL

I never knew it was possible to feel so intensely aroused and ashamed at once. With her mouth sealed and her speech halted, she looked deliciously helpless and frighteningly livid. I wanted to unhook the strap between her legs, press her against the cushioned wall and crash into her until the world ends.

I've spent a long time avoiding indulging my needs, but now I'm not sure I can. I see in her what Halloran sees; we share some proclivities, a source of constant disgust for me. Seeing Marla bound and helpless stokes my need. Watching her fight relentlessly, despite the odds, launches me into orbit. I know if I feel this way, Halloran will want her just as badly.

Marching upstairs, I think of nothing but the inferno in her eyes.

Thank god Halloran wasn't in there.

Could he see on that monitor what I saw? If so, he'll want a taste very, very soon. He'll only be patient for so long.

The question is, did he spare some attention for me? Did he pick up on the tightness in my pants? Or could he guess?

Marla noticed. An awful, selfish part of me is glad. I don't have to hide my desire from her.

What if she tries to exploit your lust?

Considering how she played Roy, I can't discount the possibility. She's going to keep fighting. If she thinks she can use my feelings for her escape, she might. I assume she'll do nearly anything to survive.

I take my time on my way to Halloran's office. I have enough questions of my own to ponder; I want to be ready for his too. Unfortunately, I don't know how he'll react to my treatment of Marla. The caning he liked, I don't doubt, but he probably wanted more. Instead I ordered the solitary confinement. Did he enjoy watching her misery, or did he find it boring? In either case, what do I do? Give him more of what he wants, or do what I think is best for Marla?

I only have so much time to gain her trust and make a plan. Once I lose control of the situation...

She'll end up like Iris. And that can't happen.

His office door buzzes open as soon as I start to bang.

"Gabriel," says Halloran. "Come in."

She's on the monitor, of course. Shaking her head, trying to dislodge the tape, cheeks puffing and blushing — eyebrows slanted inward like twin daggers.

"Enjoying the show?" I snarl.

"Why the tone?" he asks, finally tearing his eyes off of her. "I think you've done a very good job. Solitary confinement was an interesting choice, but a wise one. Like you're softening her up first. I'm assuming you'll start going harder on her from here on in."

"Yes. If necessary."

Halloran's eyes narrow. "It will be necessary, but you will punish her harshly regardless."

Is he telling me this because he wants her prepared, or out of pure sadism? Does he want Marla's limits pushed until the point where he can have his fun without her passing out from the pain? *Is that my deadline for gaining her trust?*

"Fine. I think you're right. She's far from broken. It could take weeks, maybe months."

Halloran laughs. "At this rate, maybe. Gabriel, I don't want you playing games. If she won't comply, make her regret it.

63

Leave that ass so bruised she can't sit on it for a week. If that doesn't work, find a part of her that does. This isn't complicated."

I check how she's doing on the monitor. She's still rocking back and forth slightly, but her cheeks don't glisten from tears.

"Don't forget, Gabriel: I can hand her over to Vaughn and he'll do exactly as I say. And he'll love it."

I could strangle the old man. He licks his lips, waiting to see if I lash out.

"Is that how you want her?" I ask. "So physically decimated she's barely alive?"

"No," he admits.

I press my hands on his desk and lean over him. "You want her to still have some fight in her?"

"I suppose." He meets my focus, refusing to be intimidated.

"Then let me do this my way."

Halloran studies me for a moment, trying to crack my true intent as sure as I'm hiding it.

"Compromise," he murmurs unhappily. "Be cruel, and strict. Use her defiance to justify your actions, but stop before she's too damaged. Don't worry about being consistent. It will help instill a sense of vulnerability. It will make her afraid."

He thinks she's a lab rat, susceptible to conditioning.

"All right. I'll test your theory, but I have my doubts."

Halloran smiles. "That's fine. I don't mind being wrong if you get results in the end."

"How pragmatic."

I steal another glance at Marla before I turn to go.

"Gabriel, wait. I want you to go help Vaughn with a job."

Not a fucking chance.

"Send Miller."

Halloran's voice drops an octave as he rumbles, "No, I want you to help him. He should be in the garage, so go find him. Now."

I sigh.

As long as it doesn't involve Marla, it's not worth arguing over.

"Fine."

"Thank you, Gabriel," rasps Halloran before coughing to clear his throat.

I shut the door behind me without looking back. With another sigh, I set off for the garage, resisting the urge to stop at Marla's cell as I pass by. I hate the idea of not being able to see her when Halloran can, but at least I know she's safe there. *As long as I can keep an eye on Vaughn.*

———

Odors of gasoline and pine needles mingle with a far fouler stench when I reach the garage. White cloth covers a long, lumpy form on the garage's old but sturdy work bench.

"What is that?" I ask, covering my nose with my sleeve.

Vaughn is lying in the big bucket of a wheelbarrow, limbs hanging limply off the sides. He grins and opens his eyes when I speak. "What, you don't recognize your girlfriend's handiwork?"

Grimacing, I pull back the sheet, revealing Roy's ghostlike corpse. His neck gapes like a fish's gills. I retch from the scent of death and drop the shroud, grateful the garage is fairly cold.

"Why am I here?"

Vaughn thrusts his legs to the ground, forcing the wheelbarrow to scoot out from under him. He points to a pair of shovels on a rack on the wall.

Fuck me.

"All right. All right. Let's go then," I say.

"Dirt's going to be pretty hard. Figure this is a two man job at least," Vaughn explains.

"I said all right." I lift the body by the shoulders, clasping the sheet around them. "Get the legs."

Vaughn and I load Roy into the wheelbarrow, followed by the shovels. I grab a proper coat off a peg, work gloves and a scarf. Vaughn already has his, but he finds a pick and dumps it in with Roy.

Once outside Vaughn pushes the wheelbarrow without

complaint. After a few hundred feet of silence, he starts to whistle a tune that rings a bell. I don't ask what it is. Vaughn's probably trying to annoy me, so I lose myself thinking about Marla.

I can't help the smile that breaks across my face as I imagine myself carting away Vaughn's remains after being struck down by the woman he tried to enslave. He would be so shocked, so absolutely astounded that anyone could get the drop on him, especially a woman.

I hope I'm there to see it.

After two miles I start to recognize the path we've followed through the pines. *I've been here before.* It looked different, months ago, in early fall: all green and brown, no snow on the ground. Birdsong filtered between the branches and trunks, carried by the wind. Now it's silent.

"You're fucking kidding me," I say when Vaughn stops. I know the spot. A ring of stones marks where I took Iris.

Iris...

"What the fuck happened?" I ask, applying the gauze, though I know she's beyond my help.

Halloran watches me work, his face blank, hiding whatever trace of emotion he's feeling. Anger? Annoyance? Regret? I can't tell.

"Vaughn..."

He doesn't have to say anything else.

"I'm sorry, Gabriel," he murmurs. "Will she make it?"

A tear drops down my cheek and sticks in the blood pooling on the ground. My fury breaks, leaving grief in its wake. "No."

Vaughn drives his shovel into the earth not five feet from her marker. "It's a nice spot. Very tranquil."

In a blink I've got the handle of his shovel held firm, preventing him from puncturing the earth again. "Not here. She wouldn't want him anywhere near her."

Vaughn winks, but one of his hands has traveled to the holster at his hip. "She's not gonna complain. Now fucking get to work."

It's as though he has no remorse for what happened that night. It's unfathomable.

66

You can't help her now. She's gone. Marla's not.

This isn't worth a fight, as much as I'm itching for one. I release his shovel and pick up mine. "Yeah, okay."

I'll make it up to Iris and bury you here too, Vaughn.

The work takes hours, breaking apart clods of rocky earth until we've shed our winter coats, soaked in sweat. Vaughn doesn't whistle anymore; he keeps quiet, focused on the task. He moves dirt faster than me but doesn't mind because I'm doing my best to match his pace. If being better than me at digging shallow graves strokes his ego, he can have it.

Dusk arrives before we finish. Once the grave is deep enough, Vaughn lifts the handles on the wheelbarrow and sends Roy's body tumbling out.

"You don't want to say a few words?" I ask.

"Not especially. You?"

For once, I'm fine with Vaughn's obscene lack of civility. "Nope."

Vaughn chuckles, then starts burying Roy. I join him, eager to be finished. Shoveling the loosened soil is far easier, and I know it won't be long before we're walking back.

"You gonna find a replacement for Roy?" I ask.

"Eventually." Vaughn shakes his head. "Won't be easy."

No, it won't. Gotta find a good recruit, somebody who matches the profile. Cruel. Not a lot of prospects. Dependable enough to keep a secret, but weak-willed enough to fall in line. It's nowhere near as easy as picking out a random woman at a bar and knocking her out in a parking lot.

"Don't worry about it," Vaughn adds. "That's my job."

"Yeah," I mumble, scooping more earth into the hole.

Vaughn laughs. "Unless you want to trade. I bet I can make Marla behave."

I laugh back. I haven't heard a good joke in a long time.

CHAPTER 10
MARLA

Staring at the slit in the door to my cell without blinking has become my new game. I go as long as I can. I must look insane. I wish I knew for sure. What feels like an hour of unflinching concentration could be as little as thirty seconds, but I count in my head, so I know time is passing.

Miller conducts three feedings in a row — back to disgusting oatmeal — and I start to wonder if this is some new tactic of Gabriel's. *Does he get days off? Is this a job for him?*

I expect Miller to return for the evening meal, but both he and Gabriel appear. Instead of bringing dinner, they pull me from the mattress and stand me up. Gabriel retrieves a set of handcuffs from the pocket of his low-hanging lab coat, and I wonder why until he snaps them shut around my ankles.

I guess no running, I think as they drag me out the door.

"Where are we going?"

The question earns a firm smack to the backside from Gabriel. "Quiet," he warns, though I catch a little smile on his face as he curls and uncurls his fingers. I hate that I consider giving him a reason to spank me again — something is seriously wrong with me.

I let myself be pulled along, watching the door to each cell as we pass by. For a moment I see someone, a woman on the other side looking out.

Who was that? I want to ask, but I know what will happen. I almost do it anyway. My skin stings pleasantly, like I can still feel Gabriel's hand.

Their arms pass underneath my shoulders, nearly lifting me off the ground entirely. They're both so strong, which is good because I don't know how I would have gone down the stairs with my ankles hobbled. They lifted me enough that I could let my feet touch down at the bottom and keep on going.

They bring me to a room I hadn't been to, a large space for a room located underground. It features no windows, and what dim lighting it has comes from yellowed, triangular wall sconces. An assortment of benches, tables and several strange pieces of furniture cast pale, twisted shadows. Though I can't quite tell what I am seeing, my heartbeat thumps harder.

Along the walls hang dozens of shelves, and their contents draw me into a long stare. Ropes and chains, whips and floggers, sex toys and supplies — I can hardly believe the selection available. Some of the devices look like antique torture implements, while others look polished and modern. Many of their wicked purposes are clear at a glance, but for the uses of a few I can only speculate. Those are the ones that fascinate me most, of course.

Because you're sick.

What other explanation can there be? Why else would a veritable torture chamber look and feel so intoxicating? Sure, the idea of having some of those devices used on me elicits an acute fear of pain and desperate, futile struggles — but even that fear is flavored by arousal.

The only true source of dread comes from the conspicuous security cameras interspersed throughout the room. Working in concert they would no doubt capture the scene from every angle, ensuring my treatment could be witnessed by an external observer as vividly as someone in the room.

A shiver creeps up my chest as I think of the boss, the man I only know from his commands through the asylum's PA system. I know no more about him now than when I killed Roy. Who is he? Does he want me for anything but malevolent, carnal indulgence? More questions that will only get me a harsh rebuke.

I sigh in sweet relief when Miller and Gabriel remove my straightjacket. For days I've been wearing one, granted only a short reprieve each morning during my wash. My arms ache from being wrapped around my chest, and I can see lines imprinted on my skin from where the maliciously tight straps dug in. Miller takes me by each wrist as Gabriel pulls off the jacket's sleeves. I don't attempt to break free; he's watching too closely, waiting for me to make a move.

Gabriel tosses the empty jacket aside and regards my naked form. I blush and instinctively move to cover myself, but Miller holds my arms behind my back. With a single twist he could dislocate a shoulder. I seethe and debate trying to throw a kick, but the chain between the cuffs around my ankles is too short.

The frustration of my helplessness burns straight to my core. I press my thighs together as much as I can to hide the dripping, but find it hard to stand completely still as my distraction grows. Luckily, Gabriel doesn't notice: he's scanning a shelf containing several piles of rope. He's considering the different materials and colors, finally settling on one that glows slightly of gold.

Miller follows Gabriel's instructions on how to position my arms so he can tie them. I growl at the humiliation of being manipulated like an object.

"This would be a lot easier if you weren't liable to attack us," Gabriel chides. "Someday you'll stay still because I tell you to."

I want to respond with more defiance, but I picture it in my head. Standing straight, posture perfect, arms held behind me. I keep my gaze trained on a single focal point ahead of me, not reacting as Gabriel paces in a circle, inspecting my figure. Not reacting even when the flogger makes contact with my rear…

Stop it, Marla.

"You would trust me after what I did to Roy?"

I hiss as a swat marks my bottom. It happens so quickly, and I realize the kind of skill Gabriel must have in his hands. He works the rope around my body like a chess prodigy moving pieces across the board: his moves are calculated, practiced, confident and a small piece of a grander design. I wish I could see it as well as I feel it.

"Eventually. One way or another."

What? How many ways are there?

When Gabriel finishes, my arms and chest feel like they've been vacuum sealed. The rope hugs so tightly; I can wiggle my fingers, but that's all. I moan, writhing in its untiring grip.

"Is it me, or does she like it?" asks Miller.

"Fuck you," I snap, attempting to lurch forward. Gabriel's index finger is curled up into the web of rope and arrests my momentum, causing the harness to press against my chest. It feels incredible.

My outburst is met by a series of smacks across both sides of my ass. I howl as each hit amplifies the burn from the previous one, leaving my skin singed and radiating heat.

"So feisty," Miller chuckles.

I glower at him but stay quiet. He's seen how "feisty" I can get, given the chance.

Laugh now, shithead. While you still can.

"Enough," Gabriel tells Miller. He gives the rope around my body another tug and grunts with satisfaction. "You can go."

"Sure," says Miller. "So long, doll face" he adds, winking at me.

Gabriel waits for the lock to click shut, holding my bindings carefully. "Move," he says at last, nudging me forward. He lays his hand against my back and pushes me along until we reach a long, narrow table.

"Bend over," he orders, pointing at its clean, matte surface. It looks frighteningly cold.

I whine and shimmy, not wanting to comply. Doing so would leave me more exposed and vulnerable than I could bear.

Instead of another hard spanking, Gabriel punishes my hesitation by reaching to my chest and pinching my nipples between his fingers. I'm mortified by how hard they've grown, and Gabriel's touch arcs through my breasts like an electric charge. He squeezes harder until I get the message and bend over the table. Pressed against its surface from nose to navel, I confirm that it is particularly cold.

Fuck you, Gabriel, I think as he loops another cord around my back and the underside of the table, immobilizing me. Silent invective fills my head, but not my heart. It's not letting me forget that a deeply troubled part of me is aching for more.

Even more troubling is the fact that Gabriel is just as excited. Bent over, my eyes are nearly level with the bulge in his suit pants, and my thoughts turn to all the ways he could be about to use it.

Would he put it in my mouth? Or does he assume I would jump at the chance to bite it off? And is that what I would do?

It isn't a question of courage or conviction. Were it Vaughn, I would have no choice but to try to mangle his manhood, no matter the cost. But Gabriel...

"I wish I could have gotten to know you some other way," he says. "Like a normal person. Meet you in a library, strike up a conversation."

This is odd, I think. *Where's he going with this?*

"There's no talking in the library," I reply.

"Too bad. I'd still come talk to you."

"Why's that?"

Gabriel sighs. "Because I think we'd get along. Miller told me about the video. The one with you insulting your boss. It sounds pretty funny."

"It was," I mutter.

Gabriel shakes his head. "Would it still be funny if I told you it convinced Vaughn to take you that night? That he saw it and decided you'd please our boss? If you hadn't said that on TV, you might not be here right now."

"What's your point?"

"Consequences, Marla. You did what you did because you knew some of them, but not all of them. If you'd known you'd end up here because of what you said... but you couldn't have known. My point is, most people can only work with the consequences they can see, and worry about the rest later. You don't even do that. You do what you want, consequences be damned."

He's not wrong, is he?

"So what?" I ask.

"So, from now on, this is the consequence. This is what we'll do to you to correct your behavior. Do you like being forced into this position, Marla?" he asks, rubbing my still-sore backside.

"No, sir," I reply, though I'm not sure I mean it.

"Do you find it undignified?"

"Yes, sir." This I did feel at first, though my distaste for it has dwindled.

"Does it make you want to comply, instead of resisting?" he asks, stepping away to select a flogger from one of the shelves. I recognize it from the time before my solitary confinement started.

"Yes, sir," I lie.

Gabriel doesn't buy it. "I don't believe you. I tried to make this easy, but it didn't work, did it? Solitary confinement didn't break you at all. It didn't quell your rebelliousness. Your resolve is stronger than ever. So now this is going to get really nasty."

My skin tingles. My heart races. The room spins.

"You don't scare me," I whisper. It's only half true. If he meant it when he said he could help me if I trusted him, then he wouldn't want to hurt me badly now. Should I believe him? I want to, but that's the trick: people need to trust. Sometimes we wrestle that instinct into a hole and bury it forever, but it's still there. So I'm scared of what I don't know about Gabriel.

Yet, I quiver in anticipation of what he'll do to me in this place, and I've seen twice already that he's excited about it too. Does that mean we're in sync somehow? Or is it something about Gabriel himself that elicits my reaction? I feel quite confident that I wouldn't have such slick thighs right now if I were alone with Vaughn.

"I don't scare you? Then I guess I'll have to work on that."

Gabriel looks around the room, finding a thick, egg-shaped device.

"Know what this is?"

I nod. "I think so."

He caresses my drenched pussy before he inserts the toy inside. I groan as it slides into my core.

"You devoured it, Marla. Holy shit."

He thumbs a switch on a tiny remote he found with the egg, and immediately the toy begins to vibrate. It's not very powerful, but I jerk in place anyway, stunned by how good it feels in concert with the throb from my spanking. I close my eyes and think about Gabriel holding the control, thumb held down on the button that makes the toy vibrate harder.

It has to have one that vibrates harder...

The impact of the flogger takes me by complete surprise. Gabriel provides no warmup swing, no soft slap to prime me for more. The first hit strikes my bottom hard, and my shriek echoes off the stony walls of the chamber. I stifle it as quickly as I can, but the intense agony leaves me twisting.

"No no no, Marla. The others are going to want to hear you scream. If you keep it in, they'll just keep going until you can't help it anymore. Like this."

The flogger slashes through the air three times, cracking as the lashes scour my rear. When I finish screaming, I moan; when I stop moaning, another series of swats erupts across my cheeks. Gabriel repeats the process again and again. My eyes water and I tell myself it's the sweat dripping down my forehead, but I know the pain is to blame. Even the tiny twinge of ecstasy that follows each flogging can't diminish the overwhelming agony now occupying my entire consciousness.

"If your tolerance for pain improves, all that will do is force me and the others to try harder."

Oh god, please, harder!

The vibration in my pussy mixes with my aches and I feel on the verge of coming.

Gabriel notices my distraction and thumbs the remote control, shutting off the egg. I gasp and twist, furious at the frustration.

"You're enjoying this way too much, Marla."

Maybe he's attempting to sound intimidating, but I pick up on the pity in his voice. The conflict.

I hear Gabriel's footsteps, but have shut my eyes as a way of trying to escape the pain; it does little good. When I open them again, he's standing before me and holding something to my mouth. I'm not such a prude that I don't recognize the thick, black dildo, but I've never seen one attached to a wooden rod before. Gabriel waves it slowly, evenly, like the pendulum of a metronome.

"Open."

I shake my head, though I can't take my eyes off the sex toy.

"Fine. Don't open your mouth. I'll find somewhere else to put this. Your call."

You motherfucker.

"Tick tock, Marla. Make up your mind."

I spit on the floor and buck against my bonds, but give in and open wide. Gabriel eases the cock inward just enough to keep my lips wrapped around it. The taste of rubber grows thicker as I begin to salivate. My mouth had been dry, but now it betrays me, accepting the thick toy, even to the point where I sigh and begin to suck.

"Good, Marla."

My cheeks flush, completely aghast. Glaring up into Gabriel's eyes, I see not the mirth his voice projects, but a fervent desire. I feel the need as well, intoxicated by the physical sensation of being forced into a submissive posture and having to look upward to meet Gabriel's stare. I should have found the act of using my mouth on a toy utterly demeaning, a humiliation so complete I could die of it; yet, doing it for Gabriel gives me a sense of serenity. My abduction, killing Roy, the days of isolation: none of it exists.

"Faster."

I follow Gabriel's directions without thinking.

"Hold it deep."

I choke and gag as its length goes farther than any real man's cock had ever reached. Gabriel withdraws the toy so I can catch my breath, but then presses it against my lips until I take it in again. The surface glistens with my saliva, and a line drips from my lips. My core begs for the toy, and I press my thighs together, trying to relieve myself.

Soon my head bobs in an unbroken rhythm, my tongue dancing along the ribbed rubber phallus, satisfying its imaginary needs. I only stop when Gabriel abruptly pulls the toy out and hurls it across the room. I jerk in my rope as it clatters and rolls a curved path along the floor.

"Not bad. You'll get better." Gabriel takes the remote control out of his pocket and runs his thumb over the various buttons for a second, then sets the control down on a shelf.

I groan, hating my frustration, and my need to come. *Are you serious? After all that, you're not going to fuck me?*

"Eat... shit," I croak, my chest still burning for air.

Gabriel crouches down and whispers into my ear, "I'm working on a plan. Don't let them see you enjoying any part of this." He gets up and presses the side of my face against the table. Voice booming now, he asks, "What was that? One more time, Marla. I still didn't hear you."

"I said, 'Eat shit!'"

He smacks my ass again and again. I wail incessantly, kicking my feet as much as the chain between them will allow. It goes on longer than I can imagine, leaving my rear an inferno of welts and bright red flesh. The egg is still inside my pussy too, and when I feel it, I'm overcome by the wish that maybe it will turn on accidentally and relieve my unsatisfied need.

"Fix that attitude," Gabriel says when he stops. "Or tomorrow's going to get much, much worse."

He grabs a square of white cloth from a shelf and bunches

it up, then pulls it between my teeth. Tying it off behind my head, he gives me one last spanking, then walks away. I press against the gag with my tongue but it doesn't come loose. Wailing at Gabriel I shake and scream, feeling much like I did the last time he left me in such a state. Even his cryptic claim of a plan doesn't assuage my fury.

"Say goodnight, Marla," he says, then the lights go out. The door to the dungeon clangs shut, followed by the electric buzz.

I mouth the clearest *Fuck you!* that I can through the cloth, but he doesn't hear. He's gone.

CHAPTER 11
MARLA

Tears of impotent rage wet my cheeks as I fume over the injustice.

I'm failing at communicating the severity of the situation, so I try again. "But mom, if I miss another rehearsal, they're not going to let me play Titania!"

My mother finishes applying her bold, red lipstick and smooths her clingy, white dress. "I'll call them and sort it out."

I shake my head. "I told you, this is what they said! Calling won't help, I need to be there!"

"And I need a social life, Marley."

I used to like it when she called me that, but I'm 12 and I no longer think of myself as a kid.

I want to protest that this isn't fair, but I know exactly how she'll reply. I've heard it enough times. "Why can't you just call and say you'll be late? You could drop me off, then go meet him." My logic seems more than reasonable.

"He has a reservation. I can't show up forty minutes late."

She's already running behind, but now she's finished getting ready. I follow her through the apartment, into the kitchen. I'm crying steadily, feeling the battle's lost. Titania would be reassigned to someone else. End of story.

My mother's old, tan purse rests on the kitchen table next to an open bottle of wine and a half-finished glass. She almost picks it up to drink the rest, but sees me staring and takes her purse instead.

"It'll be fine, Marley, I promise," she says, opening the front door to leave.

My eyes on the wine, I stop crying. Possessed by an idea so perfect and pure I have no choice but to obey, I pick up the glass.

"Mom."

She turns, and when she's facing me I thrust the glass in her direction, sloshing the wine in an arc that licks the front of her dress and stains it as dark as her lipstick. For a second she doesn't react, as if she can't even process what's happened. Then she drops her purse and shrieks like a banshee.

I wait until she's done. Then I say, "It'll be fine, Mom, I promise."

—

I don't remember falling asleep in the dungeon, but after a couple hours of near-constant struggling I must have given in to exhaustion.

Startled by voices, I wake suddenly. I don't know how long I've been out, but when I wake I'm bathed in the bright light of my cell. I keep my eyes shut, not wanting to give away that I'm up.

As my head clears, I register that I'm lying on my chest, but on the floor, rather than the mattress. Gone are the ropes that bound my arms behind my back, replaced instead by a simple pair of handcuffs — the cloth gag, now sodden, still rests between my teeth. My bottom throbs, an ache that is dull enough to savor fully.

When I realize the voice I hear doesn't belong to Gabriel, I turn over. It's Vaughn, and he's standing above me, straddling me, his legs spread wide.

"Look who's up," he says, smirking. "Have a fun night?"

I don't even think about it. I lift my leg, bent at the knee, then swing my foot straight up. If my ankles had still been cuffed it wouldn't have been possible, but my foot flies in an arc that ends with my shin driving into the softest spot between Vaughn's legs.

Doubled over, arms protecting his lower abdomen, Vaughn howls as spittle sprays through his teeth. Seeing the door to my cell left wide open, I sit up, plant my feet and rise, but I don't make it through: Miller steps into my path, grabs my shoulders and pushes me back into the cell.

I curse, more a grunt than an attempt at words. Miller keeps pressing until I'm backed against the wall, then holds me there. He laughs when he sees Vaughn, who's still fighting back tears.

"Shut... the fuck... up," he seethes, his face a grotesque shade of purple.

Miller shakes his head. "You dumb motherfucker, did you not think that was going to happen? You left yourself wide open."

Vaughn glares at his colleague, then straightens up. More or less recovered, he pushes Miller out of the way, then balls a fist. I'm still caught in the adrenaline high, still reveling at having kicked Vaughn in the nuts, when his fist drives into my solar plexus. In an instant I'm on the floor, coughing and choking, my lungs feeling like popped balloons.

"After last night... I didn't think you'd have... this much fight in you," Vaughn explains, still hurting. "But I bet you didn't... see that coming... either."

Rage boils up inside me and I want to strike out again, but my body is wracked by pain. I try to breathe but inhaling squeezes something that doesn't want to be squeezed.

"Come on," grouses Miller. "We're behind schedule."

What schedule? I think as they lift me to my feet. Vaughn presses me into the wall, hands on my collarbone and hip, though his eyes fell elsewhere. Miller pulls a wheelchair into the cell; on the seat is a fresh straightjacket, which he and Vaughn force me into. Carefully they uncuff my hands, but I have no opening to take another shot before the jacket is secured very, very tightly. I'm still too weakened from the punch.

Did Gabriel see that happen? Is he going to show up, livid at Vaughn? Or is he asleep, unaware of what these two goons are doing?

Soon my body is once again strung up, arms linked around my chest and straps all up my back are buckled. A band is lifted through my legs up as far as it will go, and again I have to fight the unwanted stimulation it creates.

Vaughn dumps me in the wheelchair brusquely, inflaming the throb still lingering in my bottom from the previous day's punishment. I moan as the sensation burns once more, but silence myself when I hear Vaughn's snicker.

A pair of metal braces is fitted around my ankles, locking them to the sides of the chair. This spreads my legs enough that I feel shamefully on display. A heavy, nylon band extends from the back of the seat, crossing my shoulders to buckle me into the wheelchair. The band is even threaded through two cloth rings on the front of my jacket, the purpose of which had left me wondering until now.

There is no possibility of escape, though I comfort myself knowing that they were going to bind me this thoroughly no matter what, so at least I got to take a shot at Vaughn first.

"Go on," Vaughn tells Miller. "I got this."

"Gabriel said to stay."

"Fuck Gabriel. Go. I'm not gonna break any rules. Just gonna drop her off."

Miller regards his colleague for a minute, then shrugs. "Fine. Not my problem."

I don't want to be alone with Vaughn, but Miller isn't exactly a friendly face, so I offer no reaction to their exchange. This could be some kind of test, for that matter, or Vaughn could be looking for an excuse to go a lot farther than a punch to the gut.

Vaughn turns my wheelchair to head deeper into the building while Miller veers off in the other direction, toward the stairs. We're heading to a section of the asylum I've never seen, toward a door at the far end of the corridor. Bright light pours out of a small window in the portal, and I can't help but consider that a bad sign.

"You know, I can't even stay mad at you for kicking me before," Vaughn says. He's pushing the chair along at a leisurely pace, in no hurry. "Really I'd have done the same. And I got you back pretty good there, didn't I?"

I sneer quietly.

"I'm saying we're even, Marla. The least you could do is smile. Maybe thank me."

We are not even close to even, you slimy bag of shit.

"No? We're not speaking? Is that what's going on?" Vaughn pats my shoulder. Even through the jacket, his touch is nauseating.

"That's okay, Marla. Gabriel's not going to have you to himself for much longer. Then you're going to do what I say, when I say it, or you'll wish you did."

Vaughn twists the chair around so I'm facing him. The most I could do now is try to spit in his face, which doesn't seem worth the backlash.

"You know I could kill you, right here, right now?" He reaches a hand into the collar of my jacket and curls his fingers around my neck. I want to bite him, but he grips below my jaw and I can't reach.

"This is all I have to do. You can't fight me. You can't escape. If I did it, Gabriel would be pissed, but what's he going to do? Run crying to... Ha, no. He might take a swing at me, maybe a shot, and maybe he'd come out on top, but I wouldn't bet on it. So really, your life depends on me wanting it to continue. And I do, Marla, because I haven't had any fun with you yet."

He lets go, and I gasp, desperate for oxygen.

"The next time you entertain some fantasy about escaping or injuring me, remember how easily I could end you at any moment." He grabs a fold of fabric from my jacket with one hand, and the armrest of the wheelchair with another. "This is how it's going to be from now on. There's not going to be any more mistakes with you."

"We'll see." My voice is barely a wheeze, but in the quiet hall it carries clearly.

Vaughn laughs. "You're about to."

What?

As he pushes me the rest of the way to our destination I suspect something horrible is going to happen. Vaughn's excitement instills a vicious gnawing in the pit of my stomach. I'm on the verge of throwing up when he buzzes us through the door.

Horror movie circus fun houses, haunted mansions and witches' hovels flash through my mind: spinning saw blades, red-eyed rats in cages and disfigured dolls. What meets me is as far from what I pictured as possible, and yet also somehow worse.

Before me is a wide open room brightly lit by banks of fluorescent bulbs. Sitting serenely on worn maroon couches and recliners are maybe a dozen women. As my eyes scan across them, I see immediately that they're quite attractive, though they wear blank, absent expressions. Some have on straightjackets like me, but a couple are dressed in t-shirts and pajama bottoms.

Only one of the women turns to look as we enter the room. Her face crumbles when she sees us, looking as sick as I feel, a tear rolling down her cheek.

Some cartoon plays on a TV that most of the women are facing, though they don't seem to be watching.

In case the room couldn't get more dispiriting, I notice the walls on one side are broken up by a pair of windows, but there's nothing on the other side of them. Are they real, or boarded up? I can't tell, but my heart sinks, desperate for a glance of the outside world.

How long has it been? Just days, in truth, though it feels like much more.

"Marla, meet your new friends."

"What's wrong with them?" I growl at Vaughn. "Are you drugging them?"

Vaughn laughs. "We don't have to. They've learned to behave. Someday you will too."

Good god. What if he's right?

I wouldn't be as afraid if they had one or two women in this room, but I count 11, all docile and broken. Quiet, still as statues.

"All right, Marla, I'm leaving," Vaughn says. He takes hold of my chin and forces me to look at him. "Pay attention while you're here. Maybe you'll catch on a little faster."

He winks, then pats my head.

I hope you die painfully, motherfucker.

I cannot believe how many other women are here. Did he abduct all of them? How long has it been since they were taken? None of them appear much older than me, and a few are younger.

As I take in the scene, the girl who reacted to our arrival wheels herself toward me. She's bound in her seat, but isn't wearing a jacket; she can't lift her hands, but she can nudge the wheels of her chair to move.

"You're her. The new one," she says.

"Yeah." I'm speechless. What have these women been through?

"I'm Helena. You must have a lot of questions."

"Marla." She's right: there are a million things I want to know. "Was Vaughn telling the truth? Are they really not on any drugs?"

"I don't think so. I've never been given any. I've never seen the others get any either."

For a while, I stare at a redhead who isn't bound. She's staring at the tan, linoleum floor. "Do they ever try to get out?"

Helena shakes her left wrist, the one with her security bracelet. I'd forgotten I was even wearing mine: for most of the last few days I couldn't even see my own hands.

"They do as they're told." Helena starts to cry. "You'll see. It's that or…"

"Hey," I say, not too loudly but enough to stop Helena. "I'm going to find a way out. No matter what I have to do."

Helena smiles sadly and shakes her head. "It's impossible. I'm sorry, but it is. I've been here for a year, at least."

Wait a minute. Is this…?

"Helena… Is your name Helena… Bloom?"

The girl's eyes widen, then fall. She wilts in her wheelchair like a rose cut from its stem.

"Are you from Cline University too?"

"No. But I worked for a news station, I know the story." I tell her what I remember: a year ago, college senior Helena Bloom disappeared following a political protest at her college. At first, they thought she was one of a handful of students arrested, but no one could account for her whereabouts. An ATM camera picked up a man who looked to be walking her home, but it was night time and the footage wasn't clear enough to pinpoint a suspect. With no additional leads, the investigation was suspended after six months.

"I'm so sorry," I add. "Was it Vaughn?"

Helena nods. "I met him at a party. He seemed nice."

"Yeah. He's a fucking psychopath."

Helena looks back and forth nervously, shrinking in fear. "They can hear you."

I laugh. Poor girl, she must think I'm utterly insane. "It doesn't matter what I say, trust me."

Pulling her tires backward, Helena scoots her chair away from me. I can't blame her for being afraid, but I can tell her something that might help. "You know Vaughn. What about Gabriel?"

Helena stops. She doesn't look at me, but nods.

"You know Mr. Miller?"

"Yeah…"

"And Mr. Roy?"

Confused, she replies, "Yeah, but they said he doesn't work here anymore."

I laugh. "That's what they told you?" I scan the room, finding the closest camera and looking into it. "Roy's dead. And I nearly escaped."

Helena resumes wheeling herself away. "No."

"Yes. And when I get out of here, you're all leaving with me."

CHAPTER 12
HALLORAN

"It was a momentary lapse," says Vaughn.

It's not the first time I've heard that excuse.

I haven't run anywhere in years, and the pain in my joints flares as I sprint down the hall. There was no time to wait. Already I can hear her screams.

"Vaughn, stop!" I bellow as I reach the open cell door.

When he looks at me, I see in his face a pain and emptiness so profound I can't imagine wanting to live with it for another minute.

"I'm sorry," he says to me, then looks down at her. "Oh god, I'm sorry. I'm so sorry. I didn't mean to... I couldn't help..."

"Shut the fuck up," I spit. "Is she alive?"

Vaughn nods.

"Call Gabriel. Tell him to bring a first aid kit. Then go get a gurney."

He nods again but doesn't move.

"Now!"

Gabriel is going to blame me for this, *I realize.* And he'll be right.

As I watch the pool of blood spread across the floor, I watch the shallow rise and fall of her chest. My fists clench as I realize that Gabriel is never, ever going to forgive me.

"Trust me, sir. It won't happen again."

I nod, returning to the moment. "She got you good. I know you're not going to forget it."

Vaughn sighs. I called for him to meet with me, but not to discuss his incident from the morning. He messed up, but not too badly, and he got what he got right away. No need to add insult, but I wouldn't be a responsible authority if I didn't dress him down a little. Just enough to keep him cognizant of what happens when one relaxes their guard.

You'd think Mr. Roy's recent fate would be enough.

"She's a real fighter though. She took your punch pretty well, all things considered."

Vaughn shifts in his seat uncomfortably. "I couldn't-"

I wave off his protest. "I'm not criticizing you for that. You kept away from her face, so, in fact, I thought you handled that pretty well. And you stayed within the parameters of your instruction. All I need is Gabriel having a fit because you took it too far. Again."

Vaughn nods, but darkens. I don't have to guess which part of that bothered him the most. He misses Iris too. It's perhaps the one thing he and Gabriel have in common.

"I want your opinion on Gabriel's work with Marla," I say, changing the subject. "Be honest."

Clearing his throat, Vaughn sits up and checks the monitor. Marla is where he left her: locked in her jacket and chair, watching the women around her. Most of them stare at the television disinterestedly, but some steal glances at the new inmate. Do they believe Marla's claim about killing Mr. Roy? I assume most are past caring, but Marla's too much of a wild card to discount.

It's good that I don't mind watching her very, very carefully.

"Well," Vaughn says at last. "I mean, I'm not an expert in psychology, but I know what solitary confinement does to people. I was as surprised as him that it didn't really help."

"I agree. What did you think of last night's session?"

Vaughn licks his lips. "Good times all around, right?"

I chuckle. "You think so? That wasn't too much for

Marla?"

Nostrils flaring, Vaughn snorts. "Fuck no. He could go twice as hard on that cunt, she'd still deserve every bit of it."

Though I understand his resentment, that's not what I asked. "Forget what she deserves. How much do you think she can take?"

Vaughn works his jaw like he's chewing. "Why does it matter? It hasn't been an issue in the past."

That's a fair question. "I think you, Gabriel and I recognize Marla as a unique case. I'm concerned that Gabriel is afraid of going too far in his treatment. Breaking her could require a level of intensity he's not mentally prepared for."

Vaughn sees through my euphemism. "Intensity?" he repeats.

"Cruelty."

"But that's no problem for me," Vaughn grumbles. "Because I'm a-"

"Stop, Vaughn," I interrupt. "Yes, because you have an inherent meanness that Gabriel does not. I know, I have it too. You and I are much more alike in that regard. And that is why I wanted to gauge your interest in taking over Marla's training."

Perking up, Vaughn grins like a kid. "For real?"

I hold up a finger. "Only if Gabriel can't get the job done. I promised him he would be in charge of Marla, but I'm only willing to let that go so far. He has to show me results."

Slumping back in his seat, Vaughn reclines until the chair's front legs lift off the ground and he's balanced in the air. "Fuck that. Why should he get her to himself? Why would you make such a stupid promise?"

"Because of you, Vaughn!" I thunder. "After Iris, I promised him no more women, and it upsets me that now the credibility of my word is hanging by a thread."

Vaughn rolls his eyes, though he turns away so I barely see it. "You still care what he thinks of you?"

I nod grimly. "Yes, Vaughn. I do." I exhale a deep breath and turn my attention to the monitor. "I get why you did it though. She's definitely somebody I would have told you to grab, had I known about her. You have a good instinct."

"Thanks," Vaughn says. Relief and a hint of pride soften his features, though he forces a solemn expression. "I promise, if you give me Marla, you won't be disappointed. I'll do whatever it takes to get her under control."

"I know. And I'll tell you what: Gabriel's going to have to prove he's making some progress. Tonight, in fact. Let's set up an impromptu exhibition."

Vaughn rises out of his seat, practically jumping. "Sure, no problem."

I pick up the phone and dial Gabriel's extension while Vaughn watches.

After two rings, Gabriel answers. "What is it?" he asks, voice groggy.

"I've decided to hold an exhibition tonight. Vaughn will be driving to Ravenswood right away to make arrangements. I need you to prepare Marla."

"No, she's not ready," he protests.

"Make her ready."

I hang up and smile at Vaughn. "I know it's short notice, but get everyone you can. Tell them we've got a fresh face."

CHAPTER 13
MARLA

The commotion starts when Vaughn and Miller arrive, grab Amber and Svetlana, the two women not bound, and leave. It's been a couple hours since Miller came to feed us dinner, and since then I've had nothing to do but watch the other women. After hours of begging from across the room, Helena told me their names, and I spent the entire afternoon memorizing them. But Helena refused to tell me anything else, fearful of the repercussions. I decided not to hold it against her, not after seeing what this place does to women like us.

But now I need answers. "What's going on?" I ask out loud, hoping somebody will respond.

By the time Helena wheels her way back to me, Vaughn and Miller have already returned, this time taking Lexie and Maribel.

"It's too early," says Helena. "It's not time for bed yet."

For the life of me I don't know how she can tell time in here, but I take her at her word. "What does that mean?"

Helena moans softly, shaking her head. "It's normal for one man to come in and take one of us... sometimes two of us... But for both of them to show up together... and they were in a hurry..."

I cringe when she says that taking the women is *normal* but I put that anger away for later. I expect I'll need it. "What?" I repeat. "What is it?"

The answer comes from Noriko, from her seat on the couch. "Showtime," she says, bristling in her straightjacket. She fights against it for a moment, then slides down the cushion until she's almost on the floor.

"What?"

"An exhibition," Helena says at last. "It's happened six times since I've been here. This is how they always start."

"Sweetheart, don't give away the surprise," Vaughn says. He and Miller are back for the next round.

Vaughn retrieves from his pocket a black ball with two black bands sticking out the sides of it. "No talking," he says, then shoves the gag into Helena's mouth. She screams and shakes her head, but Vaughn stays with her, pulling the bands together and buckling them behind her neck. "Look on the bright side, Helena. You're not the new girl anymore."

Her shriek ends in a sob as Vaughn wheels her away, followed by Miller and Noriko, leaving me practically alone. I wait and watch as the men come back for Fiona, Bryn, Karina, Kelly and Elise, and then I'm truly by myself. For a while I wonder if I'm not to be included in whatever is going on, but I'm not optimistic enough to believe it.

I shudder when the door opens one last time, but I sigh in relief when Gabriel kneels down in front of me.

"This is very important Marla, so listen to me."

I nod, swallowing down a surge of bile that stings my throat.

"You're really not going to like what's about to happen. I wish there was more I could do. I'm going to have to hurt you tonight, and you may not like it."

A burning rages in my chest, and an ache gathers between my thighs. I groan, attempting to deny the swelling need I feel. I should be scared, but I'm not. Not as long as Gabriel will be there.

"Marla, seriously, this is going to suck. That instinct you

have to fight us — you're going to feel it all night long. But you'll be helpless to stop anything that's happening, which will make it even harder for you to witness."

"So what am I supposed to do?"

He squeezes my shoulder through my jacket. "All eyes will be on you tonight. If you act out, you really won't like the consequences, and nor will I. So help us both and do as I say."

I nod, chills spreading out from my chest to my fingers and toes. Why won't he like the consequences? That worries me.

"What are you going to do?"

"I can't say any more."

Right. He's always watching. Whoever he is.

But I appreciate that Gabriel is trying to warn me about what's coming. It feels like he may have taken a risk to do so.

"Gabriel? Can I ask you a question?"

He looks around the room, then nods.

"The day Vaughn brought me here, you acted as though you hate him. I know why I hate him, but what did he do to you?"

Gabriel doesn't answer right away. His eyes grow distant, and for a moment I swear he's fighting back tears.

"Vaughn took something from me," Gabriel eventually answers. "And he'll never be able to give it back."

"What does that mean?"

Instead of answering, Gabriel kisses my forehead. "I'll tell you another time."

Maybe he's not ready, I figure. *Or maybe he thinks the answer will piss me off when he needs me to be calm.*

He wheels me out of the common area and through the building, past the cell block and to the lobby, where he calls us an elevator. In silence we ride up to the third floor, which I've not yet seen. I hear classical music playing through small speaker boxes hanging from the wall a few hundred feet apart.

We arrive upon a sight so bizarre I nearly laugh: Miller applying pink lipstick to Elise, who stands on a round, brown pedestal, her hands chained above her head. She wears a white bikini that emphasizes her waifish figure. She looks cold, but she lets Miller paint her lips without complaint.

Miller sees us enter the room and my bemused expression. He dumps the lipstick in a thick black suitcase and shows me the contents: mascara, foundation, concealer, gloss, nail polish and lots of creams and balms. "This was Roy's job. Now it's mine. Thanks a lot, bitch."

"Want a tip?" I ask. "Try some on yourself, but not too much. A little goes a long way on someone ugly as you."

Miller drops the case like a hot iron and shambles toward me. Gabriel quickly circles around to get between us.

"Get back to work," Gabriel orders, voice soft but no less authoritative. "Or you'll be watching the action from your room tonight."

Fist balled, Miller hesitates, weighing his options. He backs off. "All right, Gabriel. I will. You see to your girlfriend, while she's still yours."

"What's that supposed to mean?" replies Gabriel.

Miller doesn't answer him. Instead, he steps aside and blows me a kiss, then grabs the case of cosmetics. Elise must be done, because he moves onto Amber, who kneels on another pedestal.

Taking in the rest of the room, I see all of the women have been brought up and secured to pedestals in some way. Some stand, others kneel. Spotlights shine on each woman, making them practically glow against the dim surroundings. They look frightened or at least apprehensive, but not surprised by anything. If Helena's to be believed, they've been through it before. Helena herself is crying, still gagged, as she sways back and forth, her arms pulled so high up over her head that her toes barely find purchase.

Gabriel was right. This is awful. All I want to do is plunge a hot knife into Vaughn and Miller's chest and carve out their hearts. I want to shove lit sticks of dynamite down their throats. I want to kill them so painfully their screams echo over the mountains for hundreds of miles.

I close my eyes and force myself to calm down. Gabriel warned me it would be like this, which he didn't have to do.

Even if he did it to suit his own objectives, I feel certain I'd prefer his goals to Vaughn's or Miller's.

When my breathing steadies and my heart stops palpitating, I take in the rest of the room, which is some kind of old-fashioned, ornate ballroom. It's wide open, easily the largest room I've seen throughout the asylum, and it has three entrances. Rich, velvety black draperies line the walls between big, wide windows that draw my eyes immediately. It's night out, and the light of the hall is reflected in their surface, but they're windows nonetheless.

Possible way out? A security bracelet won't stop me from going through that glass, but we are on the third floor. I file the thought away as a "maybe."

"I have to get my things," Gabriel says as he wheels me toward the last pedestal. "I'll be back as soon as I can." He leans in close to whisper. "I will do everything in my power not to let anyone hurt you tonight, but I can't promise it won't happen. Help me help you, Marla. Help me get you through this night."

He doesn't give me a chance to reply. His swift footsteps clip the hardwood floor of the ballroom, leaving me to stare at the other women and wait for Miller to come do my makeup.

Before he gets here, though, someone else approaches. "Hi Marla," he says. "Ready for your big night?"

It's Vaughn. He comes into view, and like Miller, I'm stunned enough by his appearance to laugh. Wearing a white apron and toque, he smells of baking bread and garlic.

"Was that Roy's job too?" I ask, hoping speaking would disguise the rumble of my stomach. The thought of fresh bread torments me as badly as a whipping right now, and I hate that it's Vaughn I'm smelling it on. If I end up associating him with the aroma, I'll never smell it again without feeling ill.

Vaughn chuckles. "Roy couldn't cook for shit. It's always been a hobby of mine though." Taking hold of my wheelchair, Vaughn pushes me away from the empty pedestal and toward one of the windows. "I thought you might want to see this, Marla." He positions me so I can look out of them, then walks away. After a moment the ambient lighting in the room, which was already quite low, fades out completely, allowing me to see outside. However, there's nothing visible. Neither moon nor stars cast a gleam on the surrounding world. I assume clouds have obscured them, though I worry my mind is playing tricks on me, and we were in a basement, rather than the third floor.

"Do me a favor and give a shout when you see them," says Vaughn.

"Them?"

"It'll be obvious, cupcake."

I turn to look, hoping a break in the clouds will let the starlight through. I keep watching, and after a few minutes I see what Vaughn meant: little bright lights twinkling. They're low to the ground, and disappear for long stretches; when they return, they seem closer.

They're headlights. Lots of them.

I think about remaining quiet, but remember Gabriel's warning.

"Vaughn!" I call out. "I see them."

The beams of at least three vehicles bounce off the trees as the cars navigate the windy road toward the asylum. In the complete darkness the drivers are taking it slow, and I wonder if it's snowed at all in the past several days.

I allow myself a moment to fantasize that the headlights belong to a task force of police and FBI, whose lengthy investigation into the disappearances of several women has finally turned up their location. But I know it's nonsense: whoever is in those cars, they're expected.

Vaughn returns from the kitchen holding what looks like a stuffed mushroom. I can't stop eyeballing it, jaw hanging open.

"Mmm, that's the way a whore presents her mouth, you know," Vaughn taunts. He looks at the appetizer in his palm. "Tell you what: you can have this if you suck my cock."

I snarl and look away. "I've lost my appetite."

"Whatever," Vaughn replies, his voice muffled by chewing.

"What are you doing?" says Gabriel.

I softly gasp when I see him. Instead of his usual khakis,

button-down shirt and lab coat, he's wearing a full suit. The black jacket and pants contrast starkly with the crisp white shirt underneath, as well as the gorgeous, striped silver tie hanging down his chest. He looks absolutely heart-stopping, especially thanks to the intense hatred in his eyes. As he stares at Vaughn, his glare could burn a hole through a block of steel.

"Nothing. Relax," replies Vaughn, unintimidated. "Good luck tonight."

"What the fuck…" Gabriel whispers.

I agree. Vaughn is having too much fun. I'd like to think it's just the party being thrown, but dread sinks into my skin and tightens in my chest. I breathe slowly, trying to stay calm.

"Hey." Gabriel pulls me away from the window and begins unlocking the restraints on my wheelchair. He moves his hand down the sleeve of my jacket until he finds my hand and holds it a moment. "Remember what I said." He clears his throat, then pulls me out of the chair by the collar of my jacket. "Move it," he commands, voice booming.

My feet explode in pins and needles and I nearly fall, but Gabriel's grip keeps me standing. He practically drags me back to the pedestal, where Miller is waiting.

"I swear, Marla," warns Gabriel. "If you try something now, I will dig a hole in the ground and leave you there for a month."

"Yes, sir," I reply. I say it mechanically, injecting a slight hint of defiance. I'm not sure exactly what Gabriel needs from my behavior, so I walk a fine line. I can't offer too much resistance, but I expect a sharp swing into total obeisance would raise suspicion.

Together, Miller and Gabriel remove my jacket. I've grown used to the process, and the relief I feel whenever the stifling coat is taken away. As they work, Vaughn comes in from the kitchen with a large, plastic basin full of water. He sets it down, stares for a moment at my nakedness, getting a good look, then leaves again.

The men lower me to the ground. Miller holds my neck in one hand and both my wrists in the other. I moan as the icy floor chills my entire body, but after a minute Gabriel has tied my hands with rope and Miller lets me stand up. He still holds my shoulders, in case I try to run.

Gabriel retrieves a pair of white cotton panties from his kit and holds them at my feet so I can step into them. I'm surprised at how plain they look: I would have expected a thong or some kind of skimpy lingerie. Regardless, I'm glad not to be the only fully nude woman here. I don't expect that to last long, but for the moment it's nice.

Gabriel isn't finished, though: when I look again he's holding a plain white cloth. He folds it into a long strip, then ties it across my chest. The fabric is thin but soft; my hardened nipples poke through it, and for a second I almost smile, enjoying Gabriel's touch.

"Get on the pedestal," he orders. I moan as I climb up, careful to avoid a handful of metal rings sticking up through slits in the pedestal coverings. When I'm up, he adds, "Spread your legs."

I comply, letting him tie each ankle to the metal rings. When he's done, my feet are bound as far apart as possible while still allowing me to stand upright. He finishes my bindings by knotting a length of rope into the cords securing my wrists, then tying off the other end to a pedestal ring. Unable to pull my hands upward, or move my feet at all, I'm forced to stand still and wait. The thought makes me shiver, and soon I feel the crotch of my panties growing damp. Wishing I could close my legs, I pray nobody notices.

From my position facing the inside of the building, I can no longer see out the window. However, the cars' high beams pour through as the vehicles arrive, casting horrific shadows along the high walls and draperies of the ballroom.

Time stretches as the muffled sound of car doors becomes a din of male voices. I try not to look at the entrance when the double doors swing open, but I can't help glancing over. I see Gabriel approaching with seven men I don't recognize. They range in age, the youngest appearing to be as young as me, while the eldest is old enough to walk with a cane. They wear impeccable suits, no doubt bespoke, and chatter softly with easy camaraderie.

My stomach turns as I'm reminded of the night I met Vaughn. If some of these men offered to buy me a drink at a bar, I would have no doubt accepted, not knowing of the evil that lurks.

Leading the group is a man who appears to be in his late sixties, and as they fill into the center of the ballroom I hear his voice. It's the one from the intercom. The boss. He's staring right at me, pointing me out to the assembly.

Even in the relative darkness I can see this man is extraordinarily pale, but a shock of white hair covers most of his scalp and he moves gracefully. He smiles proudly as he speaks, but in his eyes I see a wolf. Though old, he leads the pack, and they are very, very hungry.

He holds up one finger and laughs at something, then turns to me. As he approaches, Vaughn and Miller burst out of the kitchen bearing trays of hors d'oeuvres.

"Hello, Marla. I'm Montgomery Halloran."

CHAPTER 14
MARLA

Halloran leans in and kisses my cheek, making me retch a little. "In a few minutes you're going to perform for us, but I wanted to introduce myself first."

His voice sounds much softer in person, and I recognize his attempt at affecting a disarming tone. "Mr. Halloran," I say, refusing to lift my gaze.

"I'll give you one piece of advice, Ms. Angel. I know you hate me, and that what you did to Roy was merciful compared to what you'd do to me."

You got that right.

"But it's not going to happen. I fucking own you. I own this place and everything inside it, including Gabriel, and Vaughn and the girls. I spent half my life building this place into what it is now, and if I think for a second you pose a threat to it, I will have Vaughn drag your ass into the woods and shoot you."

I feel the pounding in my chest as my blood turns to slush.

"As much as I'm looking forward to making you my personal fucktoy, you are not worth the risk."

"Yes, sir," I say, and for once I'm not struggling to stifle my invective. I am too inclined to believe this man's threats. I may want to kill him, but I can't bring myself to say it to his face. My cheeks burn. I'm ashamed of my cowardice.

It feels like a month ago, but it was just this morning that I gave Vaughn a good, hard shot to the testicles, and now I'm practically cowering in fear. What is it about Halloran that my bravado has vanished? Or is his warning simply compounding that which I've seen and heard to this point and making it all that much more terrifying?

"Halloran, come on, introduce us." The question comes from one of the guests, a friendly-looking, middle-aged man with a slight paunch.

"All right." Halloran straightens up and pats me on the forehead. "Gentlemen, I presume Vaughn sent you the video?"

The men laugh quietly. I fight to keep my expression passive, swallowing my rage.

"In that case, here she is: Marla Angel." Halloran grabs my hair and pulls my head back, allowing the spotlight to illuminate my face.

"Bet your boss wishes he could see you now, huh?" jokes one of the men.

Fuck you. Gerald's a jerk, not a monster.

"How long have you had her?" asks another.

"About a week," says Halloran as he pushes aside stray hairs that have fallen in front of my face. "She's still new and has much to learn."

The men collectively grumble and groan when they hear this, though I'm not sure why.

"Now now, don't worry." Halloran lets me go and strides toward the group. "I know you'd like a crack at her, but I didn't bring you out here for nothing."

"Then why did you?" asks the joker from before, the youngest of the group. Despite his quality apparel, his hair is grown overly long and wild, hanging down his back unevenly. He's wearing sneakers instead of dress shoes, and his collar's unbuttoned underneath his loose, red tie.

"Three reasons, actually. First of all, my eleven other patients need your help..." He grins. "It's time they participated in a fresh round of experimental treatments."

Halloran pauses as the guests chuckle at his euphemisms. The sound rakes at my ears like claws scraping across bone.

"Second, is to show off Marla in the hopes that you'll spread the word to the members who didn't make it out here on such short notice. And third is to show you that our hiatus is over. Halloran Asylum is open for business."

Raucous applause erupts at Halloran's last declaration, with several men stepping forward to shake his hands. I could have collapsed on the spot, but as he speaks I make eye contact with Gabriel across the room. The fury on his face could have melted a glacier. Yet, Gabriel trades it in for a smile when Halloran calls him over.

"Gabriel here is tending to Marla's training. I have great confidence that when he's done, she'll be as pliant and servile as the rest of our stock."

How Gabriel can exchange pleasant greetings with these scumbags, I'll never understand, but he goes around, shaking their hands, clapping their shoulders and laughing at small talk until they've all met.

"Are you guys ready to see the patient's progress?" he asks, stroking back my hair. The men hoot and clap in answer. "All right, let's begin."

With perfect timing, Vaughn and Miller appear with four folding chairs apiece. Halloran, Vaughn and the guests each take one and sit, ready for a show.

Gabriel doesn't waste any time: as soon as the party's attention is on us, he slips his fingers through the waistband of my panties and pulls them down. With my legs spread they don't go far, but Gabriel is content to leave them stretched between my thighs.

Halloran's speech to the guests disgusted me, turning me off, but now Gabriel's touch renews my need.

Though I'm already bound, he ties a length of rope around my waist, pulling it tight until it digs into my sides. A length of rope is left hanging in front, but he draws the cord up between my legs, sliding it between my thighs until it's parting my slick folds. I moan as he ties it off behind my back, keeping it in place. It hurts, but the pressure it exerts on my clit makes me tingle with desire.

At first I wonder why he didn't do this before, but when I look at the guests, they are watching Gabriel as if hypnotized.

With the new rope in place, he smacks my rear with his bare hand. My breath catches in my throat, then I moan and buck against the rope holding me in place, eliciting a few excited murmurs from the audience.

"It sounds like you've seen Marla's infamous video," Gabriel says to them. A few of them chuckle, while others nod. "I think I'm the only one here who hasn't."

Gabriel runs two of his fingers along my exposed entrance, rubbing back and forth with enough pressure to make me moan. "I'm feeling left out. Marla, what was it you called your boss that day?"

My mind goes blank; I can't concentrate. Closing my eyes shuts out the revolting stare of the audience, and I can imagine I'm alone with Gabriel. I quiver in my bonds, feeling his probing fingers.

Then I cry out as Gabriel spanks my backside again. "Answer me, Marla. What did you say?"

I pull myself together long enough to stammer, "A spineless... dickless... bureaucrat."

Gabriel *tsk tsks*, shaking his head. "On live television! You're lucky your boss isn't one of these guys here."

If Gabriel's trying to butter up the spectators, it's working. They're smiling as Gabriel picks out a long, black leather paddle and strikes it against my bottom. The toy is so long it catches both cheeks, fully across, letting out a booming crack that echoes through the ballroom. The pain nearly knocks me down, but I keep my balance, whining and mewling.

"It's a shame your boss can't see you now, helpless and suffering. We'll just have to enjoy it on his behalf. Now, I'm going to give you the punishment you deserve. You will count each stroke, and thank me for each one." His hand closes around my throat and forces my chin up until he's staring into my eyes. "Is that going to be a problem?"

"No, sir," I croak, shaking my head so slightly it couldn't be seen, only felt by Gabriel.

The first hit is so hard I'm propelled forward, and would have fallen off the pedestal if not for the ropes keeping me in place. "One," I moan after the intense agony subsides.

"What was that?"

I hear his disapproval, but I can't process why for a second. It's taking all of my will to bite back the pain, but also the arousal growing with each word and touch.

"You forgot to thank me," he explains, landing another hard smack.

"Two! Thank you, sir!" I scream.

"Better. Don't forget again, or we start over from one."

Trusting his threat, I focus completely on answering Gabriel properly after each swing, eroding my ability to block the pain. I feel like the center of a rope during a tug-of-war. Counting each hit of the paddle, and then thanking Gabriel for it, rides against my every instinct for resistance. A few days ago I would have gladly taken any discipline he could dish out and still spit in his face after.

However, with no choice but to let the pain wash over me, I experience a bizarre sense of freedom. I have no control over the situation, but I only have one responsibility: count, and say "Thank you, sir." As we go, obeying Gabriel leaves my pussy wetter and wetter, as I notice the animal hunger on his face. He's getting off from this too. I don't know what kind of freaks that makes us, but I feel the connection: neither of us wants to be doing this here, in front of these monsters, and yet we are enjoying ourselves.

"Twenty... thank you... sir," I say, and only then realize that I had become lost in the act. My mind hadn't fully been present, and that actually dulled the pain somewhat. Now it comes rushing back, making me whimper as heat radiates off my flesh.

Gabriel massages my tormented cheeks, then unties the band of cloth holding my breasts. A few of the men snicker as my chest is revealed, and the degradation burns me. If not for Gabriel, I no doubt would have said something regrettable.

He ties a thick, round knot into the cloth's center, then pulls it into my open mouth. I moan but don't fight as he ties off the cloth. It tastes of cheap laundry detergent, but I figure that means it's clean, at least.

Reaching into his jacket pocket, Gabriel looks at my bare chest. He retrieves a long, thin chain with two clamps at the end. "Prove to me you can be good, Marla, and I'll do something nice for you."

He takes my first breast into his hand and attaches one of the clamps to my nipple. It bites down tightly on the tender skin, but I force myself to breathe instead of screaming.

"Good, Marla."

He smiles at me, then attaches the second clamp. He keeps the chain connecting them hooked with his index finger, and tugs on it gently, lifting my breasts. The pain spirals through me like two corkscrews, but I still refuse to cry out.

"Excellent, Marla."

His fingers move toward my sopping pussy, working past the rope tied through it, penetrating my entrance just deep enough to make me tremble.

"Whether Marla knows it or not, she was born to be a slave," he tells the audience. He withdraws his fingers and shows it to the guests; in the spotlight, my fluids glisten as they drip down to his palm. "When she's learned her place, she'll be unbelievably fun to play with. Isn't that right, Marla?"

Head hanging low, I don't reply. Tears stream down my face. *Did he have to show them my wetness?* It feels like a betrayal. I try to convince myself that he did it in the name of protecting me, but the humiliation is more than I can stand.

"Marla, I didn't hear you."

I shake my head, fed up with Gabriel. Whether or not he's doing what he must to help, I can't deal with any more right now.

"This is what I'm talking about, gentlemen. She's tough, physically and mentally, but she's not received enough training.

Resilience takes time to develop."

Looking up, I see the men nod in agreement, and then I see the lashes of the flogger flying at me. I turn away, but they weren't aimed at my face: they land lower. Pain surges in my breasts as one slap after another nails my chest. I howl, my head swinging back and forth, as if that could help me escape the punishment. Each hit causes the nipple clamps to tug a little, further amplifying the torment.

As the flogging continues I feel like an animal being pushed toward the edge of a cliff, unable to stop. As the abyss draws closer, I suddenly cry out as Gabriel rips the nipple clamps off; I would have thought this would ease the pain, but as feeling returns to my tortured nips, they only hurt more.

I start to cry, feeling as though I've fallen off the side and I'm plummeting through the air.

"Look at me, Marla."

Suppressing my tears, I obey. It's as if he's reached out his hand and caught mine before I could hit the ground. *Hold on to me*, his eyes seem to say.

Gabriel is standing back a few feet, but close enough that he can still reach my chest with the lashes. He holds the hilt of the flogger in the air, pointed at me; his other hand he has bent around his back; his stance reminds me of a fencer ready for a bout.

"Thank our guests for coming tonight."

Not giving me a chance to express my repulsion or defiance, Gabriel shoots me a face that says *Do this, or else*. I've never seen such urgency in his expression. It's more than dominance; it's his own fear.

"Thanks... th-thank you... s-sirs," I say, stuttering through the cloth gag.

Gabriel drops the flogger and steps up to me. He reveals to me his other hand, which clutches the base of a long, white wand. It's a vibrating massager, one I'm familiar with. He presses it against my clit and flicks on the power, sending an intense sensation directly into my core. Immediately my pleasure centers explode like fireworks; my gasp bursts into a moan that doesn't cease until my lungs are empty.

My knees shake and I bite down hard on the cloth in my mouth. After a week of resisting climaxing because I didn't want it to be observed, I am now on the verge of an orgasm so powerful I could pass out.

"Don't come until I tell you to," orders Gabriel.

I moan furiously, trying to hold back the pressure. I'm torn between wanting to twist my hips away from the vibrating toy, or press myself harder against it, even though Gabriel keeps it tight against me. To increase the challenge, he extends his middle and index fingers, plunging them into my depths.

Begging Gabriel silently, I watch him as my need expands until it's encompassed me entirely. I tug at the ropes binding my wrists, testing their unbreakable hold, and breathe through the knot of fabric in my mouth. My hips shake of their own accord, and all I can think about is holding back the coming wave.

Maybe he sees my strength dwindling away for good, or perhaps a timer in his mind has counted to zero, but at last Gabriel says, "All right, Marla. You can come."

Euphoria explodes through my body like a chain reaction, swelling from my core and arcing outward until I feel it everywhere. My scream rings out, and I shake violently as the sensation overwhelms me. Gabriel keeps the wand lodged against my clit and pulls at the rope tied into my crotch, adding that extra dose of pain to my orgasm. I buck and squeal but he's a rock, and holds steady.

As much as I hate the stares of the audience — especially Halloran — I've never felt such ecstasy in my life. Maybe I needed the relief after a week of captivity and sexual frustration, or I could have been intuiting that my orgasm would end the demonstration. Next I know, the men have gotten up and are enjoying appetizers provided by Miller and Vaughn.

"You did well," Gabriel whispers in my ear. "Try to relax. I'll be back as soon as possible."

I nod, though I'm barely even aware of him. My heart still

races, and I tingle all over. My legs ache from standing spread, and my ass burns from the assortment of welts.

Regaining my composure takes a few minutes, but when the fog lifts, I see the guests are toying with the other women. A few are missing, and as I watch I see the oldest of the guests leaving with Svetlana. They exit out the opposite door of the one where I came in, and I don't know where it leads. Yet, I know nothing good is going to happen to Svetlana while she's with him.

Making their selections takes the guests half an hour, as the men argue over who gets to choose first. One of them even took two girls, Kelly and Bryn. I struggle not to vomit as Vaughn nabs Helena, and when I look again Miller is leading away Lexie.

Wherever they're going, it must be close, because soon I can hear a quiet orchestra of screams, slaps and groans. A cruel laugh pierces through the din from time to time, and each one infuriates me to the point that I could sob.

With none of the men present to see me, I nearly cry, but I hold it back. I want to weep openly and let it out, but I catch the stare of Maribel, the one woman left beside me. Bound and helpless, the only thing I can do now is offer her my strength.

They haven't broken me. There's still hope for us. Please believe me.

CHAPTER 15
MARLA

I've lost track of time when I feel the ropes binding my ankles coming loose. Gabriel unties the cord connecting my wrists to the pedestal, working quickly. He leaves my wrists bound, of course, and re-uses one of the ropes to make a leash around my neck. Thankfully, he pries the cloth gag out of my mouth, slips it over my head and tosses it away.

"Come on," he says, pulling me along. "Hurry." It's an order I'm happy to obey.

We rush down two flights of stairs and through the silent hall until we reach my cell. I don't wait for permission to collapse onto the mattress and let out a few tears of relief. I feel a shift in the mattress as Gabriel sits down next to me. He rubs my shoulders once, then lifts me to my feet.

"Please leave me alone," I say, totally exhausted. The ecstasy of the orgasm he gave me feels like a distant memory, consumed by the guilt of watching the other women be taken away. I wish I hadn't come; do the others know how much I enjoyed it, or did they believe it was forced out of me? Is my experience normal for this place, or did they just witness a ghoulish display from a demented slut?

"Soon," says Gabriel. He adds, whispering to me, "He

might be watching."

Lifting my arms over my head, he turns me to face the wall. He unties the rope around my neck, then uses that length to secure my wrists to a metal ring sticking out of the wall a couple feet over my head. Forced to stand, I prop my arms against the wall for added support.

Gabriel grabs my battered ass cheeks and massages them slowly. He leans against my back as he does it, sending a fresh erotic charge through my body. He's so much taller and broader than me, I feel enclosed in his warm embrace.

"If we're lucky, Halloran is still dealing with the guests."

His silk tie tickles the small of my back. He smells slightly sweaty, but it mixes appealingly with his musky cologne.

"Won't he watch the video later?" I ask, keeping my voice low.

"No, there's no video. Halloran doesn't allow recording devices of any kind. No cell phones are permitted in the asylum either," he explains.

I wonder if he's telling the truth, as usual, but I don't know what purpose lying would serve. If he's trying to trick me, what would be the point? Now I know what Halloran wants of me, and as far as he's concerned, he's got it. It's Gabriel who stands more to lose than anyone.

He lets go of me, then lands a few weak slaps on my ass. On another day they would have been too soft to bother me, but my skin is still extremely tender from before, making mild spanking far more excruciating.

"Why are you doing this?" I moan.

Gabriel says nothing for a time, then asks, "What did you think when you were in the lounge today? What ran through your mind when you saw the other girls?"

New tears collect in my eyes. "I shouldn't say."

Pain shoots through my backside as Gabriel's hand glances across. "Answer me. Were you horrified?"

"Yes!" I scream.

"Outraged?"

"Yes."

"How would you feel if one of those men had taken you to a private room?"

"Like I'd rather be dead!"

Gabriel rubs my back gently. "Exactly. So how do you think the other girls got the way they are?"

"You didn't lobotomize them?" I spit.

This earns me a hard rap at the base of my buttocks, right above my thighs. I grunt from the pain, but I'm too tired to bellow.

"Those girls have shut down inside. It's the only way they can defend themselves from what goes on here. You'll turn out just like them, given enough time. Unless..."

"What?"

Gabriel spins me around so I can face him. "I want a better fate for you, Marla. You're a natural submissive, and I want to work with that. It'll keep you sane." He caresses my breasts, then pinches my nipples cruelly. I howl and shake, but he doesn't let go. Whispering in my ear he says, "I'll prove I'm serious about helping you. It's going to get me in trouble, but I need to know you trust me."

Letting go and backing away, he asks loudly, "What'll it be?"

After what I've seen this day, I have to do more than escape. Somehow I have to break out the other girls. I can't leave them behind. What if Gabriel's idea of helping me only helps us? Though, what choice do I really have? Either I can trust Gabriel to do what's right, or not — and that's what he's already asked. *Can I trust him?*

"Do what you must," I say.

"Good. I want you to remember this night, Marla. The way you came for me on command should be burned into your brain." He takes my breasts into his hands again and for a second I flinch, expecting him to torture my nipples. Instead, he massages them. "You can pretend you didn't love it, but I know better. You liked obeying me, didn't you?"

"Yes," I say, losing my composure. I don't know whether he's acting for the sake of the cameras, or if he's being honest, but I don't have to lie: I did enjoy it, perverse as it is.

A soft slap to my face jolts me back. "Try that again," says Gabriel.

"Yes, sir."

"Good." Gabriel wraps his arms around me, and when he speaks I can feel his warm breath against my scalp. "For the next few months, you are going to learn how to derive satisfaction from serving. You will orgasm when I tell you to, and obey every command. You will become mine, and when the time comes for you to serve our guests, you will do it without reservation or contempt because I told you to do it. Do you understand?"

"Yes, sir." I tell myself it's his body pressed against mine that's affecting me. I refuse to accept that I find the idea of serving him truly arousing. I feel the hard tip poking me from within his pants, and wonder if he's wrestling with the same questions.

"Then prove it. Spread your legs."

Gabriel unbuckles his belt, and my first thought is that he's going to whip me with it, but instead he lets his pants fall around his ankles. Then he sees I haven't complied with his order and shoves his hands between my legs, splaying them. I moan as he rubs my clit for a moment, then drops his tight, black underwear.

I don't hide my interest in seeing his cock. Standing up, rigid and long, I see he's fully erect. He strokes the shaft slowly as he slips a finger into my pussy.

"Soaking," he says, voice tinged with amusement. "You're already primed to serve. You want to be owned."

"Yes, sir," I moan, cheeks burning.

"That's good, Marla. No matter what happens in this place, you will always be mine."

"Yes, sir," I whisper, tears falling. Yet, despite the pain that lies ahead, I find some comfort in the idea of being *his*. It feels right in a way I'm still just beginning to understand.

I dig my head into the cushioned wall as Gabriel slips his cock deep inside me. My jaw drops but no scream comes out.

All the air has been forced from my lungs as pleasure floods my senses. I'm so wet, his fearsomely thick cock slides in without resistance.

"Fuck," he groans. "That's tight."

"Uh huh," I grunt. I feel my inner muscles clenching on his shaft as he starts to thrust. I pull at my bonds but the ropes hold, further stoking my desire.

"You... know... the rules," he says between drives. "You come... when... I say."

"Yes... sir," I reply, my voice barely present. I'm floating away on a tide of bliss that rises like a tsunami as he pounds me faster and harder. Then he does something I don't expect: he plants his lips on mine.

I shudder and let his tongue into my mouth, tasting the peppermint on his breath and the hints of vanilla in his hair. I laugh, realizing that this is the first we've kissed; he's seen me naked plenty of times, and even brought me to orgasm already, but not before kissing. He smiles when our lips finally part, then refocuses on drilling me like a machine.

In seconds I'm so lost in the bliss, I don't even hear the hard banging on the door to my cell.

"You better come now, Marla," he says.

I hear the knocking again, but I don't care. My climax erupts and I scream, the orgasm ripping through me as the door buzzes and bursts open.

"You motherfucking piece of shit," Vaughn growls, pulling Gabriel away. Gabriel beams like a game show contestant who hit the jackpot, then shoves Vaughn off.

Not expecting to be rebuffed, Vaughn loses his balance and falls into Miller, who keeps his colleague from hitting the floor.

Gabriel pulls up his pants quickly, but not fast enough: Vaughn's swing connects with Gabriel's jaw. I watch, dumbfounded, as Gabriel twists around, landing on the ground.

I shriek in fury, kicking with my feet but missing. Miller laughs as I keep flailing anyway.

"Come on," says Vaughn, pulling Gabriel by the arm.

"Boss wants a word with you, loverboy."

"Marla, calm down," Gabriel murmurs as Vaughn and Miller lift him up. "It's all right."

For once I know for a fact he's lying.

CHAPTER 16
GABRIEL

My jaw aches from Vaughn's hook but I haven't stopped smiling by the time he and Miller dump me in the seat in Halloran's office. I can still feel her around my cock, and the whole room knows it. *Didn't see that coming, did you, fellas?*

Vaughn could have taken a few more shots at me and I wouldn't have cared. I wouldn't have even felt them. There's so much at stake right now, but the male animal in me can't help gloating. *Today you lost, Vaughn. It started with Marla kicking your ass, and it ended with me fucking her.* It's been a while that I really got one over on that motherfucker. What's even better is that I'm about to pull the rug out from under him again and beat him with it. He has no fucking clue.

Halloran does, though. He knows exactly what I've pulled, and that's probably why he's so incensed. His face is so red with rage I wouldn't be too surprised if he pops an aneurysm and keels over at any moment.

"Vaughn, go finish your report. Miller, you're dismissed. Go clean up," he says.

Miller gives a nod.

"Report's finished," Vaughn says. "I'll go get it." He glares at me one last time, then follows, leaving me alone with

Halloran.

He focuses on me, completely ignoring Marla on the monitor. "You did that to make me angry," he accuses.

"No, I had other reasons."

Halloran crosses his arms. "Such as?"

"Her training. But also because I felt like it." Of any reason I could list, that's the one he understands best. He even smiles a little when I say it, then stares at me for a while, his jaw moving like a cow chewing its cud.

"How much did you see?" I ask, morbidly curious.

"None, thankfully. Vaughn shut it off in time."

"Good." I have to admit I'm glad. I know Vaughn did it for Halloran, and not me, but I'm grateful just the same.

He finally turns to the monitor. Marla is tied where I left her, arms above her head and against the wall. Nobody went back to cut her loose or throw her in a jacket. She stares at what I think is the slot in the door to her cell. *Stay strong, Marla. I'll be back soon.*

"I was supposed to be first," Halloran says at last, breaking the silence. "You don't even touch the inmates. Now you're fucking them. Is that payback for what Vaughn did? Tell me what I'm supposed to think."

I nod and touch the spot on my jaw where a bruise has started to throb. "All right. The way I see the situation, Marla's here because Vaughn went over your head and took her without permission. That makes her a special case, and since you put her under my care, I've treated her like one."

"All right." Halloran nods.

Sorting through the threads of truth and fabrication gets difficult sometimes, and I remind myself of what I've determined to be my hierarchical needs for success:

Protect myself. Selfish as it sounds, I can't help Marla if my true intentions are discovered, and I'm either killed or stripped of my freedom.

Be patient. Be prepared. Escaping this place will mean acting at the opportune moment, so when it comes I must be ready.

Eliminate threats. If I have a chance to tip the odds in my favor by eliminating men like Vaughn or Miller, I must take it.

Put together, this means I need to be able to defend every word and action I present to Halloran and Vaughn. They're both smart men, so I keep in mind the key approach to lying: include seeds of truth.

"When I met Marla, I decided that I didn't want her personality bludgeoned out of her like all the other girls. I want her to make peace with her fate and live through it."

"Sort of like you."

Bingo, old man. "Yeah, I guess so."

"I get that, Gabriel. But I think there's more. You haven't been the same since…"

Whatever kindness is left in his heart stops him from saying her name. *It's almost as if he cares.*

"Maybe," I say. "Not that you'd understand."

Halloran sighs. "All of us understand love, Gabriel. Even if we've never known it."

I scoff. He's so gnarled and ugly, I can't believe he's got the slightest notion of love. I've known him a long time: I would have seen it by now.

On the screen, Marla's head has sunk against her chest, and I believe she's fallen asleep. After a day like today, she must be wiped out.

Halloran and I watch her for a few minutes, until a knock comes from the door. Vaughn steps into the office, and he's got a thick set of manila file folders.

"Thank you, Vaughn," says Halloran, accepting the stack. I hear a series of beeps as he punches in a combination, then the drawer to his desk opens. Halloran stuffs the documents inside and shuts it quickly. "Your timing is good. I'm going to want your input. Gabriel, now that you and Marla have… gotten to know each other better… Tell me how you're going to break her before the next exhibition."

I look to Vaughn, who's failing at hiding his excitement.

"I'm not going to break her," I admit. Vaughn's smile grows, and even Halloran's face cracks a little. "Nobody's going to break her."

"Fuck that," says Vaughn. "Give me a day. I'll wreck that bitch."

I don't take the bait. "Instead of breaking her, I will train her, and when I'm done, she will do whatever I tell her to do, and she'll like it."

Vaughn laughs out loud. "Bullshit."

Halloran regards me curiously. "How?"

I point to the monitor, "Today you put her through her personal fucking hell. The worst hours of her entire life, including everything that's happened since she met Vaughn. Yet, it ended with her having an orgasm so deep she felt it in her spleen. *I* made that happen, in spite of what you did."

Turning to Halloran, Vaughn asks, "Do you believe this shit?"

"Maybe," he says. "You're the one who saw the video. You tell me."

All the humor evaporates from Vaughn's face.

That's right, motherfucker. "She screamed so loud, my ears are still ringing," I brag. "And I've only started to shape the way she thinks. She wants to serve me, she just doesn't know it yet."

My voice is fierce, bolstered by having the truth on my side. When I cross the line into falsehood, the best polygraph in the world wouldn't have registered the change. "When I unlock her innermost desires, she will do as I say, which can include doing as *you* say. And instead of fucking dolled up zombies, you can have a living, willing woman. How does that sound, Halloran?"

"Different." Halloran pops his knuckles, then flips the channel on the TV, examining each one for a moment before moving on. Each channel displays a similar scene: one of the guests, either fully or partially undressed, is on top of one of the girls, having his way, while she limply endures.

"How can you possibly expect Marla to subject herself to this?" he asks.

"In truth, it won't be easy, but that's my problem. And if I'm wrong, and it doesn't work out, there's always your way." I watch as Halloran keeps flipping through the camera feeds. "Don't you think our guests would like someone a little more… lively?"

"I suppose, some of them, yes," Halloran replies.

That's good enough. I've got him hooked now. I resist the urge to check Vaughn's reaction.

"I have one reservation, Gabriel," Halloran continues. "What if she's playing you?"

The thought had crossed my mind, but I answer, truthfully, "I'm not worried about that."

"Neither was Roy. She appealed to his insecurities, and it got him killed."

Halloran could be right, of course. Feeling Marla's need for me helps me forget the possibility that she might be waiting for her chance to clear one more obstacle from her next escape attempt. I trust her. I have to, or she won't trust me. "I'll be careful," I say.

"Yeah right," snorts Vaughn. "You think you'll teach her to trust you, but she's the one teaching you."

"Is she? Thanks for the tip. By the way, how's your testicles, Vaughn?"

"Fuck you, Gabriel."

"Hey!" Halloran thunders. "Enough, both of you. Gabriel, you watch yourself. I don't want to send Vaughn and Miller to bury you."

"Oh, it'll be my pleasure," Vaughn growls.

"Like hell you would," I tell Halloran. "I thought you'd be relieved to have me out of the way."

Halloran looks hurt for a moment, but shakes it off. "No, not at all. Gabriel, you may not believe this, but I'm really pleased by your work with Marla. If you're successful, we all stand to get what we want. Between the three of us, that's never happened."

"I agree," I say, though I don't give a fuck if he and Vaughn like it.

"And if this works with Marla," Halloran adds, "maybe it could be repeated on others."

"Sure."

"Excellent. Okay, it's been a long day. Have a good night."

"You too," I say, getting up to go. I thought I might wait to follow Vaughn and make sure he doesn't head for Marla's cell, but he storms off without a word.

I nod to Halloran as I shut his office door behind me. I expect he plans to go through Vaughn's report on each of the guests before retiring to his quarters for the night.

Thumbing an intercom, I call Miller and tell him to meet me at Marla's. I want to get her down off the wall, jacket her and let her sleep on the mattress, but I can't do that by myself. Miller agrees so I head off to meet him.

Should I feel guilty about the lies I've told Halloran? It's hard to reconcile my history with the man and the fact that betraying him may lead to his death. Yet, I feel truly righteous.

That's because Halloran is a monster. Don't ever forget it.

CHAPTER 17
MARLA

Gabriel!

The fight between him and Vaughn hits me as I wake. I don't know what happened to him afterward. I get up off the mattress and stagger to the door of my cell. I stare out the slot but see nothing.

As my memories of last night start to surface, I realize how much I have to process. I wonder whether I'll be brought to the lounge regularly, now that I've been introduced to what really goes on at this so-called "asylum." How long have these women been imprisoned here?

And what about Gabriel?

Has he ever used any of the captives the way the other men do? Or does he just torture them while the others watch? Perhaps he's changing his ways, helping me to make up for past sins. But if he's hurt other women like me, could I ever forgive that?

I need more information. He has to tell me more, and then I'll sort out the truth.

I wait and wait until I finally hear the door to my cell buzz.

Exhaling in relief, I see it's him. Despite the punch he took, Gabriel looks all right. A dark bruise blemishes his stubbly chin, but it doesn't detract from his rugged good looks. He's wearing tight, tan slacks and a blue, button-down shirt, but he's left behind the lab coat. He carries a briefcase that I assume is a kit from the dungeon.

"Marla, how are you feeling today?" he asks.

God, where to begin? "Confused. Sir."

He sits down next to me on the mattress. I see in his expression the warning, *Be careful*, but he doesn't have to tell me that at this point.

"Can you explain?"

"Sure. Finding out what you do here… seeing the women taken… I want to cry. But then I think of what we shared afterward… and I can't pretend it wasn't important to me. And there's so much I want to know about you, and this place." I smile a little, relieved at not having to lie.

Gabriel nods. "Marla, last night you submitted to me, and you ended up liking it, as I hoped you would. It proves that the future I want for you will work, if you let it."

I can only imagine what future he really means.

"Yes, sir."

"Good." Gabriel lifts me up and guides me down to the torture chamber. Miller arrives shortly after we do and helps extricate me from my jacket. Together he and Gabriel lock my neck and wrists into a thick, wooden stock, like a relic from the Spanish Inquisition. I almost laugh, it looks so ridiculous, but once I'm unable to escape it, I see that the device is no joke. My back is bent uncomfortably, and my ass sticks out, perfect for a flogging. I can't turn my head at all, and when Gabriel stands out of sight, I realize I can get whipped at any moment and not see it coming.

The setup stirs the hunger in the pit of my stomach. I feel the churning and memories of Gabriel at the exhibition flash back at me.

He thanks Miller for his help, then paces back and forth, examining the selection of floggers and paddles on the nearest shelf. "Marla, today I want you and I to get to know each other better. I want you to ask me questions, whatever you'd like to know. Then you'll earn the answer by accepting a little discipline. I'll tell you how much. Then you can agree, or ask something else. Got it?"

"Yes, sir," I reply.

"Good. And we're going to push the envelope a little while we're at it."

Gabriel disappears for a minute, leaving me to interpret his intention. When he returns, he's holding a phallus of some kind. Made of reflective metal, it glistens brightly through a sheen of oil coating. I catch a glimpse of Gabriel's cupped hand, spying the fistful of fluid trying to escape, and then I feel it. Gabriel smears it between my lower cheeks, pressing it into my rear with a finger.

Groaning as the cold oil and his warm hand massage me, I bite my lip, waiting for the plug. I've experimented with anal in the past, but not while in bondage or while being caned or spanked. I concentrate on breathing and staying calm.

When I feel the cold metal pressing against my tight entrance I flinch, earning my bottom a quick slap. "Relax," says Gabriel.

Following his command as best I can, I unclench and let the toy dig its way inside. Gabriel goes slowly, letting me adjust to its width an inch at a time, working the plug in and out as needed. He doesn't stop, though, not until the widest part of the toy has slipped through and its flared base rests against my cheeks. I feel a jolt of pain as the plug digs in, but then it's fine, and I can enjoy the constant sensation of fullness.

Gabriel runs his hand across my backside and my skin tingles in anticipation. "Very nice. Start when you're ready."

I don't need any time to prepare. I know the most imperative question on my mind. "Gabriel... sir... before we go any further... before I start to really have feelings for you I can't take back, I need to know: have you ever taken a woman here in a way that..."

Gabriel shakes his head and cuts me off. "Absolutely not. I've doled out discipline, I've given medical examinations, but I have never forced myself on an inmate. The only time I..." He stops himself, and I see that he, too, is searching for the right words.

"What?" I ask.

"There was a woman here who… she and I…" He blinks rapidly, batting away a tear. "I'll tell you about her sometime."

I'm stunned by the admission, and already I have more questions.

Gabriel shakes his head. "Guess I gave you that one for free."

I had forgotten about the game too. "Yes, sir," I say. "Can you tell me one thing about this woman?"

"Ask."

"Where is she now?"

Gabriel chooses a cane and taps it against his palm. "Five strokes."

"Yes, sir. I accept."

He taps my bottom with the cane softly, preparing for the hard strokes. I focus on my respiration, inhaling and exhaling steadily.

"Remember what you learned last night," he says, and then delivers the first hit.

I yelp, startled by the pain and the jostling of the plug, but I say, "One. Thank you, sir."

"Good girl." He strokes my hair and cups my chin, then reels off the remaining four swings. I count each one properly. They sting, but I can tell he's starting me off slowly.

"She's gone," he says.

I had a feeling, but I had to hear it from him. "What was her name?"

"Iris. And I urge you to change the subject."

"Yes, sir," I respond, though there's much I wish to know about her. *Iris.*

Though I've learned what matters most about Gabriel, it's left me wanting more. "How long have you worked here?"

Gabriel doesn't answer right away. "Twenty strokes," he offers reluctantly.

"I accept."

He sighs, but whether he likes it or not, I obey him perfectly, counting each hit and thanking him without failure. In between strokes he maintains a steady light tapping, occasionally knocking on my plug. By the time he finishes, welts are forming across my ass and I moan in constant agony, but I feel satisfied, knowing I'm going to get my answer.

Gabriel steps around in front of me and paces for a time. "I've been here for the last five years."

Holy shit.

"Why, sir? How did you end up here?"

Gabriel puts the cane away and selects a flogger. He points it at my breasts. "Twenty."

"Yes, sir."

Gabriel swings the flogger through the air so quickly I can't track it, but it's just a warm-up for him. He stops fully before targeting my chest for the first flogging. When it starts for real he goes quickly, alternating between each breast. I fudge my words as I count, trying to keep up. With the pain rising, it's nearly impossible to think of anything else, and by the time we finish I'm in tears. My breasts throb angrily, and I half expect Gabriel to announce that I didn't count properly, and thus had to start again.

"Halloran recruited me," he says instead. "Told me I'd be helping traumatized women, which was a clever lie. They kept me in the dark at first, but soon I learned what was really going on. By then it was too late."

"Too late? For what?"

"To-" Gabriel starts, but then shakes the flogger in front of me. "Ten."

I nod and accept the punishment. My body is aching now, but I barely feel it. My mind races with each answer Gabriel gives, and it provides a potent distraction from the pain.

"To call the police. Alert the authorities. They never would have believed I wasn't complicit in what was going on. Maybe I should have called them regardless, but I didn't. That's probably the biggest mistake I've ever made in my life."

"Probably," I agree. Of course he should have, but that's a

lot easier to see in hindsight. "But why you, Gabriel?"

"What do you mean?"

"Why did Halloran recruit you?"

Gabriel stiffens, his eyes narrowing. "That's a long story for another time."

"No! You said I could ask anything."

"Fine," Gabriel growls. "One hundred strokes."

Fuck. He seriously doesn't want to answer. I'm torn about accepting because now I really have to know, but that's too much. "All right," I say, though it sounds more like, *This isn't over.* "Who were those men last night?"

"Ten strokes."

Across several inquiries and so many strokes I lose count, I learn from Gabriel that the guests are Halloran's clients.

"They pay for access to the women," he explains. "Away from the prying eyes of the outside world. Sometimes the richer ones even buy an inmate from us and take her home."

This turns my stomach, but I keep going. Now I understand how he gets the funds to operate, which isn't cheap: all the supplies are trucked in by Vaughn, who routinely travels an hour to Ravenswood. Sometimes the guests pay in favors, like getting the asylum kept out of public property records, keeping away building inspectors and managing law enforcement agencies to make sure none of the missing persons cases lead back to the asylum. By the end, my head spins, barely able to comprehend the depth of Halloran's reach.

"All right, Marla. That's enough for today."

I look down at my body, a collection of bruises and welts. My ass throbs from the presence of the plug, and I feel like a piñata. The feeling is going to get worse, too, before it gets better, once the adrenaline in my system wears off.

"You've done really well, Marla, and you've earned a reward," he adds, holding up a magic wand. "Though I'll understand if you're not in the mood."

"Please, sir," I say, eying the wand. I think back to the comfort he brought me last night and can't help wanting it again. Ever since he inserted the plug I've maintained some level of arousal, and I'm not sure I could bear the frustration of going unfulfilled.

"Very well. Remember the rules."

I sigh in relief as he holds the vibrator to my clit and turns it on. With his other hand he slips his fingers inside my pussy. Allowing the pain to infuse the growing bliss, I writhe in the stocks. I start to feel the orgasm swelling up, and I'm about to ask for permission to come when the sensation abruptly quits.

"I want you to say something while you come."

I can still hear the vibrator humming and try to thrust my hips toward it. All I can think about is relief. "Yes, sir. Whatever you want."

"I want you to say that you belong to me and that I'm your master. And you are to repeat it until I tell you to stop."

"Yes, sir. Please!"

Gabriel adjusts the vibrator to full power and plants it back against my clit. Still primed from before, I scream as the euphoria returns. My bliss is interrupted though as Gabriel pinches my nipple. "What are you supposed to be doing right now, Marla?" he warns.

"I belong to Gabriel, he is my master!" I shout. My toes curl as the words come out, and my fists clench at the air.

"Again!" Gabriel reaches around to play with the plug, pulling it in and out. The stretching brings both pain and pleasure and in the moment I can't even imagine having one without the other.

"I belong to Gabriel, he is my master!"

"Again!"

I say it over and over, louder each time. I don't mind making the declaration. I can't deny the truth to it, and if Halloran's watching — I can't imagine he's not — then I want him to know that I'm Gabriel's and no one else's. He pulls out the plug for good when I finish coming; awash in a roaring river of ecstasy, Gabriel's words are so ingrained I keep repeating them long after I come down from my peak.

Gabriel kisses my cheek and puts his finger to my lips to

get me to stop. He calls for Miller using the intercom, and a few minutes later the two of them are stuffing me back into a straightjacket.

I moan as they work, tired of the repetitive process of having each strap tightened until there's no slack, even if I do enjoy the sensation. I wonder what I would have to do for them to let me stay in my cell without being bound. Just so that I could lie flat, arms spread out, even if they would hang over the side of the mattress.

Such simple things we wish for when we can't have them, I think to myself. I add stretching to my long list of pleasures I'll never take for granted again once I get out of here.

Gabriel helps secure me to a wheelchair then strokes my hair softly. "You did well today, Marla."

"Thank you, sir," I mumble as Miller wheels me away.

—

I close my eyes, hoping to fall asleep, but then rouse myself, not wanting to be unconscious around Miller if I can help it. As the lowest rung on the totem pole, he follows his orders to the letter, but I don't want to imagine the deeds he gets away with when no one's watching.

A surge of conflicting emotions rises up within me when I realize we're headed to the lounge, where I figure I'll spend the rest of the day. I have no idea what state the other women will be in after what happened last night. I'm not sure which possibility is worse: that they're already so traumatized this won't even affect them, or that all the wounds they've accrued will be bleeding anew.

What I don't expect is for the whole group to turn and look at me when Miller brings me in. I scan their faces, but they're indecipherable.

Except for Helena, who glares at me so hatefully I nearly break down on the spot.

Miller spins my chair around so I can see the television, pats my shoulder and then walks off. I watch until the door shuts behind him, and then turn to the TV.

It's then that I figure out why the room is as quiet as a morgue. Instead of cartoons, the TV shows what at first appears to be a still image: it's the torture chamber. After a moment, Gabriel comes through, wiping down the floor underneath the stock I'd been locked in.

"Oh my god," I say.

I hear footsteps. In a straightjacket instead of a wheelchair, Helena walks up to me and looks like she's about to sob. "H-have a g-good t-time?"

"How much did you see?" I ask, unable to make eye contact.

"There was no sound, but we saw everything. Not hard to figure out the rest."

"I'm sorry," I say. "But Gabriel and I-"

"Save it," Helena snarls. "I thought you were fighting them. But now you're turning into their pathetic pet."

Is she wrong? I don't know.

"Gabriel's not like the others." I have no doubt we're being watched intently by Halloran, and probably Vaughn. I don't want to hurt Helena, but adhering to Gabriel's plan comes first. "We talked. About who he is and what he's been through, and I believe him."

Helena's laugh is a choked rasp. "You're an idiot, Marla. You don't know Gabriel at all. What did he tell you about? His lost love Iris? How he was tricked into working here?"

I'm starting to get angry, either at Helena or Gabriel or both. "Yeah."

"Did he confess he made a huge mistake not going to the police when he found out the truth?"

I nod, though a cold snap spreads outward from my stomach until the icy stab leaves me shivering. "Because nobody would believe he was innocent."

"Yeah, that's a load of shit, Marla," Helena snarls. "He didn't go to the police because he wanted to protect Halloran. His father."

CHAPTER 18
MARLA

I spend the rest of the day in a self-induced stupor. I must look indistinguishable from the other girls, just sitting there staring blankly in one direction or another. Forcing myself into numbness is the only way I can keep from sobbing in front of everybody.

It's not so much what Helena told me about Gabriel — even if it is true, he deserves a chance to explain. If anything, it makes his story more believable: if Halloran is his father, then it is unlikely the authorities would believe in Gabriel's innocence.

No, what kills me is Helena's reaction. I don't blame her: when all she's known is misery for the last year, watching my ecstasy must have felt like a dagger in her back. Hopefully someday she'll trust that I didn't wish to hurt her, but now I have to give her time.

And prove myself. Help them escape like I said I would.

I hold onto that notion until Miller returns me to my cell, where I've never been so relieved to be alone. As soon as the door closes I let it out, sobbing in the corner. With the jacket on I can't even wipe my tears, adding to my sense of futility, but when I finish crying I feel better. Eventually I drift off to sleep.

—

The buzz of my cell door wakes me hours later. I feel rested. Opening my eyes, I see it's Gabriel, dressed down a little in khakis and a tight, black polo shirt. He sits next to me on the mattress and strokes my hair for a while before speaking.

"I almost came right away, last night, when I heard what happened."

I nod. My eyes still feel raw. I want to ask him about what Helena said, but don't feel ready yet.

"You were asleep, so I decided to let you rest. But I had some choice words for Vaughn."

"It was him?"

"Of course." Gabriel helps lift me to my feet and takes me from the cell. He leads me down to the washroom, where Miller is waiting. They clean me thoroughly and carefully, and when they finish, Gabriel opens a cupboard and takes out a plastic bag. "This is for you."

I'm handcuffed and can't open it myself, so Gabriel reaches in and pulls out a bra and panties. "You've earned a little something to make you feel more like yourself."

"Thank you, sir," I say, though in my head alarm bells clang. I feel like the housewife receiving a bouquet of flowers the day after finding foreign lipstick on her husband's collar. Is he attempting to buy my trust, or is this gift sincere?

As if reading my mind, he whispers in my ear, "I'm sorry. I should have told you."

I nod, then put on the underwear with the help of the men. Admittedly, having on real clothes of any kind is a relief after going so long without. I still groan as the straightjacket is replaced, but I can feel the soft cotton of the undergarments against my sensitive skin instead of the coarse canvas.

Once they finish, Gabriel fastens a black, leather collar around my neck and attaches a matching leash. He leads me from the washroom to the torture chamber but tells me, "Don't get comfortable. We're not staying."

Comfortable, right.

Working quickly, Gabriel picks out a set of chained ankle cuffs and locks them. At his instruction I walk around, listening to the metal links scrape the concrete floor. With the cuffs on I can walk, but not quickly; running is out of the question. When I've finished a circuit of the room, Gabriel has chosen a white ball gag and dangles it in front of me.

"Open."

The sight of it makes me shy away, but only because I know I'll enjoy it, stirring up the guilt I felt throughout the day yesterday.

"It won't be for long, Marla. But you have to obey me now."

I don't know what he has planned, but I comply, allowing him to gag me. He pulls the straps tight before buckling them, and I groan angrily. "I know, I know," he whispers. "Miller, you can go."

When he's done and Miller's departed, Gabriel takes my leash and positions himself behind me. "We're going for a walk. There's a place I want you to see."

Following his direction, we ride the elevator to the ground floor; I appreciated not having to climb the stairs with my ankles chained together.

I didn't understand at first that when Gabriel spoke of a walk, he meant we were going out. My excitement skyrockets when I see the entrance to the building; I haven't been outside the asylum's walls since we arrived. My heart races at the idea of smelling a scent other than disinfectant, sweat and fear. Maybe I'll hear birds returning north for the spring, or feel the rustle of the wind in my hair.

Vaughn is waiting for us in the lobby, blocking the exit. I don't care about deference: I glare at him with more hate than I've ever felt for a living soul. Only the gag keeps me from saying something regrettable.

"Umm, what the fuck are you doing?" he asks Gabriel.

"Hobble training. Should take a few hours."

Vaughn notices the chain connecting my ankles. "You don't need to go outside for that."

"You're right. But I want to, so get out of the way."

Vaughn sneers and steps aside. "Watch her," he says, pointing at me. "She's going to be looking for a way to kill you. I wouldn't be surprised if she finds one."

"Duly noted."

"Nice gag, by the way," Vaughn says. He pinches my cheek until I turn away from his touch. "It looks very pretty on you."

I growl, but stop when it causes a line of drool to escape my lip. Vaughn chuckles, winks at me and walks off.

Gabriel watches for him to disappear from view, then opens a small cabinet by the door. He takes out a pair of tan, leather moccasins and tosses them at my feet. "Put 'em on."

Smiling through the gag I slip my feet inside the shoes, the first I've worn since arriving at the asylum. They're a little loose, but I'm not going to complain. When I'm ready, Gabriel presses his thumb into the security panel and the thick, metal doors click open.

Stepping outside, I smell soil and the fresh air. It's sweeter than any freshly baked dessert, and tears immediately splash my cheek. A slight breeze tosses my hair and cools my bare legs, but I don't mind: it feels amazing, and when it dies down the temperature is warm and comfortable. Looking around I see small piles of snow, but most of it is gone, revealing the crushed, green grass below. And I do hear birds, and their song is the most beautiful music ever sung.

Gabriel takes the lead, heading for a path into the forest. Though I hadn't let myself actively fantasize that Gabriel was breaking me out, I'm still disappointed to find we're walking away from the road and Vaughn's truck.

It occurs to me that, if this is an escape attempt, I don't know what to do. I don't want to leave unless the rest of the women are coming with me, but... if I could go, right now, would I be a fool to say no? What if I never get another chance?

I eventually dismiss the dilemma, remembering what I saw when Vaughn brought me here: there's only the one road to the asylum. Unless Gabriel has a helicopter hidden in the forest, escape lies in the other direction. We're going somewhere else.

When the asylum is completely out of sight, lost in a sea of pines, Gabriel speaks. "I'm sorry for what happened yesterday. You have my word, Vaughn will pay for his cruelty."

He hasn't taken out my gag yet, so I nod.

"And I'm sorry I didn't tell you about Halloran. He is, biologically, my father, but I don't think of myself as his son. I grew up with my Aunt Janice, who told me my parents were dead. I asked about them both; she told me my mother was an saint, but that Halloran was a monster. She refused to say much more. Years after she passed away, Halloran found me through a private investigator. We met a few times, but I was already an adult, and didn't feel any sort bond to him. When he asked me to come work at his 'private facility,' he was alone. I felt bad, and I needed a job, so I agreed. At the time I thought maybe wasn't so bad after all, but I was mistaken. He's not a loving man, even if sometimes he acts like he wants to be. And I don't call him 'dad,' or 'father.' Just 'Halloran.' I hate that I'm related to him — hate to admit it — so I didn't. It was wrong, but that's why."

Now he takes out my gag and stuffs it in his pocket.

"Thank you," I say, working my jaw. "I understand not wanting to be associated with that man."

"Yes. I think he feels a greater kinship to Vaughn. He's done everything but adopt him."

I laugh. "They were made for each other."

I'm still walking and taking in the scenery, and don't notice that Gabriel has stopped and stepped into my path. I barely avoid colliding with him, but instead he pulls me into a kiss. Tasting the salt of his lips, my legs feel weak. I want to wrap my arms around his thick chest, but settle for him embracing me. A pang of guilt encroaches as Helena's fury flashes in my vision, but I shut it out.

Someday she'll know the truth, I promise myself.

With my eyes closed, I let myself fall into the moment completely. The world stands still as we kiss, surrounded by the tranquility of the mountain. It reminds me that the world is still there waiting for me. Halloran Asylum isn't forever. I could have let the kiss go on and on and not grown tired. I take comfort in the dual clutch of Gabriel and the jacket.

Eventually we separate, though, and Gabriel's eyes grow wide with excitement. "Come on, I've got a gift for you."

CHAPTER 19
MARLA

Eager for the surprise, I walk as fast as I can, careful not to trip over the chain or extend myself too far. We travel down a narrow path, where I see a heavy set of tracks: three lines are imprinted in the dirt. However, Gabriel steers me aside, following fresh footprints into a copse of trees forming a semi-circle around a small clearing. In the center is a pile of rocks, branches and pine needles, which Gabriel brushes away, revealing a small, gray cardboard box.

"Ready?"

"Yes, sir." My smile is miles wide.

Grinning too, he opens the box, revealing a blue, striped, folded up lawn towel. He digs his hand inside, and when it emerges he's holding a bag of chocolates and a container of fresh strawberries.

I nearly collapse. I can hardly wait for him to spread out the towel and help me to the ground, but when he feeds me the first strawberry, I moan so loud, birds shoot from the trees in panic.

"Oh my god," I mumble, mouth full of the succulent fruit. "Where did these come from?"

"I put them on Vaughn's shopping list. Said they were for

me."

I laugh, and Gabriel quickly unwraps a chocolate and holds it to my lips. I suck it onto my tongue, where the sweet candy starts to melt. I let it all linger in my mouth until I realize I'm crying.

Gabriel pulls me into a hug, and I rest against his shoulder. Behind me I feel his hands tugging at the straps of my jacket, but instead of getting tighter, they begin to loosen.

"Tell me what you're feeling," he says softly. "If you want to."

"I'm not sure. After what I've been through, this is…"

Gabriel kisses my cheek. "I wanted to give you a… a day off, I guess. Something to lift your spirits."

"Thank you," I say, though I'm interrupted by my growling stomach.

Gabriel laughs. "Hungry for more?"

"Yes, please."

Standing, but leaning against Gabriel's chest, I eat strawberries and chocolate until my teeth ache. When I sadly have to say no to any more, Gabriel eats a little, but leaves some in case I change my mind.

"If anybody asks you what we did out here, you're going to say we just walked."

"Yes, sir."

"And you're definitely not going to tell them about this." Gabriel reaches around and continues the job he started with my jacket. With only one pair of hands, the work takes longer, but I don't mind. Soon the straps are undone, and Gabriel pulls the jacket loose.

The breeze cools the sweat on my body rapidly, and I shiver from the sudden exposure, but I don't care. For the first time in more than a week, my hands are completely free. I stretch my arms, head tossed back, and revel in liberation. Though my ankles are still locked together, and the plastic security band encircles my wrist, for a moment I feel free.

"You're not worried I'll run?" I ask Gabriel.

"No, not really. This place is like Alcatraz. You can get out of the building, but then you've got an even bigger problem."

"How bad is it?"

Gabriel looks around, and then points past the trees. "Ravenswood is 20 miles that way, through dangerous terrain. Impassible ridges, high cliffs. The forests are thick, and it's possible to run into bears. The only safe route is the road, but that makes you easy to find."

"Shit."

"Yeah."

I take a deep breath, tasting the lingering milk chocolate on my tongue. "So, what's the plan then? How do we get out of here?"

Gabriel frowns. "I have one idea, but you're not going to like it."

"Tell me."

"We wait until the next exhibition. When the guests are busy with the girls, I'll get us out. We'll steal one of their cars and go while everyone else is distracted. We'll be halfway to Ravenswood before they notice we're gone."

He's right. I don't like that plan. "This is bigger than us, Gabriel. We need to get out all the girls."

Frustration creeps into his features as he nods. "Yeah, I want that too, but I don't see how. Once we get to town we can call the police and guide them back here. That's what I've got. If you have a better plan, I'm listening."

I sit down and pull my knees against my chest. "I don't have a better plan at the moment, no."

Gabriel crouches down, takes my hand and squeezes it. "We'll figure it out. I know this is tough. You're a reporter, not a soldier. And yet you're handling this better than anyone has any right to expect."

"Thanks," I say.

He sighs and looks up through the trees to the overcast sky. "Marla, can you tell me something?"

"Yeah?"

Gabriel grins a little, lowering himself to sit. "When you insulted your boss on TV, why did you do that?"

I laugh, thinking back. How long ago was that? A month? It feels like decades. "He fired me for some bullshit."

"Why am I not surprised?"

I punch his shoulder and shake my head at him.

"All right, all right," he chuckles. "But what was the bullshit? What did he do?"

Remembering that day still makes me mad.

"I was out covering a story, nothing serious. We — me and Bob, my cameraman — were the only news team there. A truck had gotten stuck on an old road above a creek. The day before, there had been a huge thunderstorm, and the winter snow was melting, so the creek was roaring, deteriorating the bank underneath the road. A chunk of it collapsed under the truck. The driver got out safely, but the truck had to be lifted before it could be towed. We were there filming, wrapping up, when more of the road gave way and a city worker fell into the creek."

"Geez."

"Yeah. The other workers were all on the road too; they had no chance to help the guy. But Bob and I were farther back, so I did what I think anybody would have done: I ran down to the creek and grabbed him. Bob came too, and together we pulled him out of the water. He had some scrapes and bruises, but was fine."

"That's amazing," says Gabriel, smiling and rubbing my back. "But wait, you were fired? Why?"

I snort. "Gerald claimed it was an insurance issue, I don't know exactly — it was what he told me instead of the truth, which is that he wanted a video of a man drowning. You know, for the ratings."

"Fucking hell." Gabriel kisses my forehead, holding me tight. "I think he's lucky you only insulted him."

"Yeah."

"I know you know this, but you did the right thing."

Smiling, I ask, "Helping the guy, or insulting Gerald on TV?"

"Both," says Gabriel. He kisses my cheek again, and I don't

resist when he turns my chin so he can take my lips in his. I let go of my knees and lie back, allowing him to shift into position above me. He plants his hands on the towel, straddling me, and I feel trapped below his massive frame, but in a good way. I love being within his control, tied up or not.

I snicker as the bulge in his pants pokes my belly, then reach for his belt buckle. Fumbling around, I work it loose and pull the khakis down.

Gabriel laughs too. "You want to do this here? It's a little cold."

Using both hands I slip my panties down to my knees. "Then keep me warm."

"You want my cock, Marla? Take it."

Reaching for his rigid shaft, I suck on my lip. I take hold of his cock and guide it to my pussy. Drenched and ready, he slips inside me with ease. I gasp as his length seems to fill my whole body, and when his thrusting starts I quickly lose control.

Sorry, Gabriel, I think. *If anyone's listening, they're gonna know what we were up to.* He doesn't care, apparently, because he lets out his own satisfied groans.

Feeling his cock driving into me, I throw my arms back against the ground. Seeing them there, Gabriel grabs them and pins them with his steely grip. I tug against his hold instinctively, but his grip is too firm. I moan, savoring his dominance, and that for once it is being achieved with only his hands and body, rather than restraints of fabric or metal.

As Gabriel's rhythm gets faster, I feel his teeth on my shoulder. I nibble at his earlobe, sucking on it until I run out of breath and my head falls back to the ground. I clench down hard on his cock, causing both of us to moan. Gabriel releases one of my hands, but it's so he could slap my breasts. Squealing from the unexpected pain, I swivel my hips, but Gabriel stays with me. He gives each nipple a pinch until I scream, then lets go.

"Oh god," I mutter, again and again.

"You can come," he tells me between drives. I had been waiting for him to say that, so as soon as the words are out I let go. Bliss consumes me. I try to lift my legs to curl them around Gabriel, but the chain prevents it.

"Stop," he says. I comply immediately, letting myself go limp. Gabriel lifts my shoulder and flips me over. Cackling, I spread my arms on the ground and lift my ass invitingly.

I hear a jingle of metal, and then the cuffs around my ankles slide away.

"Spread 'em," Gabriel commands. Obeying happily, I move my legs as far apart as I can, offering myself for his use. His hand caresses my pussy, and then I feel his slick fingers probing my rear.

"Nice and soaked," he mumbles, appreciating how hot I've gotten for him. After a second, I feel his thick cock pressing into my ass. I gasp at the size of the intrusion, but after a quick twinge of pain he slides in. Moaning as a second orgasm starts to build, Gabriel thrusts wildly. He smacks my ass hard every few pumps, stoking the intensity of the orgasm on the verge of breaking through.

"Keep holding it," he orders. "Wait for me."

"Yes, sir," I say, gasping for air and struggling to control the volcano of bliss boiling inside. The coupling of pain and pleasure meets the joy of serving the man I've called my master, and I scream in fury, attempting to hold in the orgasm as long as I can.

Gabriel, on the cusp of his own climax, begins pounding like a machine flying out of control. At last he says, "Marla, you can come."

I wail as his hot seed bursts inside me. The world around me feels as though it's drifting away while I cry from the sheer bliss. I've never felt a relief so pure and necessary, a result of my captivity, I'm sure. For the moment, the fear, uncertainty and danger of Halloran Asylum don't truly exist. It's only temporary, I know, but it doesn't feel that way. Time stretches in my perception. I'm being pulled into Gabriel's lap so he can hold me — so he can keep me warm — and all I have to do is be there with him. It won't last, but I don't think about it, not for a long time.

—

My sublime state holds together long after Gabriel pulls up my panties and lifts me to my feet. We've left behind the lawn towel, my jacket, and the rest. The breeze has picked up and I'm a bit cool, but Gabriel holds me close as we walk.

"Where are we going?" I ask.

"You'll see. It's not far."

He's right: after a few minutes we've reached the end of the trail. Standing at the base of a cliff several stories high, I look around, wondering what it is I'm supposed to be seeing.

"Look down, Marla." Gabriel points at a couple of rocks, but I don't see anything. Not too far from them though is a spot where the grass is broken up, freshly dug.

"Is that where they put Roy?" I ask, indicating where I'm looking.

Gabriel gives me a look. "They? No, it was me. And Vaughn. I had to help him do it. But forget that. Look over there." He indicates the stones again, and when I look closer, I notice they form a rectangle with its corners rounded off.

"Is somebody buried there too?" I ask, though I've answered the question in my head even before I finish asking it. "Iris?"

Gabriel nods. "Yeah. I didn't want to put Roy down here with her, but I didn't have a choice."

"I'm sorry."

"Thanks. Marla, I brought you here because I wanted you to know what happened. Come on, it's cold. I'll tell you on the way back." He takes a last look at Iris's plot, then leads me back.

As we walk, he tells me the story. Iris was taken, much like me, because she defied her boss. She blew the whistle on his discriminatory hiring at his factories, and when he tried to fire her, she sued him and went to the press. She had collected evidence, recorded conversations — the whole deal. She won her case. It was a nice story, most people agreed. For once the

141

underdog beat an unscrupulous bully who thought himself untouchable.

But then Iris disappeared — fell off the face of the earth, it seemed. They obviously thought her old boss had had her killed, but there wasn't enough evidence to convict. Of course, in this case he was innocent. Iris had caught the attention of Halloran's clients, who hired Vaughn to bring her to the asylum.

"You remind me of her in so many ways, Marla. And I think Vaughn sees it too. That's the problem."

"Huh?"

Gabriel hears me shiver and rubs my body vigorously, hoping the friction will keep me warm. "She didn't hate Vaughn the same way we do. She didn't really hate anybody. She managed to get him to admit his personal fears and insecurities, and listened to them with sympathy. She cared for him. It was just her way. And I'm positive he loved her."

"I find that hard to believe." *How could such a monster be capable of love?*

"I know," says Gabriel. "I guess you had to see it in person. The way he acted while she was around, like a smitten teenager." A tear falls from Gabriel's cheek. More are coming. "So I ask myself, if I'd gotten out of the way, maybe she'd still be here."

My stomach knots in grief, as I think I know what he's about to say. "You loved her too."

"I did. And she loved me. I wanted to help her. I told her I'd try to find a way, but before I could…"

Gabriel breaks off and covers his mouth. His body convulses, so I hold him tight. I'm crying now too, sharing his grief.

"Vaughn must have heard us planning, or maybe he hated that she wanted me instead. Either way, before we could break free, Vaughn snuck into her room late and…"

I take his hand and pull it to my chest; his fingers are cold against my skin but I don't care.

"I'm glad I didn't see it happen. Halloran saw, and to his

credit he spared me the details. But Vaughn... that fucking animal. After what he did, Iris lost too much blood. I did my best, but without a transfusion, there was no hope. She was unconscious when she slipped away. My last words to her was a promise to keep her safe."

We walk in silence for a while when he finishes. We've reached the copse from before, but we don't lie back down or sit, as if too paralyzed to continue on. When the tears stop, and I regain my composure, I say, "I'm so sorry."

"Thanks, Marla. I know. After that night, when sadness became rage, I contemplated going on a rampage. Try to kill Vaughn, then the others. But they were watching me. They knew I might snap. They've never fully trusted me since. Instead, I extracted from Halloran a promise that this wouldn't happen again. No more women would be taken, no more lives ruined. I thought it was the least I could do for Iris. Halloran got Vaughn to agree, and I did my best at making peace with fate, as awful as it was. But then Vaughn met you, and now it's happening all over again."

Blood boiling, I break away from Gabriel, my hands balled into tight fists. "Vaughn doesn't love me. But he knows you do."

Gabriel nods. "I know. I do love you, Marla. That's why this time is going to be different." He picks up the straightjacket and holds it open for me. "But for now I have to get you back inside, or they'll come looking for us."

I walk toward him, holding my arms up so I can guide them into the sleeves, but at the last second I pull them back. Before Gabriel can react, my fist flies out in a right hook with my entire weight behind it. My knuckles connect squarely with his nose, and Gabriel falls onto his backside.

The entirety of Gabriel's story made me realize that if Vaughn hadn't abducted me, nothing would have changed at Halloran Asylum. Gabriel would have continued biding his time, serving Vaughn and Halloran and their guests. Iris would rot in the ground, never knowing justice. If I were the one in that grave, I couldn't bear the idea of my murder going unpunished. That should have been the last straw for Gabriel; he should have gone to the authorities months ago, no matter what the cost to himself.

If he couldn't do what was right for Iris, how do I know he will for me? I don't.

When he hits the ground he falls into the fetal position, so I follow up my punch with a swift, moccasined kick to his abdomen. He gasps in pain, but his lungs are already emptied, and his cry makes no sound.

Seeing him writhing in agony, I don't wait another second. I run and I don't look back.

CHAPTER 20
MARLA

My first thought is that when I was locked in my cell, I should have spent more time jogging in place and stretching my legs. I'm sprinting so fast that the muscles in my legs cry out in open revolt, burning painfully. I know every drop of adrenaline my body can make is being pumped into me, but it's not enough to dull the throbbing completely.

This was a terrible idea, Marla, I think as I follow the path back to the asylum, and from there, the road. I consider trying to move through the terrain, but one look at the rocky bluffs tells me it would be suicide. I have neither climbing gear nor experience. I'd either fall to my death or get stuck on a ledge, where I'd either succumb to exposure or get "rescued" by Vaughn and Miller. So I head for the road. At least there I won't leave tracks.

I try not to let my fears distract me from the moment. How long would it take Gabriel to recover and come after me? He could be seconds behind me, or maybe he's still rolling around in pain. I have no idea. In the meantime, I'm stuck trying to run in moccasins that barely fit, in panties that offer little protection from the elements, and I have nothing I can use to defend myself. My plan is to find help, and hope the first person I encounter, whoever it ends up being, isn't a monster.

Twenty miles, Marla. That's going to take hours! And that's just as the crow flies, not traversed along a winding road. Night would fall, bringing bone-chilling cold, long before I reached Ravenswood. I'd need shelter for the night. *Worry about that later. It won't matter if you don't get away.*

I hide in the trees as I get close to the asylum, checking to make sure no one happened to be outside, watching for mine and Gabriel's return. I hear quiet, however, so I keep going, making for the road.

My memory of being taken comes back to me when I reach the narrow segment of the asylum's driveway, and my heart races when I see Vaughn's truck parked at the end.

You have to try it. I nearly pass it by, worried about wasting time, but I stop and tug on the door. It's locked, it won't budge. I'm about to move on when I hear a noise. I hold my breath and listen: footsteps echoing in the distance. It sounds like someone running.

Gabriel.

I jump off the truck, intending to hit the ground running, but I misjudge the drop and stumble, losing a moccasin.

"Hey! Marla!"

I hear him; he's coming. In a panic, I don't stop. I get up and keep running.

Maybe if you go back now he won't tell the others.

No, I can't go back.

You'll never make it.

Maybe. But I can't go back.

You'd rather be dead?

Maybe.

Fuck you, Marla. You didn't survive this long to give up now.

Arguments bounce around my head, and Gabriel's calls continue to carry through the breeze. I feel a window closing — if I feel I have to go back, I have to decide posthaste.

I keep going.

With a moccasin missing, it doesn't take long for me to step on a rock that leaves a nice cut on the sole of my foot. I stifle the scream, but when I look behind me there are clearly visible drops of blood gleaming on the pavement.

Fucking perfect. You're leaving them a handy trail to follow.

Each step I take with the injured foot is agony, but I refuse to quit. I put as little weight on it as I can and watch my step, but running keeps my heart pounding, meaning the blood keeps flowing. I should try to calm down to slow the bleeding, but I can't stop.

I refuse to believe that there's nothing between here and town. There has to be some other residence — a farm, a cabin, something! Even if there's nobody there, it could be a place to hide, or find supplies.

Vaughn will know about it. He'll find you there.

Yes, but what else can I do? Where else can I go?

Maybe you can find a cave. Or you could climb a tree. Or you could stop being an idiot and go-

No.

Go back.

No! I'm not going back without a fight.

A fight? You're already wounded.

The pain in my foot is getting worse, it's true. I take some time to hop on my good foot. Doing so leaves a gap in my blood trail, but I'm following the road, so it's not like it really matters.

In the distance, I hear the rumble of an engine. I'd recognize that sound anywhere. It's the truck.

Think they'll have your moccasin? That would be nice of them.

I've run for what feels like a long time, but that's the stress and adrenaline distorting my perception. I've gone a mile, at best. The truck is going to catch up to me at any second. I finally admit I can't outrun them.

They'll have to find me.

I hop to the edge of the road and hide behind the pines, getting low to the ground. I wipe off my foot, getting blood on my hand, then smear that below my eyes. I tell myself it's for camouflage, but it feels more like war paint.

The van flies down the road, and for a minute I wonder if

they think I've gotten a lot farther than I actually have. Does Gabriel not know how long it took him to get back? Do they suspect him of giving me a head start? If they think I've been gone since Gabriel first walked me out, then indeed I could have gone several miles by now. It depends on how much he told them, and what they believe.

I keep my attention on listening for the van, but since I can't hear it, I start back out again. The short rest has eased the pain in my foot, but it wells up again immediately, worse than before. I'm still bleeding. I contemplate trying to put my remaining moccasin on that foot, but it won't fit, and I'd most likely soon end up with two injured feet instead of one.

Rounding the edge of a cliff and a sharp curve in the road, I again hear the engine of the truck. It's coming back.

This is it. You're not getting away, Marla.

I know, I know. I can only hide for so much longer.

Gazing out over the cliff, I lean on the rusted guardrail for support. Looking down, I imagine taking a wild, desperate chance and hoping for the best. There are lots of pine trees below, with thick branches. The drop would only be a few stories — if they broke my fall, maybe I would survive.

Big if.

Blood is starting to puddle at my foot. As soon as they slow down to follow my trail, they'll know that I stopped here. They'll know I'm close.

There's no going back.

No, there isn't. But that's what they'll be expecting, isn't it?

There is one wild, desperate chance I'm willing to take. Hearing the engine louder now, I know I don't have much time. I pull off my bra without unhooking it, then drop it over the edge. I'd like to watch it float down and see where it lands, but I can't. I plant my wounded foot on the guard rail, leaving a nice, wet mark against the dry rust. I then hop away, ducking behind the trees on the other side of the road and hoping I have enough cover.

As I watch, the truck goes by once more, but this time it's crawling up the road agonizingly slowly. I freeze, breath held, as it rumbles on by, but it only goes a little ways before I see the brake lights illuminate. A second later the motor putters away and I hear the truck doors opening.

"Yeah, that's definitely blood." It's Vaughn. "She won't be far. I'll go south, you go north."

"Got it," says Miller.

"Marla!" Vaughn shouts. "Come out now and I promise we won't torture you! Not after you kicked Gabriel's ass! How could I be mad at you?"

I chuckle, enjoying the morbidity of the situation. I remind myself of what he did to Iris so I don't forget there are fates worse than death.

Miller comes into my field of vision; my eyes are drawn to the gun in his hands. He's keeping the weapon up, ready to fire, but taking frequent glances at the ground, following the blood.

"Seriously, Marla, the longer you make us stay out here, the worse you're going to get it."

Chuckling softly, Miller turns toward the ridge, noticing the trail's change in direction. He moves even faster when he spots my print on the guard rail. He looks over the edge, scanning back and forth.

I loosen the laces on my other moccasin and leave it behind as I creep out of hiding. My heart is pounding, but I can feel the space between each beat. I'm moving fast, but the world slides past me in slow motion. Every detail is sharp in my mind, from the barely audible tap of my feet on the pavement, to the barely perceivable twist of Miller's body as he turns.

He looks in Vaughn's direction up the road. "Hey, I think she jumped!" he shouts. He keeps turning, and he's going to see me. His gun rises back up, but it's too late: running at top speed, I've crossed the road. My hands shoot out in front of me, jamming into Miller's shoulder. My feet go out from under me and I can feel my momentum transferring through my arms into Miller, knocking him down.

If he hadn't been standing against the guardrail, he wouldn't have gone over the edge. I hear the clatter of metal, a sudden shout and then a wet crunch.

When it's done, I don't believe for a second that it's real. I feel like I'm about to snap out of a reverie, backed up to where Miller was following the trail and I was still hiding in the brush. But it's real: Miller is gone.

The moment comes roaring back. The truck. Vaughn. I remember hearing a clatter, and I see Miller's gun lying by the guardrail. Rubber souls pound pavement close by.

I lunge for the gun. My hand fits around the grip, but at the same time a heavy boot lands on my wrist.

"Stop."

Looking up, I see the gaping maw of a gun barrel pointed inches from my face. Vaughn's chest is heaving, but he smiles. "Fuck, that was close."

He pulls me to my feet and keeps his gun lodged against my neck. Miller's gun he sends plummeting off the cliff with one quick kick. He pulls me toward the ledge, as if to throw me off, but I know he won't be letting me off the hook that easily.

"Miller!" he shouts. "You alive?" He waits for a response, but none comes.

I laugh.

"What?" Vaughn asks.

"I told him he'd be next."

CHAPTER 21
HALLORAN

My toys look scared; they pace about the lounge instead of sitting and watching TV.

I shouldn't have used the intercom. The urgency in my voice in calling Vaughn and Miller meant something was wrong. Coupled with Marla's absence… Now they want to know what happened. Did she escape? Has she been hurt, or killed? They want to know, as do I.

My eyes have been glued to the monitor ever since Gabriel shot through the door, nose and chin covered in blood. While he waits in the lobby, I watch the feed from outside, waiting for the men to return. I don't even want to contemplate the worst case scenario: Marla has escaped, and it's only a matter of time before an army of investigators crashes through our doors.

It's impossible, I remind myself. It will take her more than a day to get to town, assuming she gets to one at all, which she won't. The only reason I entertain the possibility is that she's surprised me a few times already; I'd be foolish to not be slightly concerned.

At last, I see movement on the screen, and Vaughn comes into view with Marla in tow. Her hands are behind her back, presumably cuffed, with Vaughn's arm linked through her's, keeping her close. Though he walks, she's hopping on one foot. She's got on a pair of panties but no bra, and there's blood smeared across her face. The rest of her body is covered in dirt and grime. Miller is nowhere in sight.

Gabriel, Gabriel, Gabriel. What did you do?

When Vaughn gets the girl through the front door, Gabriel rushes to them, but Marla tries to bolt at him. While I watch, the men take her and practically drag her downstairs to the torture room. Fighting non-stop, she swings her cuffed fists in arcs that Gabriel and Vaughn dodge long enough to subdue her, forcing her into a straightjacket. They tie it so tightly she can barely breathe. She still kicks out her feet, trying to connect, but she knows she's lost this fight. There's no getting out of the jacket.

I press the call button on the intercom. Speaking as though nothing unusual has happened, I say, "Miller."

Vaughn turns and looks into the security camera. With a grim look on his face, he holds out his index finger and draws it in a line across his neck, then points to Marla.

Unbelievable. That fucking cunt.

The crystal whiskey glass on my desk bears the brunt of my rage, shattering against the wall of my office as drops of rye soak into the floor.

If Gabriel wasn't my son, I would kill him.

Is he still your son if he doesn't think of you as his father? And how many chances am I supposed to give him?

When I turn back to the monitor, Gabriel has wedged a thick, round gag between Marla's teeth, and Vaughn is buckling it in place. The fury in her expression gives way to fear as they drag her across the room to a small, iron cage. Barely big enough for a person, it forces her to sit, legs crossed, and keep her head bowed. She shakes her head as Vaughn shuts the door and Gabriel fastens it with a padlock.

They start to leave, but then turn around. Marla has stuck her foot through the bars of the cage. Vaughn stands there, but Gabriel grabs a cloth meant for either a gag or a blindfold and instead ties it around Marla's foot, which looks as bloodied as her face. She nods, then pulls her foot back inside. She watches the men leave the chamber, then looks up to the camera. Knowing I'm watching, she curls up her gagged lips, smiling at me.

Marla, when I'm finished with you, I promise you'll never smile again.

—

I'm still seething, staring back at the girl, when Vaughn and Gabriel reach my office.

"How did she do it?"

"Pushed him off the edge of the road," says Vaughn.

I'm watching Gabriel, who manages to keep a grin off his face. "You're certain he's dead?"

"If not, he's in a bad way. Not much we could do for him."

"I see. How did this happen?"

Gabriel stares at the ground, lips trembling.

"Answer me. Now."

"It was part of her training," he says at last, shaking his head. "I told Vaughn it was for hobble walk, but there was more. She was submitting to me. She was mine, I knew it. I wanted to show you. When we came back, she was going to walk in here without her bindings, totally of her own volition. Just because I told her to."

Interesting. Is that really true? Was he that confident of her progress?

"Why didn't it work?" I ask, assuming, for now, that he's telling the truth.

Gabriel sighs. "I'm not sure, but I think... because I told her about Iris. The whole story. Maybe it freaked her out enough to run."

Vaughn bristles; he hates being reminded of Iris as much as any of us. I wait a second, giving Gabriel a chance to continue, but he says nothing.

After a beat, I holler, "Does she look scared?" I point at the screen: Marla's still grinning, rocking back and forth in the cage. She could be shaking from the adrenaline, but I don't think so. She's enjoying herself, reveling. And why not? She killed a man twice her size. She's a gazelle that bested a lion.

"I had to tell her," Gabriel says. "She needed to trust me."

"No. She needed to fear you, and me. That's all. And that's what she's going to do from now on. No more of this master and submissive nonsense. You hear me?"

Gabriel nods, though a tear falls from his cheek.

"Starting with a stint in solitary, you will spend the next month torturing her. And not in ways that she enjoys."

"Fine."

"Do you have a problem with that?"

"No." Gabriel shakes his head. "You were right. I misjudged her."

His admission is refreshing. "Yes, you did. So now you'll do things our way until she's unquestionably and irreversibly broken. Understood?"

"Yes, Halloran."

Truthfully, I expected more resistance on this from Gabriel. Ever since Iris, he's fought me at every opportunity, so much so that I assumed his objections came solely for the sake of opposition. Of course, he may be going along with my edict because I haven't told Vaughn to kill Marla, and keeping her alive is all Gabriel wants.

The fact that he's not fighting me makes me think I should reconsider sparing her. Is she really worth the trouble? Losing Roy made operations difficult enough. Without Miller, the asylum could quickly fall apart.

"And Gabriel, you will assist Vaughn with Miller's duties. Vaughn, I need you to find replacements immediately. Even if they're only temporary."

"No problem," says Vaughn, sounding like a man ready to step up. He obviously senses a chance to gain my favor over Gabriel, considering the severity of my son's failures. It's a fair thought to consider.

"Gabriel, go back and dress her wound properly. If you say to her anything off the topic of her foot, I will have Vaughn beat her senseless."

"Understood."

"Good. You're both dismissed."

Seeing the broken remains of my whiskey glass on the floor, my first instinct is to open a line on the intercom and call for Miller. Growling, I go and get the broom, wastebasket and dust buster myself. I haven't cleaned a floor in decades, and when I kneel, shards of glass get caught in my trousers, poking at my knees.

When I finish I open my oak cabinet and take out the decanter and my other glass. I pour a double and down it in a single gulp.

I've studied history's great leaders, and golden ages. The downfall of empires, the collapse of civilizations — no one ever thinks Rome is burning from the smoke. Even when the conflagration melts stone, some people deny the obvious, desperate to hold onto what they have. Denial is a powerful force.

Maybe I should have Vaughn shoot Marla now, while she's locked in a cage. I could have him wait until Gabriel is asleep, then do it quickly.

I could have him do it right now, I think, watching Gabriel leave the building, heading for the road to retrieve the truck.

She's already killed two of my men. She fought off Gabriel pretty well. Even with Gabriel now on board, my organization is less capable of maintaining order, not more. An outside observer would recommend cutting my losses.

But they're not here, and they're not me. If I have her killed now, she wins. She will have forced my hand, and that is utterly unacceptable.

So I'm going to do what I love most: I'm going to break her. And if she dies in the process, so be it.

CHAPTER 22
MARLA

Aside from the fact that they haven't killed me, the days following my escape attempt are worse than I could have predicted. Many times I ask myself if I wouldn't have been better jumping that day. I question whether Gabriel's plan would have worked, or if he even meant to go through with it. I wonder if his actions now are forced by Halloran, or if he no longer needs to disguise his intentions. He says nothing to clue me in; he gives me no signs.

I haven't been back to the common room since the other women saw me on camera in the dungeon. Surely they will have figured that Miller is gone now, but do they assume I am too? Do they think I'm dead, or do they know I'm here? Are my sessions in the torture chamber being shown to them? Am I being made a daily example of what happens to the defiant? Is that my role from now on?

Day after day, it's all the same. Gabriel and Vaughn wash and feed me each morning. They never, ever speak to me. Even Vaughn doesn't bother taunting me like he used to, though if he thinks I miss it, he's delusional.

Following each meal, they torture me. Working together, their plans communicated before they arrive, they whip or flog or cane me until my entire body throbs. They've used cattle prods, they've used clamps. They've dunked my head in ice water and dripped hot candle wax on my bare skin. They tighten nooses until I nearly pass out, and contort my body in bondage so stringent I start to go numb.

Sometimes I enjoy it, even though it disgusts me, but I turn that revulsion into strength. I've picked up on the pattern: if I like some new form of torture, they either don't do it again, or they make it more intense, hoping that I won't be able to take it. They don't want me to enjoy anything, and that allows me to find ways to like everything, especially when I think about how angry that must make Halloran.

When I feel the shards of agony coalesce into a mountain of ecstasy, I hope the other women are watching. Let them see me enjoy my torment. Let them see that I can take it and either come or laugh. Let them see the crazy bitch who has killed two able-bodied men, who has to be kept locked up constantly because otherwise she's too dangerous.

I can keep this up as long as you. Just try me.

The solitary confinement messes with my head, I admit. I try to count the days. I think it's been two weeks. But sometimes I ask myself, did I already add to the tally today, or was that the day before? I wish I could scratch lines into the walls to keep count like they do in prisons in the movies, though that wouldn't help. I consider asking Gabriel how long it's been, but I know he won't answer. I've taunted Vaughn a handful of times, but the only response I've ever gotten was a gag. Sometimes I come up with a fresh insult so that they have to gag me. I like that I can get them to do it. If they ever figure it out, they'll stop, but they haven't yet.

On the last morning of my solitary confinement, I laugh so hard my sides hurt when I realize that Vaughn and Gabriel look worse than me. Though they are diligent in keeping me bound and helpless, they appear sleep-deprived and chronically fatigued. I'm sure with Miller and Roy gone, all the work at the asylum has fallen to them. Feeding and cleaning the women, the maintenance and supply runs — it's amazing they're pulling it off. On top of that, they have to concoct new ways to try and break me, a war they are losing daily.

The next day, I sleep and sleep, uninterrupted in the morning — the men don't come for me. Sometime in the afternoon, Vaughn and Gabriel — now looking well-rested — take me for feeding and cleaning, but then dump me in the lounge without a word.

When the women see me, it's like they've witnessed a resurrection. They just stare, and I'm not sure what to say. I notice that all of the women are now fully bound in jackets. Most are also locked to wheelchairs; those who are not have had their ankles restrained by chains and cuffs.

They're not taking any chances anymore.

This is my fault, and I'm sorry, though I don't know how to tell them this right now. In fact, I don't even know if the women have permission to speak with me. Did Vaughn threaten to punish them? I wouldn't be surprised.

I opt for caution. I sit and wait, maintaining an active alertness, keeping quiet. I don't avoid eye contact with the others, but I don't stare. When I see that Helena looks away when I catch her watching me, I stop turning in her direction. She doesn't appear angry at me, but she's jumpy. Fearful.

And yet, after what feels like a few hours, she says, "Marla. Are you okay?"

I nod.

"They were showing us what they were doing to you, but they stopped a week ago. We thought… we thought you…"

I smile at her and wink. *No, I'm not dead. But they didn't want to you to see me standing up to them.*

"I'm sorry for what I said to you. About Gabriel."

Fuck it.

"It's okay," I reply. "You were right."

"They didn't tell us what happened. Is Miller dead? Did you kill him?"

"I did."

Several of the women smile; for some, it's the first facial expression I've ever seen them make.

"And if I'd been a little faster, or a little luckier, I would have killed Vaughn too."

It's then, after all the time I've spent refusing to cry in front of them, that the tears come.

"This would be over, if I'd just-"

"Stop," says Helena, interrupting me. "It's okay."

"No, because now they're being too careful and I won't get another chance and-"

"Marla, stop!" Helena takes a deep breath. "Nobody expected you to take them down on your own. But now we see what you've done and we're going to do the same, so don't give up hope now. That goes for all of us. We outnumber them. Vaughn and Gabriel are exhausted. They're going to make a mistake."

"I've got a different theory," says Vaughn.

We were so wrapped up listening to Helena, none of us noticed the door opening behind us. Now Vaughn is looming over me, hands on my shoulders, while Gabriel stands with his arms crossed in front of his chest. He doesn't make eye contact.

"That was inspiring, Helena. And you made a good point: we've been really overworked lately. So we're going to make some changes until the place gets back to normal. All right?"

Vaughn strides over to Helena and grabs the handles of her wheelchair. Dragging it behind him, he pulls her chair until Helena is directly across from me. Frozen vipers bite hard in my stomach, because whatever Vaughn's about to do, he wants me to see it.

While everyone else watches, Vaughn releases the straps binding Helena to her wheelchair. When he finishes, he lifts her out and sits down in her place, then lays her across his knees, ass up.

"Pay attention, Marla."

I would have gladly taken her place. I'd like to think everyone knows this now. The spanking makes her howl, tears streaming freely. If he'd done that to me, I think it would have tickled a little, but Helena isn't used to it — fond of it — like me.

"Okay, Vaughn!" I shout. "We get it!"

"Oh, the fuck you do!" Vaughn keeps pounding Helena's rear as he speaks. Her screams are earsplitting. "And even if you do, Marla, it sounds like Helena here doesn't. So this is as much on her as it is on you. But that's the good news. Gabriel, take her."

He moves in and yanks Helena to her feet, holding her in place.

Vaughn gets up and crouches in front of me. "Forget bad behavior. If you even *talk* about acting out in any way, we are going to punish Helena. And I don't just mean you, Marla. This goes for all of you, but double for Marla. If you do as you're told, we won't have a problem. But if you make trouble, Gabriel and I will take Helena to the torture room and give you a real show."

I know what I want to say to Vaughn, but if I do he'll hurt Helena. *It isn't worth it.*

Helena, however, feels differently. She snorts, and takes the words out of my mouth: "That didn't go so well last time."

Vaughn laughs. "You poor thing, you're learning all the wrong lessons from Marla. Gabriel, take her downstairs."

Helena doesn't protest. She looks to me with icy determination in her eyes.

Then I feel a pull and my chair swings around. "Don't worry, Marla," says Vaughn. "You're coming too."

CHAPTER 23
MARLA

For the first time since my abduction, I've been drugged.

Vaughn tossed the pill, making me catch it in my mouth. He threatened to spank Helena until I swallowed. He spanks her anyway.

After an hour, however, I realize the pill isn't a sedative. It's a stimulant. Maybe even straight caffeine. Even though time is crawling by, I don't feel drowsy; in fact, my mind races.

In addition to my usual straightjacket, a thick, leather hood has been fitted over my head, enclosing me in total darkness. The only sound comes from my pounding heart; I breathe through two holes cut out by my nostrils. I sit on the mattress in my cell, afraid if I get up I'll lose my bearings, and I refuse to let that happen. The sensory deprivation and confinement will rapidly bend my mind in half if I don't keep myself grounded — literally.

So why give me drugs to keep me awake? The only explanation I come up with is Vaughn's twisted sense of sadism: each second I'm awake, all I can do is fume about what they did to Helena, coupled with my total inability to prevent it. Vaughn's finally found a torture I can't learn to enjoy.

Bravo, you twisted fuck.

Helena looked at me and said "It's not your fault" three times before Vaughn gagged her. I know she meant well, but it *was* my fault. And each time she said it, Vaughn laughed and Gabriel whipped her extra hard.

What really kills me is how quickly Gabriel has fallen into lockstep with Vaughn and Halloran. I tell myself that he's going along with the charade and that his plan for our escape is still possible, though I don't see how. The next time there's an exhibition, I have no doubt I'm going to be the star of the show. There won't be any opportunity to sneak me out, even if Gabriel can, or still wants to.

I can't even stand to think about escaping right now. The fact is, I've struck out each time, and now if I try and fail, the brunt of the consequences will fall on Helena and the other women. How can I gamble with their pain and misery? I won't do it. Maybe I should, but it feels wrong.

At least being locked in my cell, hooded and bound, means that I can't bring further wrath down upon Helena. Yet, even this gets taken away from me when Vaughn enters my cell and rips away the hood.

"Morning, sunshine."

He buckles a leash around my neck and pulls me to my feet. "Do I have to tell you what will happen if you don't behave?"

"No."

He tugs the leash, cutting off my breath for a second and yanking me forward. "What was that?"

"No, sir."

Vaughn grins and pinches my cheek. A couple weeks ago, I would have bitten off his fingers without thinking twice. "That's better. You know, Gabriel was always the one who enjoyed this kinky stuff, but it's starting to grow on me too."

Wonderful.

I don't speak as Vaughn leads me upstairs to Halloran's office. The floor is freezing. Though it's healing, I still limp a little from the wound on my foot.

When we reach the office, Gabriel and the old man are

waiting quietly. I've never been to this part of the building before, and I can't help observing everything. It smells of tobacco, liquor and sweat, and I come close to vomiting imagining what must happen in this room when Halloran's alone, eyes glued to the wall-spanning, flat-screen monitor.

Currently he's watching Helena languish in the dungeon. Strapped to a wooden chair by her arms, legs and neck, she's blinking rapidly, fighting back tears. How long has she been there? What else have they done to her? I feel the fury rising in my gut, but choke it back down, knowing I'm only going to make matters worse.

As we enter, Gabriel doesn't look at me. He stands in the corner, looking down at his feet.

You goddamn coward, I think, wishing I could strangle the life out of everyone in this room.

"Thank you, Vaughn," says Halloran. "Sit her down. Marla, I think it's time we spoke."

He hasn't asked a question, so I don't respond, other than to give him my full attention.

"Please, I want you to speak honestly. I promise, nothing you say right now, in private, will be punished. We won't harm Helena, as long as you participate fully in this conversation."

My presence in the room shows how little his promises are worth, but what can I do?

"Fine."

"Good." He pours himself a double of some kind of whiskey, taking his time. I feel Vaughn's eyes on my back, but Gabriel may as well be a ghost, or a statue. I can't get a read on what he's feeling, assuming he has any emotions at all.

"I'll start by asking a dumb question: have you enjoyed the past couple weeks?"

"No, I haven't."

"Because you don't like seeing your friend get hurt?"

"That's correct. I don't think it's fair to punish her for what I've done."

Halloran nods and sips his drink. "Perfectly understandable, Marla. It's a gross injustice, without question. By now, though, you've seen that appealing to our sense of fairness is beyond foolish, haven't you?"

"Yes." And because he told me to speak freely, I add, "You don't have any conscience whatsoever."

"No, not for you," he agrees. "Vaughn and Gabriel, on the other hand, I care about. And I care about my home. With Roy and Miller gone, Vaughn and Gabriel have been picking up the slack, but at great personal cost. I would like to lessen that burden."

I can't help myself. "You could let us go. That would make life easier."

Vaughn laughs. "Shit, why didn't we think of that?"

Halloran smiles. "You know Marla, I've thought about selling off the lot of you to my clients. I know enough who would gladly take you off my hands, and then Vaughn could find us some more fresh faces."

"It's fun and I'm good at it," Vaughn adds. "When this place is fully booked, I miss the hunt."

"And I like variety," Halloran continues. "But that's why I've enjoyed watching your time here, Marla. You've surprised us in so many ways. I think we've only scratched the surface of the fun we could have with you. I've owned this asylum for a long time, Marla, and the things I want to do with you... I have a list, and I will not let you go without crossing off every item on it."

Gabriel still refuses to look at me. I wonder if he's even listening to his father.

"So I dismissed the idea of selling my toys. I'm keeping you. But I can't have Vaughn and Gabriel wasting hours of their day torturing you and Helena. I want my girls to behave themselves without a daily show of force. Is this not a win-win? I get a little peace, and you don't have to watch your friends suffer. What do you think?"

"I think that I should turn down any offer you make on principle, but I need to consider it."

Halloran downs the rest of his drink and pours another. "Take your time, Marla, though don't be surprised if the offer gets taken off the table. As soon as Vaughn finds some new orderlies, I'm giving him a week's vacation to do whatever he pleases. I have a feeling he's going to spend much of it with you."

I ignore Vaughn's quiet snickers. "Thanks for the warning. Got anything else?"

"I do, actually." Halloran gets up and steps around his desk. He props himself up against it and looks at me from the higher vantage point. "Since you've been here, Gabriel has tried to tame you and Vaughn has tried to break you, both unsuccessfully. But if you take my deal, then it will show them, the other girls and my clients, that I'm in charge here for a reason. Reputation is always a good investment, so if you take my deal, I'll see to it that Helena is granted leniency. She'll no longer be held responsible for your transgressions."

Fuck me.

Isn't that what I want? To have her be left alone?

His promises are meaningless, Marla! You know this!

"How do I know you'll keep your word on that?"

Halloran sighs. "There's no way to be sure, but I'll have what I want. I'll have you, kneeling before me, doing anything I say. Helena's a strong, attractive woman, but she's nothing compared to you."

"You're a fucking bastard." I turn to Gabriel. "And you, how can you stand being related to this psychopath?"

Finally, he speaks. His voice is raw and soft, as if the syllables are stabbing his own chest. "I wish I hadn't taken you out that day. Maybe things would have been different."

"Yeah," I spit. "It would have taken me longer to see you're just like your father." As I say it, I recall the way I felt with him that day, before I ran. I remember how, for a minute, my hopes felt like more than wishful thinking. I could see myself having a future that didn't involve padded walls and floors, or tears and cries of lost souls. But was any of it real? Losing the trust I put in Gabriel hurt, and I wanted him to feel it. From the look on his face, I figure I've succeeded.

Nodding and rising to his feet, Halloran looks to Vaughn.

"Get her out of here."

"With pleasure," he says, taking the handlebars of my wheelchair.

"I don't make deals with my possessions often, Marla," Halloran says as I'm dragged from the room. "You won't get another."

CHAPTER 24
GABRIEL

Halloran follows Vaughn and Marla on the monitor, clicking to cycle through the hallway monitors until they reach her cell. He and I watch as Vaughn removes her from the wheelchair and dumps her onto the mattress.

Vaughn is speaking, but the sound is muted. Cursing, Halloran jams his thumb on the button to raise the volume. "Hey, my next stop is the dungeon to get Helena and take her back to the lounge, but I can leave her there all night long if that's what you want."

"Okay!" she snaps. "I'll have an answer for you in the morning."

"Atta girl." Vaughn winks, then slowly pulls the cell door closed behind him.

Halloran mutes the TV again and turns to me. "I thought that went much better than expected, overall. What do you think?"

In the past five years, I've lost count of the number of times I'd felt positive that if there was a Hell, I would spend eternity there for sure. There have also been times that I've thought, morbidly, that after a lifetime spent in this asylum, the real Hell would pale in comparison. But listening to the meeting here made me wish, if there is a Hell, I could head on down right now and spare myself the wait.

The betrayal on her face, the venom in her voice... For Halloran, being hated by his women is normal. I'm pretty well-accustomed to it too, but not from Marla.

On the monitor she sobs violently, shaking so hard it looks like a seizure. I'm grateful Halloran cut the sound again, because if I had to listen there's no way I could keep it together.

"I think you should rescind that offer immediately."

This catches the old man off guard. "Really? Explain."

God this is fucked up.

"Ostensibly, your goal is to control Marla, get her following the rules and accepting her lot, correct?"

Halloran nods, but there's a calculating menace behind his eyes that could crack a steel girder.

"Well, that's never going to happen. She'll behave if Helena's well-being is at stake, but once that's off the table, Marla will risk her own safety without hesitation. If you make this deal, she might act compliant at first, but eventually she'll see an opportunity to lash out. Maybe I'll get careless with her again. It could be you or Vaughn, or a guest. Especially a guest. They're so used to the women here being irrevocably broken. They will definitely misjudge Marla and she will take full advantage. That won't be good for your reputation."

I wish more than anything to witness a future where my prediction comes true, and Halloran finds himself at the center of a real shitstorm caused by Marla. A dead billionaire killed by a sex slave at a hidden prison asylum? The investigation would be national news for years; it would be the end of the madness Halloran has built.

Instead, he's nodding and watching Marla bawl. "You're probably right, Gabriel."

"I *am* right. But if you keep Helena as a carrot, you won't need the stick. Marla needs a purpose, such as protecting Helena."

I have no illusion that Marla would drive a dagger right

through my sternum if she could hear me right now. I'm telling the absolute truth, and it will help Halloran, if he listens to me.

"Gabriel, that's quite insightful, and I believe you're correct. However, you've missed something critical." Halloran walks to the monitor as if he could get physically closer to Marla. Maybe that's how he feels, watching her trembling image.

"What's that?"

He smirks to himself. "I don't want her to have a purpose, I want her broken. That's what I enjoy, Gabriel. That's *my* purpose. The journey is fun, but the destination must always be the same. Marla has shown me that more than ever. I can't explain why it has to be that way, any more than you can identify why you like tying girls up and spanking them."

I know this already. "You're not the only one to have monstrous desires, Halloran. People who are otherwise decent don't act on them."

Halloran sighs and sits back down. He hits the remote and turns off the monitor, which I rarely see him do.

"You're right. If I were a good man, I would bury that part of myself. I would think about it, masturbate to it, maybe even hire prostitutes willing to role-play it. I have done all of that in the past. It kept me satisfied for a time, but it wasn't enough. Not for me. Have I told you about your grandfather, Gibson Halloran?"

"You've tried," I snarl. Is he really going to try and justify himself? Or is this just for my edification? Maybe he wants to tell somebody. I know how that feels.

"Don't worry, I'm not going pretend he was misunderstood or a product of his time. He loved me, like I love you, but he was an even worse monster than me. He was the principal at the local high school, and he ran a tight ship. When I was a student there, he encouraged me to use my status as the principal's son to intimidate women into getting what I wanted from them."

"That's demented."

Halloran laughs. "I was way ahead of him. I acted as if I hadn't already been doing it. And when I saw how thrilled he was, I happily bragged about each girl. He memorized the names, and one-by-one called them into his office. Told them what he knew. Disciplined them, as you can imagine."

Rising from my chair I sway in place, my stomach on the verge of a violent purge. "Okay, that's enough, I don't want to hear this."

"Sit down!" Halloran roars. "You're going to listen, because this is your history, and you need to know it."

Sneering, I sit. Hearing him out might be what I need to end this horror show once and for all. If Halloran thinks I'll embrace his legacy, he's insane.

"Good. Now, you can imagine the effect this had on the girls. They were afraid of me, but even more afraid of my father. Some of them changed schools. A few had breakdowns. One killed herself, that I know of. I was having the time of my life until I met a girl named Joanna Philips."

Joanna? My mother was named Joanna. *It can't be the same person. That's impossible. There's no way.*

"She was so beautiful, but she wasn't intimidated by me. I may have been the principal's son, but she was the mayor's daughter. When I told my father, he said he'd speak with her."

As I watch, Halloran balls his fists and bares his teeth.

"Of course Joanna told her father about what mine did. Gibson was arrested immediately, but he used his connections to get out on bond. Maybe he should have stayed in jail, but how could he have known that the mother of one of our victims worked as a typist at the court? She was there at his hearing, and later that night she was there at his front door. She stabbed him nineteen times in the stomach and chest, and he bled out on his own porch while I slept upstairs in my room."

Halloran refills his whiskey glass and raises it into the air in tribute. He drinks nearly the entire glass and slams the rest down on his desk.

"Gabriel, I learned two lasting lessons from your grandfather's death. The first is that our lives aren't stories — or if they are, then they're not all especially good. They can end suddenly, and unhappily. Look at Roy and Miller. Did they think their stories were over? Did they know they were living their last days on earth? Of course not. So a man must be aware that his world can come crashing down, and do everything in his power to prevent it."

"And what was the other?" I ask, wanting this to be over already.

Halloran smiles nostalgically. "The same thing the whole world's parents try to impart on their children: do what makes you happy! Gibson did. He knew that you only get one life, and so you may as well do with it what you please."

"Even if that means ruining dozens of other lives?"

"I didn't choose to be this way, Gabriel. I'm not going to let bad luck stop me from living the life I want, even if it took me decades to build it, which it did. I decided this when I was your age."

I'm speechless. What is there to say to this? I wish I'd let Halloran tell me the story earlier. I don't know what I would have done in response, but at least I would have done it a long time ago.

Finally, I get up. "So, that's it then? No compromise. You want Marla broken, so that's how it has to be? Have I got that right?"

"You do."

In a way, I'm relieved. Halloran's immutable need to destroy women, no matter what, has made my decision easy. If he had opted to let Marla be the exception, it would have meant years of living with the guilt. For years I would have to watch Marla endure Vaughn and Halloran's cruelty while fearing to fight because it would hurt the other girls. But now that's not going to happen.

I'm done. I've had enough. I can see that now.

"Fine," I say. "I'll break her. But you know that pain and torture aren't enough. She needs to lose hope for good. When she truly believes that what we shared is gone forever, and that I will be of no help to her ever again, she will be lost. I'm the only one who can do that to her, so I want something in return."

Seeing Halloran's intrigued grin makes me want to punch through the wall, but I hold my nerve. *Just a little longer, and then this will be done.*

"What's that?" he asks.

"After I break Marla, I'm leaving. For good. I'm going somewhere, I don't know where, and I'm starting a new life. You won't come looking for me, and Vaughn won't show up someday to tie up loose ends. I'll keep your secret, but I'll have a so-called insurance policy, in case I die suspiciously. All I ask is to be left alone."

Halloran stiffens, and his grin evaporates. "I'm your father, Gabriel. I want to be in your life."

My heart goes out to you, pops. "You've got Vaughn. He worships you."

"He's a dog, not a son."

I laugh. "Maybe so. But I want out of here. I can wait until you replace Roy and Miller, but there won't be any need. With Marla under control, the others will fall in line. So can you live with that?"

After a beat, Halloran nods. "Yeah. If that's how it has to be, then fine. But you better figure Marla out before I change my mind."

"Don't worry," I reply as I throw open the door to his office. "I know exactly what I have to do."

This is it, I think to myself as I march to my quarters to prepare. *This is how the end begins.*

CHAPTER 25
MARLA

"You can't do this," says Helena.

The look in her eyes devastates me. If I hadn't cried enough for one lifetime, I would still be sobbing now.

"Think about it, Marla! Obeying them isn't going to help us! They'll still do whatever they want. Promises mean nothing to them."

I shake my head. "I can't be the one to bring you more pain." I sniff and shake in my jacket. "If it was only me taking the heat, then I could live with whatever happens. But not if one of you could end up hurt, or killed."

"I think we're willing to take that chance," Helena says, looking around the room.

We're together in the lounge, just us women. I know at any moment Vaughn or Gabriel will bust in and break up our discussion. Vaughn wanted a decision, and I've made it. Halloran will probably have some fun basking in his victory over me, and that's fine. Let him. I'd rather endure the humiliation knowing Helena wasn't being tortured for my recalcitrance.

I've never believed in fate. I don't assume life will turn out one way or the other. Yet, I always believed that escape from the asylum would happen. There was no way I could end up here forever. It was inconceivable. Now, though, it's sinking in. I tell myself the cards were stacked against me from the start, and this was inevitable. I feel as though that's supposed to comfort me, but it doesn't really.

"Marla, you do what you feel is right, but we're still going to resist them, whatever the cost. Somebody has to."

Shaking my head, I nearly lose my composure when Gabriel and Vaughn enter the lounge. I'm actually glad; I'd rather deal with whatever they want than listen to Helena condemn herself to more suffering.

"Good afternoon, ladies," says Vaughn. "Have you been behaving? Marla, I know you have. What about the others?"

"We've been good," I reply, staring down at my crossed arms. The fabric of my jacket is splotched with spots where tears are still drying.

"That's fantastic. Really, it is. Keep it that way, ladies, or I'll be back for you." Vaughn grabs the handles of Helena's wheelchair and pushes her out.

"Wait, where are they going?" I ask, trying to twist around enough to see.

"Torture chamber," Gabriel mutters. He takes my chair and we depart as well.

"Why? I haven't done anything, I swear!"

We head for the cell block. "Doesn't matter. Did you think you could really make a deal with us, Marla? We own you."

We?

Oh, no. Gabriel...

I could scream, but I keep my voice level. "What's going on? Where are we going?"

"Quiet."

"What's Vaughn doing to Helena?"

"Whatever the fuck he wants, Marla. Now be quiet."

Gabriel buzzes us into my cell and shuts the door. As it clangs shut, and the lock clicks, I'm close to giving in to despair. There's nothing I can do for Helena, or for myself. Gabriel, who I once thought could help me, is not the man I thought. He's a monster like the rest.

I should have killed him too. That day in the woods I left him on the ground, wrenched in pain. I should have found a heavy rock and bashed in his skull. Then I could have run and gotten a much bigger head start. If I knew then what I know now…

Helena was right. We may as well fight.

After releasing me from the wheelchair, Gabriel folds it up and leaves it in the corner. He lifts me up by my jacket, turns me to face the wall and pushes me up against it. His hot breath warms my ear as he squeezes my ass. I hiss angrily, hating that his touch still feels good.

"This is going to be over soon," he whispers in my ear.

Is that supposed to be a threat?

"Go to Hell, Gabriel," I snap, though my voice is like a wisp of smoke, dissolving into the air.

"Actually, that's the plan."

In my cell he has left his duffel bag and supplies. From it he takes out a pair of thick chains and threads them through the D-rings on my jacket's shoulders. He lifts each chain until he can fasten them to hooks high up on the wall.

While he binds me I wonder what he meant. How is he going to Hell? And how is this ending soon? What is he doing? And does Halloran know about it? What the fuck is going on?

Gabriel opens the strap running up between my thighs and spreads my legs. He runs his fingers through my lips. "I still make you wet. That's fucked up, Marla."

"You're one to talk, you piece of shit."

Pain explodes across my backside from the slap of a thick, wooden paddle. The sound booms in the tiny chamber, matched only by my anguished cry.

When I stop gasping and regain my composure, Gabriel draws his hand across the skin he punished. "Did you think of Helena when you said that? Did it cross your mind that Vaughn may be watching? That he could be doing the same to her?"

His words hit me harder than any whip or paddle.

"You have no control, Marla! None!"

I feel my resolve start to slip away as tears pool in my vision.

"You can't help anyone, because none of us are going to be stupid enough to let you outside ever again. And Halloran's not going to hire two new orderlies. He's going to get four. In a month, this place will be a fortress."

No no no no no...

"Vaughn is going to start taking more women because there's no real reason you need to have private cells."

Please, no...

"The women who witnessed your rebellion will be sold off to our clients. Eventually, the only girl here who knows about it will be you. Halloran is going to keep you here until one of you dies, and make no mistake: that is the only way to leave this place."

No!

Gabriel hooks a finger around my chin and pulls until our faces are close enough to touch. I shut my eyes, not wanting to see him. I could smash my forehead into the bridge of his nose, or try to bite his cheek, but I can't bring myself to do either. There's no point.

"Open your eyes, Marla."

"Go away." Tears are finding their way through my eyelids now. "Just leave me alone."

"Open your eyes," he repeats, angrier.

Get it over with. I do as asked, but the face I see is not what I expect. His skin is puffy and pink, eyes bloodshot. He looks as grief-stricken as me. Tortured and dead inside. In a flash, our conversation replays from my memory.

This is going to be over soon.

Go to Hell, Gabriel. Actually, that's the plan.

That is the only way to leave this place.

"Gabriel?" I sniff.

"Your training is over. Tonight there's going to be a special presentation. Vaughn and Halloran will do to you whatever they want. And I'm going to do what I should have a long time ago."

I shake my head frantically. "Please, Gabriel, no. Please don't."

"I have to, Marla."

Then he leans in close and whispers in my ear.

He says, "For Iris."

What?

He backs away and when I look again he's unbuckling the belt of his trousers.

For Iris?

That doesn't make any sense. How would him dying *now* be for Iris?

"But before I leave you, I'm going to give you one parting gift."

My mind races, trying to piece together what he said. A fire burns in my chest, and my core warms as I watched him spread lube across his hardening cock. After all that's happened, I still want him, and now there's a feeling spreading through my body that maybe I'm not wrong. Something is going on.

"Remember who your master is, Marla. When you're being used by the others, tell yourself it's me, and maybe you'll enjoy it."

"Do what you want," I say, turning away from him, hoping he can hear the intended invitation. "I don't care."

"Perfect."

I feel a pulling and tugging at my back. It takes a minute for me to realize that my straightjacket is getting looser. Soon my sleeves come free, and then the jacket is coming off completely. I slump to the floor, no longer supported by the chains binding me to the wall.

"On your feet!" Gabriel commands.

Pushing myself up with all fours, I steady my legs and stand before him, nude and unbound, staring into his gaze. His pants are down around his ankles; he'd have trouble pursuing me if I could run away. I could take a swing, try to knock him out, but I don't. I place my hands behind my back and bow my head.

"Stand on the mattress."

I do as he says.

"Get down on your knees."

I obey his command.

"Serve your master."

He holds his cock up to my mouth. I open wide, take in his length. Sealing my lips around him I try not to think. Just act. Suck hard. Go up. Go down. Let him guide me.

I try not to think, but I still do. Does he really trust me not to maim him? I could do it at any time, but I don't. It doesn't matter.

Tonight he might die, leaving me here alone in Hell, in which case I want to give myself to him one last time.

But if he means something else... and he needs my cooperation... then I'm with him.

And if this is a game — if he's lied from the moment we met, then there's no point to anything. Then I'm lost, forever, and nothing anyone does to me will ever matter, because I won't even really be there anymore. I'll be gone, like the other girls. And that'll be all right.

Gabriel twitches as my tongue dances around his shaft; he fists my hair, holding me against his hard body. His grip sends a shiver of desire through me, and I don't complain when he abruptly pulls out and pushes me back into the mattress. I watch calmly as he finishes undressing, taking in the site of his heaving chest and still rock hard erection.

"Normally this is the part where I'd tie your hands at least," he says. He motions at his supplies. "I still could."

"Whatever you want," I reply.

"I'll make an exception."

He drops down onto the mattress; as he does I spread my legs and cast my arms backward. My breasts rise and fall quickly as I feel Gabriel's hands clasp around my wrists, pinning them against the wall until they sink as far as they can into the padding. He drives his lips into mine, and my core surges with warmth.

I hadn't expected a kiss. It feels too intimate. That isn't what this is about, is it? Or is Gabriel as confused as me? Does his mind tell him one thing and his body another? That's the effect he has on me; it's only fitting if he came here looking for gratification, but found love instead.

Still, though, when we've tasted one another long enough, Gabriel drives his cock deep into my soaked chasm, eliciting a euphoric moan from me — the first I've made in what feels like a year. His lips find my breast and then my nipple, sucking the hard pebble until my eyes shut and I'm thrust into a state of bliss I haven't experienced since that day in the forest.

Gabriel's rhythmic pounding shoots waves of ecstasy through me. With each drive of his cock, with every new touch of his tongue or exploration from his fingers, I become less and less a captive of monsters. I become free and fulfilled, and though it's only for a little while, in my state, time stretches on endlessly.

Am I supposed to be asking permission to climax? Some part of my brain is functioning enough to vaguely remember doing that, but Gabriel doesn't ask. He, too, is enraptured, lost in the moment. What's going through his mind, I don't want to know.

By the time Gabriel climaxes, I'm long gone, deep in subspace. I pant and writhe when Gabriel lifts my body and lays me out on my stomach. I ignore the cool spots on the mattress where sweat has soaked in. Gabriel pours lube between my cheeks and spreads it around, though I already feel so wet it hardly seems necessary. I hear him rooting through his bag for a moment, then I groan as a cool, hard object presses into my ass. Gabriel eases it in without resistance, my hole hungry for the intrusion and twinge of pain.

"Marla," he whispers.

His cock slips through my folds once again, and his fingers rub my clit as he thrusts vigorously.

"I want you to come so hard," he says. "Like it will be the last time."

I can't tell if his words are more ominous or sexy, but I have no trouble doing exactly what he says. He pinches my nipples, and I howl as I orgasm, drunk on pain and love, on hate and fear. Gabriel's fingers trace a path from my chest to my thighs, and their electric touch keeps me gasping until his cock begins to hammer anew.

What are you doing, Gabriel? How can you do this to me and then leave me? Is that what you're going to do? If it is, it'll be the meanest thing you've done to me yet.

If this is the last I'll ever feel Gabriel against me, the last I'll ever smell his musk or taste his salt, the last I'll ever scream his name as I come, then the sensations and details have been seared into my memory. Like a canyon gouged into the earth by an eternally flowing river, Gabriel has permanently carved himself into my mind. Nothing will ever make me forget this day.

He lies with me on the mattress, arms wrapped around me, for at least an hour. Then he dresses in silence and collects the toys and restraints in his bag.

"You don't have to do this," I say before he can leave.

"I'm sorry, but I do," he replies. As he shuts the cell door, he adds, "You know why."

Yes, I know.

For Iris.

CHAPTER 26
MARLA

It figures. For the first time since I arrived at Halloran Asylum, no restraints of any kind bind my body. No cuffs, or chains — no straightjacket — Gabriel took all of them. After weeks of being bound, I dreamed of a moment of semi-freedom. Now that it's come, I'm paralyzed.

For hours I lie on the mattress, body and mind both exhausted. I want to shut down, but I can't. I'm worried about Gabriel. Is there more I could have done? Would it have been any different if I'd not tried to run that day, or would I have reached this point in another way?

I could question each decision I've made and imagine alternate outcomes and busy my mind for weeks. I might just do that. Go well beyond the night I met Vaughn, imagine life if I had never insulted Gerald on TV — I'd have the same reporter job at a different station, most likely. Maybe even in the same town.

Joining us now is the newest member of our news team, Marla Angel. Marla, what's the story?

Thanks, Pat. As you can see, there was a lot of anticipation for a Paco's Tacos truck to arrive in Hunter's Valley. The line extended down two blocks of East Main Street and caused a serious traffic backup.

Customers waited up to an hour to try one of the signature dishes, but many said it was worth the wait.

Did you get to try one, Marla?

I sure did!

I'm dreaming of strips of beef marinated in tomatillo salsa verde when the door to my cell buzzes open. Vaughn stands in the portal, blocking it, fists clenched and ready to fight if he has to. Halloran peers around Vaughn tentatively, like a visitor at the zoo who's afraid of a caged animal.

Vaughn steps in and links his arm behind his back. "Come, take your best shot."

I look up at him for a second, then go back to staring at the wall.

"Total freebie. No repercussions."

No thanks, Vaughn.

He widens the stance of his feet, spreading his legs. "Come on, go for the balls. I won't try to stop you."

"I don't think she's interested," Halloran observes.

"You think this is for real?" asks Vaughn.

I'm not even sure myself.

"We'll see," says Halloran as he hands Vaughn a flat, gray cardboard box. "Be careful until she's bound."

Vaughn flicks the top off the box and takes out a lacy, black bra and matching thong. "Put them on," he orders, throwing the garments at me.

I don't scramble into motion, but I don't dawdle either. Acting mechanically, I dress, finding the bra and panties to fit perfectly. They're fancier than any I ever bought for myself, and in another context I'd feel devastatingly sexy.

"See, this is nice," says Vaughn, taking a good long look. "I really owe you an apology, Marla. You've got such great tits. Keeping them hidden in a straightjacket was wrong, and I'm sorry."

He laughs at his own line, leaning against the frame of the door like a model in a menswear catalog. I look straight ahead, arms limp at my sides.

"Vaughn just apologized to you, Marla. What do you say?"

asks Halloran.

"Thank you, sir," I mumble.

The old man steps forward, no longer skittish. "Are you behaving now to protect the other women?"

"I can't protect them."

"Oh screw this," Vaughn says, unzipping his jeans. "I know one way to find out the truth."

"Stop." Halloran holds out his hand. "Put it away. Save it for the ceremony. When she sees the girls watching, that's when we'll have our answer. Got it?"

"Yeah, sure," Vaughn replies, though the disappointment in his voice is clear. He winks at me as he zips back up. "Soon, sweetheart."

"Get her ready," Halloran orders, disappearing from view.

Vaughn produces a pair of handcuffs from his pocket and tosses them at my feet. "Behind the back."

I do as told, tightening the cuffs until they dig into the skin of my wrists. Vaughn checks them anyway, and I cringe as he tries to squeeze the cuffs a little tighter, but I don't fight. Satisfied, he swats me on the backside and tells me to move.

Following his directions, I walk ahead of him, always in his field of view. Soon we've reached the third floor and the ballroom. I recall the first time I saw it, the night of the exhibition; it feels like another age. Not much has changed, except the pedestal nearest the window has been stacked atop two other pedestals, rising a few feet off the ground. Vaughn instructs me to climb on and get on my knees, then uses a chain to bind my cuffed wrists to the pedestal.

In the past, I'd have lamented being bound facing into the room, wanting to gaze out the window, but now I'm actually glad not to have to face the outside world. I know they won't take me outside again — not alive, anyway.

"Think the old man is watching right now? Is he making sure I don't cheat and have a little fun with you before the big show?"

"I don't know," I mumble.

"I bet he is. Where else would he be?"

Vaughn cups my breasts through the bra and squeezes gently.

"What do you think he'd do if I whipped it out and made you suck it? Think he'd be mad?"

I feel an urge to remind Vaughn he's too much of a bitch to try it, but it only tickles at the periphery of my heart. A month ago I'd have let it out and laughed.

"Yes, he'd be mad."

Vaughn nods. He lets go of my chest and strokes my hair. "I know, you're right. It's fine. I've waited this long, what's another hour or two?"

His touch draws out a shiver and I don't try to hide it — not out of any sense of defiance, but nothing makes me try to stop it.

"Ooh, frigid." Vaughn chuckles. "Didn't Gabriel tell you to think of him?"

Of course they were watching.

"Yes," I say.

"Then think of him. I don't care. You can scream his name when you come, it won't bother me. It's only fair, right? You think Bryn and Noriko mind when I call out *your* name?"

Fuck you, I think, a trace of my old self surfacing.

Laughing to himself again, Vaughn adds, "Speaking of the others, I'm their lift to the party, so excuse me for a bit. I'll bring up Helena first so she can be first to see the new you. How does that sound?"

"Whatever you want, sir."

Winking, Vaughn turns and leaves.

For twenty minutes I'm completely alone in the hall, waiting for Vaughn to return. When he takes longer than I expect, I imagine what he's telling the other girls about what's going on. He could be held up, having to bind each of the girls himself, but I know he won't pass up an opportunity to hear himself speak.

As promised, Vaughn returns with Helena. She's locked in her jacket, and a ball gag hangs below her chin like a necklace, ready for use should anyone want to silence her. Her expression remains unchanged when she sees me; her face is an impassive mask. Vaughn pushes her wheelchair until Helena's only a couple feet from me, positioned front and center, facing me directly. Neither of us speak.

Vaughn looks back and forth at us. "Marla, don't be rude. Say hello to your friend."

"Hi, Helena."

"Hi, Marla," she replies before Vaughn can goad her. Helena's words, however, are sharp as fangs.

"Oh, she's pretty mad, Marla. I'm going to go get Maribel. Convince your friend to be civil, okay?"

"Yes, sir."

Helena watches Vaughn until he's out the door, then turns to me. "What did they do to you?"

Not they. Gabriel.

Helena hides it well but she's terrified. Marla the Unbreakable is a changed woman and that's a good reason to be afraid.

"Talk to me, Marla!" Her facade gives, and tears start to fall.

"We're never getting out of here."

Helena shakes her head. "Don't say that. We'll find a way!"

"No," I whisper. "Gabriel told me. They're going to hire more men. They're going to sell you off, bring in newer girls."

"We'll still outnumber them," Helena argues, refusing to accept the truth. "And Gabriel…"

"What about Gabriel?" I snap, though I regret it instantly. I doubt my time with Gabriel yesterday was broadcast to the girls. Helena doesn't know what I do. She doesn't know what he said.

Though it does occur to me that with him gone, Vaughn's going to have a real problem trying to take care of this place himself. But what will that mean for me and the girls? Maybe he'll save time by skipping some of our meals, or our showers. Maybe he'll be less picky when it comes to finding replacements for Roy and Miller, leaving the girls at the mercy of some truly malicious individuals.

Helena doesn't know it, but they're about to need me to be myself more than ever. I wish I could.

Vaughn exaggerates huffing and puffing from exertion when he brings in the last of the girls; each one required a separate trip, as they are all bound in jackets. Like a drive-in show from Hell, they are parked in their wheelchairs in rows facing me.

In the midst of Vaughn's shuttling, Halloran shows up. Like a fussy host preparing for a lavish gala, he sets about preparing the space: he starts by pacing the length of the room, lighting dozens of brass candelabras and floor holders. He loads a half-dozen logs into a wood-burning stove, warming the room.

He then drags a dining table close to my pedestal. He sets out an arrangement of restraints, floggers, canes, plugs and more. He hoists a thick metal case onto the table and unloads several more devices I've never seen before. They can hardly be called toys. These don't look designed for sadistic games for discerning adults. They look meant for torture.

I don't see Halloran finish his chores, but when he does, he climbs onto the pedestal and sits down next to me. "What does it feel like for you, Marla?"

"What does what feel like?"

"Defeat. Surrender. Whatever you want to call it."

A small voice inside implores me not to answer. As if stalling this conversation could delay what's about to happen. "I don't know," I say.

Halloran nods. "Are you past the point of feeling anything? Or are you unable to articulate?"

"No, I feel it. An emptiness." Like a cavern so dark and massive one could shout into it and not hear the echo for a year.

"Elaborate."

I sigh. "I guess it's… I mean, I want to hate you. But it's just not there. It's like a phantom limb. Once in a while I can feel it, but most of the time it's gone."

"Fascinating, Marla. However, emotions can come back,

even if we think they're gone forever. Why can't your hate return?"

Return? That's the wrong word.

"Maybe it can't return because it hasn't truly left. I know I hate you, but I don't feel it. Is that not being broken?"

Halloran slips a finger into the waistband of my panties. I should be convulsing with disgust, but nothing comes.

"Yes, you do sound a little broken to me. Maybe not in the way Gabriel set out for, but that's fine. It's a good start. We'll finish the rest in the future, with or without Gabriel."

Huh? What does that mean? Does he know what Gabriel is about to do? Why did he say that?

My mind races as Halloran slaps my ass a few times. I hardly even feel it.

"My son better get here soon," he says. "We're really tired of waiting."

I look to Helena, who has watched and listened with great interest. In her face, the message is clear: *Hold on, Marla. Please, hold on.*

But in my head, I'm also wondering about Gabriel. Where is he? I think, *What if he's not coming? What if he's already gone?*

CHAPTER 27
MARLA

"We've waited long enough," Halloran says. "I really thought he'd be here."

Vaughn shakes his head. "I'm not surprised. He didn't want to see what we'd do with his precious pet."

"He doesn't need to see it. He can imagine it just fine." Halloran turns to me. "Maybe he'll show up later in some misguided, guilt-stricken attempt to comfort her."

"I'd pay to see that," Vaughn snorts.

They don't have any idea, do they?

They act as if Gabriel is merely leaving. Is that what he told them?

They're right about one thing, though: there's no way Gabriel would have wanted to witness any of this, if just out of hatred for Vaughn and Halloran.

When the presentation starts, Vaughn draws his gun from the waistband of his pants and jams the barrel against my forehead. "If I think you're going to try anything, I will shoot you in the gut and watch you bleed out," he warns. There is no need to tell me, but it has the desired effect on the other girls. Though silent, they are actively watching.

He puts the weapon away and picks out a whip from the

collection of toys. He steps around the pedestals, getting in position to swing at my exposed backside. "I know I'm not as skilled with this as Gabriel, so imagining he's the one doing this to you might be tough. I think I'll get lots of practice though, and soon you won't even be able to tell the difference."

I don't react to his taunt, but when the whip cracks across my backside I do howl in pain. Vaughn swings so hard, he may not realize how much it really hurts. Gabriel would have started off much more slowly, building his way up to the harder strokes — Gabriel wanted me to suffer the right way, and get off from it. Vaughn is just a pure sadist.

I'll always be able to tell the difference, you bastard.

Vaughn lands one stroke after another, and soon my skin burns. Welts are rising, and my eyes water from the pain.

Setting the whip aside, he runs his fingers over my thong, finding his way up between my legs.

"You weren't thinking about Gabriel, were you?" he asks. "You're not wet at all."

Halloran watches from the audience. Sitting in a high-backed, black king's chair, he strokes Amber's hair absentmindedly. During the whipping he smirked, enjoying Vaughn's performance, but now he glares.

"I'm sorry, sir," I say loud enough for Halloran to hear.

Barking a raucous laugh, Vaughn turns to the other girls. "Did you hear what she called me? Tell me you heard that."

"We heard," grumbles Helena.

Vaughn lifts the cups of my bra, then yanks them apart with his bare hands. He fondles my breasts, sighing to himself. "Let's see what else we can get her to do."

He leaves the remains of my bra hanging at my sides while searching the table. He picks out a set of nipple clamps connected by a thin chain. He attaches them gingerly, as though worried he might do it incorrectly. Though unimposing in appearance, the clamps pinch tightly, sending twin rivers of electric anguish through my chest.

"Gabriel really liked using these on you. They hurt, but you like them, huh?"

Gabriel liked them, and that's why I did, you ass clown.

Vaughn lifts the clamps' chain to my mouth and sets it between my teeth. "Don't let go." He picks out a short-tailed flogger and swats at my breasts with it, aiming carefully to not hit the chain. Still, the blitz of lashes leaves me shaking and dry as ever. During the flogging I held my mouth open, not wanting to bite the metal chain too hard, and now a line of drool escapes my lips and lands on my chest. Feeling humiliated, my cheeks begin to blush.

Wait…

Something isn't right.

Why does the drool bother me?

It shouldn't have mattered. I was supposed to be past caring about pain and humiliation, but I'm not. Far from it.

Gabriel, what's going on?

I wish he could answer me.

Halloran rises from his throne, his face frozen in fear. "Vaughn, what are you doing?"

I feel his hands brush against mine, pulling them back, and then there's a click as the handcuffs come loose.

"This position's no good. I want her on all fours."

"Fix her cuffs," Halloran orders.

Vaughn pulls my ankles backward, forcing me to plant my hands on the pedestal to break my fall. I lose my hold on the nipple clamps' chain, but if Vaughn sees, he doesn't care. I hear a zipper and squeeze my eyes shut.

"I'm not kidding, Vaughn!" shouts Halloran. "Tie her down, now!"

I look back at him, and though I don't mean to, I realize I've issued a challenge.

As I watch, Vaughn slips the gun from his pants in one fluid motion and aims it right at Halloran's heart. "Old man, shut the fuck up. I got this."

Halloran fumes, but his caution out-duels his rage, and he lowers himself into his seat slowly.

"I've been waiting for this for far too long. She wouldn't

even be here if not for me. Next time I'll have myself a little fun on the drive. That was my mistake."

Vaughn's fingers slide along my ass, and then I feel the thong slipping down my thighs.

"If I'd known Gabriel would get attached to someone so soon after…"

Come on, say her name, you son of a bitch.

"Please, Vaughn!" cries Halloran. "She looks like she's about to snap."

Vaughn groans in frustration. "Seriously, shut up." He rubs my lower lips. "Marla isn't going to give us any trouble, isn't that right?"

"That's right."

Helena and the other girls gasp. I do too, because I'm not the one who spoke. I turn to the source of the voice.

"Isn't that right, Marla?" asks Gabriel, repeating Vaughn.

I mean to say "Yes, sir," but I can't even get out the words. My lip quivers in relief and joy.

"Gabriel!" calls his father. "What happened? Where were you?"

He drops to the floor a black duffel bag. "Packing. But I couldn't go without saying goodbye."

"You couldn't have packed a little faster?" Vaughn grouses. "Look what you interrupted."

Gabriel strides over to us and brushes my pussy with his thumb like a contractor checking a fresh coat of paint. "Totally dry," he says, though that's changing now, thanks to his touch.

"How do you still not know how to punish an ass properly?" Gabriel asks, picking up the whip Vaughn used. Gabriel points to my ass and says, "Look at those bruises. You went way too hard."

Vaughn rolls his eyes. "Gabriel, what makes you think I care?"

Chuckling, Gabriel massages my cheeks, causing me to yelp from the sudden jolts. "This ass is far too gorgeous to fuck up, and that's exactly what you're going to do. So, do you want some tips or not?"

Vaughn grins and zips up his pants. "Fine, yeah. If it'll get you to leave already, then why not?"

"Great. Watch me, okay?"

My attention shoots around the room in disbelief. *What is Gabriel doing?*

Halloran has the same question, I can tell. The trepidation about my lack of bindings is still there, but now he seems transfixed by the unlikely display. Helena looks equally confused, especially since she's been taking her cues from me, and even I'm stumped.

Is Gabriel really invested in teaching Vaughn the fine art of whipping? Or is he desperate to keep Vaughn from finally fucking me? Anyone's guess would be as good as mine.

When the whip makes contact, it inflames the soreness left by Vaughn, but the impact is spread out, and I can handle the pain without feeling overwhelmed.

"See that? See how she jumped a little, then moaned? Yeah, she dug that."

Vaughn laughs. "No, I didn't see. I was watching you."

"Okay, well watch her this time, all right?"

He whips me again, eliciting a deep moan. I can feel my wetness growing.

"See that?"

Vaughn laughs. "Yeah. But could you do it again, just so I know I've got it?"

Gabriel chuckles too. "Sure."

I turn around to see Vaughn staring at my ass, and in the corner of my eye Gabriel is winding up to swing with his full weight and strength. I flinch so violently I practically leap from the pedestal, but the whip never touches me. Instead it connects with the bridge of Vaughn's nose with such force that it knocks him straight to the ground.

"Fuck!" Halloran shouts, launching from his seat toward us.

Gabriel is already on top of Vaughn, pummeling his face, but Vaughn's hand is still reaching under his body for the gun wedged in his pants.

Do something, Marla!

The world moves in slow motion again. Halloran is closing in on the men. Gabriel's fist is about to find Vaughn's nose. Blood is streaming from Vaughn's eyes and mouth, but his hand is still creeping along.

Fucking snap out of it, you bitch!

Before Halloran can get past my pedestal I stick out my leg, catching the old man's ankles and sending him flying. "Gabriel, gun!" I scream.

Vaughn's hand comes up with the weapon, but Gabriel intercepts it, slamming Vaughn's arm back to the floor and sending the gun skittering away.

Stepping off the pedestal, I head for Gabriel, picking up the fallen whip along the way.

"Move. Get the gun," I tell him.

I lower myself onto my knees, straddling Vaughn's body. He coughs and wails, spitting blood as I knot the whip around his neck and pull it tight. I whisper into his ears, "Remember when you had your fist around my throat and you bragged that you could have killed me?"

His hands fly up, grabbing at my thighs and stomach, so I slap him hard across the face. "Not much fun, huh?"

I pull the noose tighter. He gurgles like a clogged drain as his arms and legs spasm. "Rot in Hell, Vaughn. This is for Iris."

The light in his eyes fades. His mouth hangs open, unable to voice his final protest. I check his neck for a pulse, but there's none. He's gone.

I remove the nipple clamps with a shriek, then turn to Gabriel. He's pointing the gun at Halloran, who's walking backward, hands raised in the air. "Please, just take Marla and go!" he pleads. "You'll never see me again."

"No one *on earth* is ever going to see you again," Gabriel growls.

"Son, no-"

Whatever Halloran was about to say next, it dies in his throat, startled when he walks backward into one of the floor candelabras. Toppling over, it lands against the hall's draperies, catching it on fire.

"No no no no no!" Halloran screams, trying to get to this feet. "Run, get an extinguisher!"

I search Vaughn's pants pockets and find a ring of keys. There are several, but after a month of watching him, I know which key turns which lock. Rushing over to Helena, I release her from her wheelchair, then set to work on her jacket.

"Please, Gabriel!" Halloran yells, watching the flames. "Before it spreads!"

"Move," his son replies, waving the gun at the doors. "Marla, get everyone free. I left the front door propped open, you can get out that way."

As he says it Helena's arms emerge from the jacket sleeves.

"Can you free the others?" I ask her.

"Sure. Go," she says, taking the keys.

"Where are we going?" Halloran asks as Gabriel grabs him by his shirt collar.

"Your office."

I follow them even as the smell of smoke grows thicker, and soon the alarm klaxons sound. The building is old: it doesn't have sprinkler systems, and I realize that we won't have long to get out once the fire gets past the ballroom.

"Open the desk," Gabriel commands once we reach his office. On the monitor I see Helena through a haze of smoke. As she frees the last of the girls from their chairs, one of the big windows shatters, startling the girls and letting in fresh oxygen to feed the inferno. Helena waves her arm and the girls run as a flock from the ballroom.

Halloran puts his thumb to the keypad but shakes his head. "Gabriel, please don't. If they find out-"

"Open it."

Halloran punches in the code to open the drawer and pulls out a large, metal briefcase.

"If who finds out?" I ask.

"The guests. The clients," says Gabriel. "He's kept files on all of them. For insurance. Are they in there?"

Halloran nods.

"Marla, could you check?"

With a smile, I turn the case around and snap the latches. Inside are dozens of manilla folders; the case practically overflows there's so many. "It's full," I say.

"Good. Now we can go."

Gabriel and I turn to leave, but as I take the case, Halloran sits down at his desk. Out of habit he looks at the monitor, but the feed has gone dark.

"What are you doing?" asks Gabriel. "This place is going up."

Halloran shakes his head. "What's the point? You know what will happen to me out there."

"Gabriel," I say, starting to sweat from the rising heat. "If he wants to die here, I say we let him."

"He deserves to spend the rest of his life alone in a prison cell. He's coming with us."

Halloran laughs darkly. "What are you going to do, drag me? You won't make it out. Just go."

"He's right," I say. Maybe Gabriel's dreamed of watching his father rot in jail, but he's going to have to forget about it. "We need to leave!"

Gabriel points the gun at his father for a second. I hold my hand over my mouth, not wanting to inhale as the room grows murky.

Spitting on the floor, Gabriel shakes his head. "Fine. He gets to win one last time. Goodbye, Halloran."

He nods. "Son."

Gabriel takes my hand as we exit the office. He stops at the door unexpectedly, and I nearly slip. Gabriel checks the gun, then aims carefully at the office door's security panel. When he fires, the bullet tears through the device, sending pieces flying as sparks and smoke crackle. The gunshot booms like a cannon in the narrow hallway, replacing the sound of crackling flames with a ringing tone.

Gabriel yanks my hand. *Let's go*, he mouths.

And with that, Gabriel and I run.

CHAPTER 28
MARLA

Oppressive and thick, the heat is sweltering as we escape the asylum through the front door. I thought the lower floors would be less engulfed in flames, but as I'd thought, the blaze spread rapidly.

As soon as we're clear of the structure, the sudden switch to cool spring air causes us to shiver uncontrollably. The last time I was outside, Vaughn was dragging me back with a gun to my head. I laugh, now able to draw some enjoyment from the memory. What was going through his head at the time? I doubt he considered that in a few weeks he would be dead, burned to ash as the world crumbled around him.

Skidding to a stop, my knees buckle beneath me and I collapse in the grass. Gabriel drops down next to me, pulling me against his body and shielding mine from the cold. I turn over so I can face him, and as he smiles I feel something break, and tears erupt at the same time as laughter and need.

Not content to just hug, I raise my lips to Gabriel's and quell my sobs. Wet drops land on my cheeks; he's crying too.

"I thought you were dead," I whisper. "When you said..."

"I'm sorry. I had to make you think I was gone, and that there was no hope for you. I needed them to believe you were broken. It was the only way to get enough of their trust. And it wouldn't have been possible if you hadn't killed Roy and Miller."

"Glad I could help."

Laughing, Gabriel kisses my forehead and brushes back my hair.

"Was this your plan all along?"

"No. The plan was still to steal a car, and you, during an exhibition. But after that day in the woods… I was prepared to die tonight, Marla. I might have if not for you."

"I'd be dead inside without you."

We kiss again as the asylum disintegrates. The flames light up the night sky and cast an orange glow on the surrounding forest. Pops and crackles elicit continuous satisfaction as the structure collapses, though I do feel a twinge of regret for the evidence being destroyed.

We're still making out, totally lost in one another, when we're interrupted by a clearing throat. Standing together on the path away from the asylum are Helena and the girls. Wearing their straightjackets, though the sleeves are not bound to their torsos, they lean against each other, perhaps in shock.

"I'm sorry, but it's freezing out here," says Helena. "And we're hungry. Can we go?" She holds up Vaughn's keys, singling one out. "I'm pretty sure this one is for the truck. But can we fit?"

"It'll be tight, but I think so." Gabriel helps me to my feet. "Okay, let's go."

As a group we march toward the truck, all of us taking last looks at the roaring fire. When we reach the vehicle, he helps the girls into the back. They flinch at the sight of the chair bolted to the floor, but there's no way to get rid of it.

"It'll be fine," Helena assures the girls, though most line themselves against the wall to stay away from it.

As they get in, I unlock the truck's front doors and throw the briefcase onto the passenger seat.

"We're an hour from town," notes Gabriel. "Helena, keep everyone sitting down and try to hold on. I'll drive carefully, but it might be bumpy."

"Thanks," she says, nodding. "Just get us there."

"Knock if you need anything," I say. "We'll stop."

"Will do. And Marla… thank you, again."

I climb up and pull her into a hug, holding her tight. "Thank you for believing."

"Always."

Gabriel nods to her as I hop out and he draws the back door shut. Around the front, he helps me up into the truck. Once I'm in, he gets into the driver's seat and starts the ignition. I move the briefcase to my feet and fold my legs beneath me to keep them warm.

"I'll turn on the heater once the engine gets going," he says.

"Thanks."

"If you want my shirt, in the meantime…"

I look down and notice the ruined bra and my bare breasts. I'd grown so used to being deprived of clothes, I hadn't noticed. "It's fine, let's go."

Gabriel flicks on the headlights, shifts into gear and then we start to move. I can hardly believe it. I could almost imagine this never happened, and that I'm still on that pedestal as Vaughn finally gets his way. But when I hold out my hand to Gabriel he takes it, and I know this is real.

"So where are we going?" I ask. "Once we get to town."

"I figured we'd find a hospital. You're all going to need full examinations and blood work. Marla, I wish I could say you'll be yourselves again someday, but some of you might not find peace again."

"I know."

Depending on the direction of the road, I can sometimes see the glow of the fire in the distance. I didn't think about it before, but what if the fire spreads to the surrounding forest?

"What about the police?" I ask. "And fire? Shouldn't we tell them what happened as soon as possible?"

Gabriel nods. "The hospital will call the police, and the police are probably going to call in every agency in the country when they see what we have."

Curious, I set the briefcase down on my lap and open it. I choose a file at random and flip through the documents. I can't read them without light, but there are pages of information. I sift around through the files, digging my fingers through them to reach the bottom of the briefcase. As I do, I feel something different: a block of papers with a distinctive texture.

"Oh my god," I say, shifting the files to one side.

"What?"

Below the files, fitted in tight rows and bundled up, are several dozen stacks of currency. Twenties, I think. "Halloran's money. I'm guessing all of it. How much do you think he had?"

Gabriel shrugs. "He wasn't doing this to get rich. He put most of his money back into keeping this place operating. But it sounds like tens of thousands."

It's more money than I've seen in one place at one time, for sure.

"Marla, I just wanted the files. As far as I'm concerned, you can do whatever you want with the money."

The van climbs and descends as we go traverse the hills. I wish I could recall the mental catalog I made of turns Vaughn made on our way in, but that was too long ago. When escape seemed like a ludicrous fantasy, I stopped trying to remember the journey here, and it mostly slipped away.

As we drive, I consider the options. The first one that comes to mind — to my slight shame — is using the money to disappear with Gabriel. We could forge new identities for ourselves and put the past behind us as much as possible. Would anyone recognize me as that girl from the news who insulted her boss? In the time since my abduction, has that video become yesterday's news? How many people have really seen it? If it's mostly the populace of Hunter's Valley, it will be okay. But if it's spread...

It doesn't matter. The idea of taking the money for ourselves is unconscionable, and I dismiss it. The only moral option is to donate the money to treating Helena and the other victims. Years of therapy won't be cheap, nor will it be easy to reintegrate into society. Every dime will help. It might even be worthwhile to set aside some of the money to establish a charitable foundation to help raise more. Spread across 12 women, even tens of thousands of dollars won't go far.

Briefly I consider using the money to hire the best lawyers to sue Halloran's guests; that could help raise millions. However, these are the kind of men who can drop hundreds of thousands — maybe millions — on their defense. Throwing our money away on legal fees might get us nowhere.

My lips curl up in a malicious grin.

We could hire hitmen to kill those motherfuckers.

"Marla, you've got a look. What's up?"

I sigh. "Nothing. Just a little fantasy of what I'd do to the guests. But we should probably let the police handle it."

"I think so too. We'll all testify. We'll get them, Marla. I promise."

Testify…

I'd like to think that my background as a reporter might give credence to my testimony. Not that I was breaking news stories of any significance in a place like Hunter's Valley, but still…

Although… What if…

Possibilities explode in my mind. It would be bold, and dishonest — I laugh at the irony that such a move never would have occurred to me if not for Halloran. I savor the idea that somewhere in Hell a note was passed to him with my thanks.

I know how I can help all the women, and Gabriel and myself. Only Gabriel has to be told. Maybe Helena, but not right away. We would have to lie to a lot of people, again and again, possibly for years to come. We'd need to have our stories straight, for sure, but I think we can do it.

"Gabriel."

"Yeah?"

"I've got an idea."

CHAPTER 29
MARLA

The sequence of events that begin when we step foot into the Ravenswood General emergency room is so vast and rapid, I can't even follow all of it.

In the waiting area, people forget the ailments that brought them to seek medical attention. They stare at the twelve barely clad women. The hushed conversations sound like they're pointed at us, and I'm sure many are.

I explain to the nurse at the reception desk who we are in a calm voice, but after one look at us she calls for a social worker immediately. Soon the local police are on the line. Then the crime victim's assistance center and CPEP — emergency psychiatric care — who the social worker asks to send everybody within a hundred miles.

The hospital staff gets involved in the meantime, starting with finding gowns for us to wear. After a few minutes they arrive, allowing me and the others to cover up. "Hang onto those jackets," I tell the others. "The police will want them for evidence." I don't know that that's true, but I imagine it is.

When the nurses bring out wheelchairs for moving the patients, I quietly intercept them and explain that wheelchairs are a no-no for us. I'm no psychologist, but it strikes me as the right call. We can walk anyway, and the nurses lead the way for us in soft voices.

I make a scene when the officers attempt to separate me and Gabriel, though it's partially an act. I don't want to go anywhere without him right now, but he did tell me this would happen.

"Actually it'll be better," he said while we discussed the plan. "Having our stories match up, even while we're apart, will be more convincing."

It made sense, especially because the first line of questions I face focuses around him.

The police bring me and Gabriel down to the station in separate cars. I wish I could have ridden with him, but I focus on the goal.

The other cops in the station stare as I go by, the conversations in the room coming to an abrupt halt. A phone rings unanswered until one officer, who strikes me as the one in charge, reminds his staff to get back to work.

They take me to an interrogation room but make it clear I'm only supposed to give a brief, preliminary deposition. I doubt it will be brief, but I don't say so. Instead, I ask about Gabriel.

"We're questioning him. Ms. Angel, right now he can't hear you. Anything you need to tell us about him, you can do so safely. If he poses a threat to you in any way, we'll protect you," promises James Green, a police chief facing the kind of situation no small-town cop ever expects will happen in their jurisdiction.

For that matter, he's not even sure it is his jurisdiction. I tell him approximately the way we came, but I was too busy planning to pay much attention to the roads. He'll have to ask Gabriel for proper directions.

"Everything he did was to help and protect me."

"What about the other girls?"

"Gabriel would never do that. I'm sure he'll tell you that he is a victim too. It's the truth."

"I hope you'll forgive us if that's difficult to believe," he says. "Please don't get the wrong idea: I don't think you're lying to me. But it can't be overstated that in here you don't have to feel intimidated by anyone. You can talk to us. The people who held you can't hurt you anymore."

"They can't hurt me because they're all dead."

Chief Green exhales deeply, and I can smell the coffee on his breath. "I'll be back, Ms. Angel. I need to call in a few people."

"Wait. Before you go, can you tell me something?"

He nods.

"Did anyone know I was missing? Did anyone file a report?"

"I'm sorry, I don't know. I'll find out." He points to a phone on the wall. "Listen, you go ahead and pick that up if you need anything. This could take a while."

He's correct: it takes an hour to touch base with representatives from the state and federal law enforcement agencies. A momentary uneasiness comes and goes, as the interrogation room reminds me of my cell, but I remember how I got here and feel better.

I'm accustomed to waiting, but I am hungry, so I use the phone to call for a bite to eat. It took a long time for my empty stomach to command enough of my attention, but now that it has I realize I can ask for whatever I want.

"A bacon cheeseburger. I don't care from where. Fries too, please. Cola, regular. And mint ice cream. Oh and cigarettes. Any kind."

We'll see if they honor that last one. This is a government building, after all.

When the food comes, I tell myself to take it slow, but I can't really help scarfing it down. After a month of lumpy goop, the meal is the greatest I have ever or will ever eat. My only regret is not getting to share it with Gabriel.

I should have asked for a phone, I realize. *Or a computer.*

I want to e-mail my family and friends to let them know I'm alive. They may not even know I was in any danger. I'd like to know what's happened since I've been gone.

What if I went missing, and after firing me, poor Gerald was brought in as a suspect?

I shouldn't laugh at the idea. It's not supposed to be funny. Of course, if it caused him to spend a few nights in jail, I wouldn't be totally heartbroken.

While I'm eating an officer comes in and sets up a video camera and a digital voice recorder. She smiles at me but says nothing. Soon after that, Chief Green returns with a couple other officers whom he identifies as representatives of the county and state police.

"At this point the full scope of the investigation is unknown. I've put in calls to alert the federal agencies," says Green. "Ms. Angel, we know you've been through hell. Take your time, okay? Try to remember everything you can."

"Okay."

"You're not under oath. We just want to know what happened. And if you need anything, please ask."

I hold up the pack of cigarettes brought with my meal. "A lighter, or some matches, please?" I suppose I should have mentioned that, as a kidnapping victim, I didn't have any.

Green fumbles through his pockets and tosses one my way.

"Thank you," I say, scooping it up. The first drag I take fills my lungs and I feel a surge of relief I'd almost forgotten existed.

I can quit again later, I tell myself.

"Ms. Angel, if you could start at the beginning. The night you were taken?"

I shake my head and ash the cigarette into an empty soda can. "That's not the beginning."

"How so?"

Here we go.

"It started a year ago, with the disappearance of Helena Bloom. You're all aware she was with us, I assume?"

The cops nod, sorting through a series of papers, including the original report of Helena's disappearance.

I remind myself, *The best lies contain a morsel of truth.*

"When I heard about her case, I started looking into it.

There were others. Women vanishing. Especially ones who had pissed off a powerful man. I decided to investigate further, look for other links, but the cases were spread out around the state. There wasn't much to go on. I decided that if I wanted to get anywhere, I needed to try to draw them out. I ended up getting fired from my reporter job, but I thought I may as well use the opportunity. So I insulted my boss on live TV and got myself a little famous."

"Excuse me," says Green. "Did you honestly think that would work?"

"I thought it had a chance, yes. I had other ideas, though, in case it didn't."

He looks unconvinced. "So your plan was to be bait, get yourself taken?"

I shake my head. "No no no. I said I wanted to draw them out. My plan was to put myself out there and see what turns up, but I was always careful. I know how to defend myself."

And here's the truth:

"That night I got unlucky, is all."

Unlucky that Vaughn chose Hunter's Valley, and Tommy's Place, and me. That's how life is sometimes: a series of lucky or unlucky events.

"And you didn't mind potentially putting yourself in harm's way?" he asks.

If it hadn't been me Vaughn met that night, eventually he would have found someone else to fill Iris's cell. While I would be living in another town reporting on traffic jams and town board meetings, she'd be suffering and waking up each day in Hell. I let that thought fill my mind.

"Look, I'm not close with my family," I say, a tear dripping down to the table below me. "I don't have many friends. I thought, if somebody were to take a risk to expose these people, why not me?"

Green nods. "That was very brave of you, Ms. Angel."

"Thank you."

He hands me a tissue, and I wipe my eyes and blow my nose.

"Ms. Angel, your abductor — while conversing with him at the bar, were you aware that he was part of the operation you were investigating?"

"No, I wasn't. I knew I didn't like the vibe he gave off, I felt endangered, so I left. While I was waiting for a taxi, that was when he knocked me out."

"I see. In that case, what would your next step have been if you weren't taken that night?"

That's a good question, but it is amongst those I thought up with Gabriel. "I would have done some research on him the next day, see if he sounded like somebody who might be involved. If not, I'd move on."

"I see. Continue, please."

I tell them the rest as it happened: the ride to the asylum; meeting Gabriel, Roy and Miller. I burn through half the pack of cigarettes. Green blushes when I tell him about me and Gabriel, but laughs heartily at how I killed Roy, Miller and Vaughn. For a moment I worry that they might want to charge me for killing those men, even if it was in self-defense, but they make no mention of it. I cry for real when I recall thinking Gabriel was gone. Soon I'm explaining how the asylum burned down, with Halloran still inside. I omit the part about Gabriel shooting through the lock, however.

"Thank you, Ms. Angel," says Green, passing me a fresh cup of coffee. "I think your account will be instrumental in prosecuting Halloran's associates."

"Thank you, Chief, but I hope that the others can provide more meaningful testimony than me. They were there longer, and suffered worse. They deserve justice."

"For sure."

I wipe my face with another tissue, soaking up new tears. "When I saw them for the first time I could have died. Knowing that I'd gotten caught and probably wouldn't be able to help them... I wish I could have told them about my investigation. To let them know that if I saw the pattern, others would too. But I couldn't tell them. If Halloran found out..."

"He probably would have killed you," Green finishes.

"Yeah."

Green stands up, his knees popping. "I think we could use a little break. That okay?"

The other cops nod, rising from their seats as well.

"Ms. Angel. Marla," says Green. "You don't need to sit there. Come with me and I'll set you up with whatever you need. We'll wrap this up later."

"Thanks," I say, making a list of what I could use now. A phone, a pen, paper.

A shower.

A very long, very hot shower.

Green smiles at me as he holds open the door to the interrogation room.

You did it, I think to myself. I told the story right.

I just hope Gabriel did too.

CHAPTER 30
MARLA

A police helicopter found the site of the asylum, but by the time firefighters arrived, there was nothing left to save. Cinders continued to smolder, but the building burned down to its foundation. Following Gabriel's directions, police recovered the bodies of Roy and Iris. Authorities searched the area for Miller's corpse, but were unsuccessful, they assume due to wild animals finding it first.

Gabriel's interview with the agents is taking a long time, although after living there for five years, it is understandable that he'd have to account for much more. They don't let me listen in, and I don't press the matter.

Having little else to do, I ask for a ride back to the hospital, to see if I can help the other girls in the meantime. I end up in Helena's room; she's asleep, and soon I doze off as well.

We wake when a middle-aged man and woman burst into the room. They look exhausted and on the verge of tears, but that melts away the second they see Helena.

"Mom!" she shouts, shooting to her feet. "Dad!"

She bowls them over jumping into their arms. All three cry without an inkling of self-consciousness. I watch them for a second but then turn away, not wanting to be rude.

"I never stopped thinking of you guys," says Helena at last.

"We… we came as fast… as soon as we heard…" her father replies, barely able to get out the words.

I try not to feel a pang of jealousy. When I called them, my folks were relieved to hear I was okay. Though they had been made aware that I was missing, they didn't believe it was a serious matter — they assumed I'd picked up and left, like I have in the past. When I heard that, I mentioned having to go and hung up.

The call left a sour taste in my mouth, and I'm still thinking about it when I hear Helena call my name.

"Marla? Please, come meet my parents."

"We're so grateful," says Helena's mother. "You brought us back our girl."

"If there's anything we can ever do for you," her father adds, "It would be our honor."

"Thanks," I wheeze as I join the three of them in a hug. When we finally let go, I turn to Helena. "Actually, I could use your help in telling the world what happened here. I'll understand if you don't want to relive it now that it's over, but I'm going to share my own story."

Helena nods. "I'm interested. Can we talk about it later?"

"Of course."

Her parents give me their contact information, and after one last hug, take their daughter home.

—

I'm snoozing again when Gabriel enters the room. "Marla," he says, nudging my shoulder. I wake with a shot; it's the first time in a month that I'm not waking up bound, locked in a padded cell or a torture chamber.

"Hey, hey, it's okay."

"Sorry. I was back there and-"

He draws me into his body and clutches me tightly. I feel his warm lips kiss my forehead. "If it's fine with you, they'd like to move us to a hotel room. Your examination came back mostly clean. Bruising to your… ah, your buttocks. That'll heal. You're also a little malnourished — no surprise — but you'll be all right if you get back to a regular diet. So there's no real medical reason to stay in the hospital. It's your call, though."

Thinking of a bigger, more comfortable bed, I say, "Okay, let's go."

A pair of officers gives us a ride to the hotel, with a quick stop at a superstore to buy snacks, clothes, toothbrushes and paste, pre-paid phones, a notebook and pens — as well as a box of condoms.

Before we leave the store, Gabriel leads us through the hardware section with a glint in his eyes and a smirk on his face. Into our cart he throws a roll of duct tape, a few lengths of rope, a multitool and some zip ties.

"You can't be serious," I say.

"Of course I am. You think our first night of freedom should be spent sleeping, or watching TV?"

My cheeks flush and there's no question the desire is there, but I play coy. "I haven't watched TV in a month, Gabriel. That sounds really good."

"Tell you what. I'll leave the TV on so you can watch to your heart's content after I fall asleep."

"You know I can turn the TV on myself."

"Not if you're still tied to the bed," he jokes, giving my ass a quick slap.

My yelp draws looks from the other late night shoppers, though I suspect our behavior isn't unusual for this hour. I punch Gabriel's arm in retaliation, but he grabs my wrist and starts pulling me in the direction of the checkout line.

"Gabriel?" I say as we wait.

"Yeah?"

"I'm sorry I kicked you and knocked you down in the woods that day."

He chuckles. "It's okay. I understand you had to."

"Thanks."

After paying with cash from a white envelope stuffed into his pocket, Gabriel carries our purchases back to the police car.

It's only a couple minutes on the highway to the hotel.

"We'll see you in the morning, Mr. Halloran," one says to Gabriel. His face falls a little, taken out of the moment. I don't blame him. My month at the asylum was hell, but he was there for years. It will be impossible to truly put it behind us until the investigation concludes and we can move on. Plus, I know he hates being called by his father's name.

"See you then," he tells them. Taking my hand, he leads us to our room, practically jogging, he's walking so fast. "I don't want to waste a second."

"Me neither," I say.

We take one look around once we get inside: the carpet is forest green, and the sheets are a creamy café au lait. There's a TV on a dresser and a desk with a mirror. Gabriel puts out the "Do not disturb" sign while I shut the window blinds, and just like that our shopping bags are strewn across the floor and he's tossing me like a doll onto the bed. True to his word, he takes off his shirt by pulling it apart, blowing the buttons across the room. I shriek as one hits me in the stomach, bouncing off harmlessly, and then Gabriel is on top of me, lips locked to mine. With our bodies pressed against each other, I can feel the stiffness in his pants, and I even imagine I can feel the pounding in his heart.

I groan as he lifts my t-shirt up over my head, letting it tangle in my arms, covering my eyes and exposing my chest.

"Who needs cuffs?" he mutters as he presses my shirt into the mattress. I laugh, then sigh as I feel Gabriel's tongue on my nipple. It hardens to a pebble as I clutch the blanket in my fists. Everything about the moment is perfect, from the way Gabriel stimulates my body to the soft, soft mattress below me. I'd forgotten how fresh a clean mattress could smell.

"Oh god, Gabriel," I moan as he pulls down the pink pajama bottoms I was provided at the hospital.

"You sure you don't want to watch TV instead?" he taunts, throwing off his jeans and boxers. Looking up I see his cock is practically swollen.

"Depends on what's on," I shoot back. I bite my lip,

SANSA RAYNE

wanting to feel his rigid shaft driving into me.

"We'll find out later," he says, pushing me down onto the bed. My head lands on the pillow, and I gasp at how far it sinks in.

Gabriel gets up, but comes back quickly with a package of zip ties. "We're in luck," he says, running his hand across the headboard, which is cut out in the middle. A pair of wooden columns are built into the gap, and Gabriel uses the ties to secure my wrists to each one.

"How's that feel?"

"It's tight, but good."

"Exactly." Gabriel climbs on top of me, straddling my body, and kisses me again. When I taste his lips I wish that the moment could go on forever. It's ironic, but even after escaping from an asylum, I feel as though I could spend the rest of my life in this hotel room, as long as Gabriel is there too.

Of course, he would have to go out and replace his toys: we don't have any floggers or canes, handcuffs or gags. For tonight that's okay — all we really need is each other. And, as I find out with a pinch of my nipple, there's plenty Gabriel can do with his hands.

"Gabriel?"

He lifts his tongue from my breast long enough to answer, "Yeah?"

"I forgot... oh... to ask. How did it go... with the... police?"

He kisses me on the cheek. "Fine," he says. He slides down the bed until his head rests over my crotch. I can't lift my head, with my arms in the way, so I can't see what he's doing, but then I feel his tongue exploring my crevice.

"Oh god," I moan, writhing on the bed, tugging at my restraints.

While his tongue circles my clit, his hands reach for my breasts, massaging them and occasionally pinching the nipples. The ebb and flow of pain and pleasure make my head spin. My entire body feels like it's glowing. I could focus on one sensation — Gabriel's tongue making long, hard strokes — only to have it stolen away with a caress of my lips. I open my mouth and suck on his finger.

When I'd licked it until I could no longer taste the salt of his skin, he takes it from my mouth and presses it gently into my pussy. I shudder blissfully, breathing deeply as an orgasm starts to build. My warmth closes down on his finger, hungry for more, and Gabriel doesn't let his tongue stray far from my clit.

"Can I come?" I ask. I don't know why exactly it occurs to me to ask, but I like it. It feels good, like having my hands tied. I may have learned to submit in the asylum, but it wasn't about the place — it was about the man. I never truly gave in to Vaughn — my body wouldn't allow it. I belong to Gabriel, at least sexually.

"Just once for now," he says. "We have all night. I don't want to wear you out too soon."

"Yes, sir," I say in a soft, demure voice. As soon as I do, Gabriel dips another finger into my pussy and brings his mouth back down. I squeal and shake, overwhelmed by the flood of euphoria erupting inside me. Spreading from my core, it soon occupies all of me, and I feel as though I'm floating away, like I'm made of pure pleasure.

I'm reminded of being back in the forest with Gabriel, outside the asylum. For a time, the world felt perfect — all the horrors of the asylum faded away as I experienced Gabriel's love. Now I'm launched back to that same place; even though a world of horror and stress wait for me outside this hotel, there is another world that's now a smoking ruin thanks to us, and as I climax I don't forget about what our love eventually accomplished.

"I'm coming!" I scream. "Oh god I'm coming!" I don't know if anyone can hear me through the hotel walls, but I don't care. Gabriel laughs as his fingers drive in and out. If my ecstasy comes in waves, it is Gabriel creating the tide, working every last blissful moment out of the orgasm. He only stops when he sees my body go limp and my eyes shut, drowning in the lingering afterglow.

———

When I finally regain my composure, my arms rest at my sides and the zip ties lie split apart next to the multitool Gabriel bought. The TV is on. He's watching a late-night comedy show.

"Hey," he says when he sees I'm awake. He opens the minifridge, takes out a bottle of water and tosses it to me. I drink half of it in one pull.

"Feeling good?" Gabriel asks.

"Oh yes. That was incredible." I point to the TV. "It's nice, isn't it?"

Gabriel laughs. "I have no idea what the fuck they're talking about. I've been away for too long."

"You'll have to catch up. They're going to want us on those shows."

"What?"

I shake my head. "Well, not that show. But the news, when the story breaks? They're going to want interviews."

"You're right," he murmurs, voice distant.

"I could probably raise a decent amount of money for the victims' fund by selling an exclusive to some show or another."

"That's a good idea," says Gabriel. "Honestly, I find the idea pretty intimidating. I've always disliked public speaking."

"Really? I thought you handled yourself well at the exhibition. Sorry, I don't mean that in a bad way. You were acting, but you seemed comfortable."

Gabriel turns off the TV and sits down next to me on the bed. "I was comfortable with you."

He reaches down to the foot of the bed and when he comes back up he's got a package of chewy chocolate chip cookies.

"Fuck yeah," I say. "How did you know I like chewy?"

"Everyone likes chewy. But I got regular too."

I laugh. "You're a saint, Gabriel."

He kisses my cheek. "And you're my angel, Marla."

"Oh, that's bad," I say, wincing.

"Shut up. Eat the cookies. I want you on a sugar high for what comes next."

I scoff, but I do as I'm told, groaning as the chocolate chips melt on my tongue. Gabriel has a few, but he opens a bag of fresh baby carrots. He washes them in the bathroom sink, then snaps one in half in his teeth.

"That motherfucker Vaughn never bought these. Most of our food was canned — I missed fresh, crunchy produce."

"Better than oatmeal," I say.

"No doubt. Want some carrots?"

I held out my hand and took a few. I wanted my strength, and that meant having more than cookies.

Once we'd eaten our fill, Gabriel cleaned up, then got out the rope. "I hope you can still taste the chocolate."

Smirking, I think I know what he has in mind.

He pulls one end of the bundle of rope, causing it to fall apart in a pile. "On your knees, hands behind your back."

I get into the position, and soon I feel him bend my arms to form a square behind my back, followed by the smooth cords tightening around my wrists. The binding renews my arousal, which grows further still as Gabriel ties a band of rope around my forearms, forming a knot at the center of my back. It locks my arms into position tightly, making them feel fused and worthless. I can wiggle my fingers, but can do little else with them; the tie is too stringent. It feels incredible.

Gabriel pulls me to the edge of the bed, then slips out of his boxers. His cock is already hard, standing firm. I don't have to be told what to do: I lean down and take the tip into my mouth. I start there, sucking hard until Gabriel groans, then I open wide and take as much of his cock as I can. I feel it fill my mouth, pressed against my tongue.

The salty taste of his skin mixes with the sweet chocolate from before, causing me to moan from my own pleasure. I look up into his eyes, loving to imagine how I must look and feel. Serving him brings me an intense satisfaction, one that's as good as any orgasm.

Not being able to use my hands adds an extra challenge to the task, meaning I must be that much more adept with my mouth. I love it, though maybe not as much as Gabriel. Face contorted with bliss, he fists my hair, keeping me in place so I can keep sucking.

However, before he climaxes, he pulls out. As I gasp he pulls me onto the bed, then flips me over so I'm facing the ceiling. He climbs over me on the bed, then lowers himself until his cock is back in my mouth, this time going deeper. I see his thick thigh muscles tensing as he holds himself above me. Having his body imposing on me, helpless and small, emphasizes his sexual, physical and mental domination, and I can't get enough of it. I suck as hard as I can, moaning as his cock grows slick with my saliva.

The harder we go, the more it feels like he's fucking my mouth than I'm sucking his cock, but the difference doesn't matter. All I care about is tasting his essence as it comes shooting out in hot, milky spurts.

When that happens, I hold my mouth open obediently, allowing Gabriel to shake off every last drop. He jams his cock inside one last time so I can clean him off.

"That was perfect, Marla."

"Thank you, sir."

He turns me onto my stomach, relieving my arms, which had grown a little numb from the weight of my body. Gabriel traces his fingers over the curvature of my backside. "I really wish I had a flogger right now."

I shriek as I feel the spank, a hard slap that catches me directly on the ass. "That still feels good," I say.

"Oh does it?" he laughs, peppering my bottom with a series of quick swats. I shake and squeal, trying to get away from the bombardment, but Gabriel holds me down with his other hand. "Still feel good?"

"Yes, sir," I moan. Obviously my skin burns from the onslaught, but I hunger for it. My body craves the fight, the resistance. You can tie me up and punish me, but I will take that and turn it into pleasure.

Gabriel massages my pussy with a hand, feeling my wetness, then squeezes my ass cheeks, inflaming their soreness. Then I scream as the world falls away; Gabriel has picked me up in his arms and slung me over his shoulder. I feel like a sack of potatoes. I cackle as he marches around the room, spanking my bottom with his free hand.

"Stop, oh god!" I shout.

Gabriel halts but doesn't put me down. "Someday you and I are going to have to work out a safeword," he says. "Because in our world, sometimes people say 'stop' and don't mean it."

"Sure, we can do that."

"Good, now did you really want me to stop?"

Oh you bastard…

"No, sir," I say sheepishly. "Please, continue."

Gabriel kisses my thigh, then resumes his circuit around the hotel room, smacking my rear until I can see how red it is in the mirror above the desk. After several circuits I'm tearing up from laughing and the pain. "Please put me down," I beg.

"Only since you asked nicely, Marla," he says. He sets me down, keeping me steady until I'm feeling the strength in my knees again.

Grinning, he jogs to the bathroom. I hear the sink running for a minute, then the sound of dripping water for few seconds at a time, and finally a single slow snap. When he returns, he's holding a soaked, white towel, which he's pulling taught between his fists.

"Oh god," I mutter, seeing him heading straight for me. With smiles a mile wide across our faces, Gabriel chases me around the room, occasionally taking a shot with the towel. A few of his swings land, stinging my rear, but a wet towel is no substitute for a proper flogger. Still, I loved being chased, and fall, breathless, on the bed.

"Do you give up?" Gabriel asks.

"Never," I growl.

"Damn straight." He drops down onto me and kisses me again. I drink it in, though my ass throbs.

"Here, let me help," says Gabriel, turning me back onto my stomach. "And I've got something else for you."

I can't see what he's doing, but after a second I feel it: more rope, which he ties around my ankles. He pulls the rope down, tying them tight to the legs on either side of the bed, causing my legs to spread far apart. Shaking against the bonds I try to close my legs, but I can't.

The lights in the room dim, and after a moment I feel Gabriel's fingers dig into my pussy. He doesn't keep them in long. Feeling my drenched entrance, he gets into bed, directs his cock into my eager pussy, and begins to thrust.

Each drive is like a firecracker of euphoria bursting. Together in the dark, our passion ignites fully. I'm completely at his mercy, the way we both like it — subservient and willing. He is gentle when necessary but dominant and commanding. His stamina also seems endless, as his rhythmic motion goes on and on, getting faster, rather than slower, as if Gabriel cannot tire. He bites my shoulder and reaches underneath me to grasp my nipples, as though he wants to consume me completely in a single night, leaving no inch of my body unstimulated.

"I'm going to come!" I shout. My toes dig into the blanket Gabriel didn't bother to remove, and my fingers claw at the air. Gabriel spanks my ass a few times to bring the pain back into the forefront of my perception; like a car shifting into a higher gear, it unleashes my orgasm with even more power. I scream so loud that somebody in the next room bangs on the wall.

"Sorry!" Gabriel shouts.

To my utter dismay, he stops and gets off the bed, leaving me. "What the fuck!" I shout, but Gabriel's only gone for a moment. He comes back with the roll of duct tape he bought. He pulls loose a strip several inches long and tears it off with his teeth.

"I'm sorry! I'll be quiet," I say, my words pouring out so fast they run together.

"I know you will," Gabriel replies as he fixes the tape to my lips. He presses it down, smoothing it out. "Just until we're finished," he adds.

I moan through the tape, glaring it him angrily as he adds a few more pieces. However, by the time he finishes I'm so horny I wouldn't care if he used the whole roll as long as he let me come first.

Thankfully he does — he tosses the roll away and gets right back to where he left off, plowing into me. Muffled by the gag, I shriek as loud as I need, quaking in place as his full length invades my hungry orifice.

He doesn't stop after my first orgasm. He's not yet finished, and though he's sweating he shows no signs of fatigue. He smiles, enjoying my symphony of wails as the biggest wave of all crests and breaks.

Pausing for a moment, he kneads my bottom a little, running his thumb over the welts. I scream and cry, but the pain does its job, setting me up for another staggeringly powerful orgasm. As I gasp blissfully, Gabriel digs his fingers into my pussy, feeling me and his cock at the same time.

When he pulls them out they reflect the single shaft of light coming through the window blinds. Seeing them glisten, he presses them into my ass, probing at my tight rear entrance. Even through the tape my moans are deafening, but I can't help it. His fingers dig deeper, penetrating me in a way that adds pain and pleasure together.

Soon he's thrusting his fingers in rhythm with his cock, driving into one hole at a time — it's so overwhelming I don't even have a chance to mumble the announcement that I'm coming. I writhe and spasm with total abandon, and while I scream I hear his orgasmic groan too.

Gabriel strips off his condom and throws it in the waste bin with the others. He strokes his cock a few times, then begins untying all the rope.

"Are you tired now?" he asks.

I don't know why he's left the tape on and started with my ankles, but I'm too blissed out to care. "Mmm hmm," I mumble.

"Do you want to watch some TV before bed?"

I shake my head.

"Are you hungry, or thirsty?"

"Some more water, please," I say, when he rips off the tape.

He gets bottles for the both of us after he finishes untying me, and then throws off the blanket.

"Do you want me to hold you for the rest of the night?" he asks.

"For the rest of my life," I say.

Gabriel nods. "I'll always be yours, Marla. My angel."

"And I'll always belong to you. I love you."

"I love you too," he says.

He pulls me into his body and wraps me in his arms, and then the night takes us both.

CHAPTER 31
MARLA

Noises make me stir, but I fall back asleep. I'm so wiped out, I feel like I could rest for days. I hear the kinds of sounds one expects in a hotel: running water, footsteps, knocking on doors.

When I finally wake, I reach for Gabriel to find the bed empty. Gathering a sheet around me like a gown, I get up and check the bathroom. The haze of sleep evaporates immediately as my heart starts to race. I check the dresser for a note, in case he left to get coffee, but there's nothing. His shopping bag, his clothes — it's all gone.

What the fuck, Gabriel?

I throw open the blinds to let some light into the room, and when I look out to the road and lot below, I see him. He's walking toward a pair of police patrol cars parked outside. Four officers are waiting for him, and as he gets close he drops his bag to the pavement.

I pound on the glass as hard as I can. "Gabriel!"

He turns toward me and our eyes meet. He waves, then puts his hand over his heart. After that, he nods to the cops.

Numb, I watch as they cuff him and seat him in the back of one of their cars. The same officer takes Gabriel's bag and throws it in the trunk, and then they drive off. As I watch, the other two cops head for the hotel.

I dress as fast as I can, finishing as the knock sounds on my door. I throw it open. "What's going on?" I ask them.

One of the cops hands me a thick white envelope. It's heavy, and I recognize it as the one Gabriel kept his cash in at the store.

"He asked us to give that to you, Ms. Angel. We'll take you to the station when you're ready. We have some forms for you to fill out. Okay?"

"Sure," I say, shutting the door in their faces. I rush back to the bed and open the envelope. Inside I find a wad of cash, a folded piece of paper and a chain necklace with a round, metal locket. I examine the piece, which looks antique, then set it down.

I open the note.

Marla,

I told the police everything we discussed. I also told them everything that I could have left out. Even if I was trapped in the asylum, you were right that day in the forest. I should never have let Halloran continue after Iris died.

In the short time I've known you, you've always done the right thing. I wanted to follow your example, and take responsibility for my mistakes. If I had acted to stop Halloran back then, you wouldn't have had to go through this. I'll never be able to apologize for that enough.

I agreed to turn myself in, plead guilty and turn over any information I could. I asked in return one night with you, which they granted. It was a perfect night, Marla. I couldn't ask for more.

Please forgive me for leaving you like this. If I tried this in person, I would have failed. I would have felt unworthy.

I don't know how long I'll be gone. I want you to go on and have a good life, the one you were meant to have, before all this. I hope that's possible. But I know you will continue to make a difference.

I've enclosed a locket belonging to my mother, Joanna. I didn't know her, and this is the only possession of her's I have. I want you to keep it. Please take good care of it.

I love you, Marla. I hope one day to be yours again.
—Gabriel

—

I cry in bed for an hour after reading it. I cry for another hour after re-reading it.

Gabriel, you bastard.

I feel like I'm back in my cell at the asylum, hopeless and alone.

I feel that way for a long time.

CHAPTER 32
MARLA
TWO YEARS LATER

A squadron of SWAT units stands ready in a line outside the warehouse, waiting for the signal. I watch from the perimeter, which is made of stanchions and patrol cars lining around an entire block. Most non-essential personnel have been evacuated from the scene.

"Be ready," I say. "This is it."

Helena points the digital video camera at the loading docks of the warehouse, already recording. "I'm set," she replies.

The squad leader gives the signal, and the men breach through the side. On the other end of the building, another attack begins simultaneously. Gunfire sounds from inside almost immediately.

Then I see it: the door for the main dock is opening.

"Here we go," Helena and I say in unison. She chuckles at the timing; I grin.

When the door rises about two feet, men start tumbling sideways through it, hitting the ground and looking around. A dozen spill out in short succession, and only a couple carry guns.

They see some of the cars of the perimeter and turn in the other direction, but as soon as they take two steps a dozen uniformed officers pop out from cover, screaming for everyone to get on the ground. The suspects are completely trapped; they drop their guns and get down.

Helena and I watch as the men are arrested. Several other officers emerge from the warehouse with other suspects in tow. The whole scene is caught on tape.

"Ms. Angel, Ms. Bloom," says a voice from behind us. Helena keeps filming, but I turn around.

The man facing me is the agent in charge of the operation. He's tall and handsome — well built. I'd have some interesting thoughts about him if not for the gold band on his finger.

"The tip you gave us was accurate. The operation was a success."

I nod, stripping off my armored vest. "Have you got a count?"

"Twenty women were found in a cargo container inside. Medical is already responding."

Twenty, I think. *Our best result yet.*

"Thank you, Agent Cole. You'll give a statement later?"

"Of course," he says. "I've gotta get back. Thanks again, ladies. Call me when you've got another."

"We will."

Helena and I stare as he heads for the command center; we have pretty different thoughts on what we'd like to do with him. After her experiences, Helena still hasn't felt ready to enter the dating pool, but for a well-dressed federal agent she might take a second look. That's what we're each doing when he suddenly turns around and catches us.

Shit. Busted.

The agent smiles. He calls out, "Ms. Angel! I almost forgot, there's someone at the south end of the perimeter. Says he knows you."

"Okay, thanks!" I call out, trying to sound extra professional.

"Think he saw us?" mumbles Helena.

"Come on."

We follow the barriers cordoning off the block until we reach the southern end. Helena and I see him at the same time.

"Gabriel!" I scream, breaking into a sprint.

He beams as I close the gap and catches me when I leap into his arms. I have millions of questions, but when I see him all I want to do is kiss him. Despite my somewhat tight blue jeans and leather jacket, I wrap my arms and legs around him and kiss him so hard he nearly falls over.

Ignoring the snickers of detectives passing by, Gabriel squeezes me tightly and runs his hand through my hair. We only stop kissing because we run out of breath, but neither of us lets go.

"Hi," he says.

"Hi."

"Hey Helena," he calls out, over my shoulder.

"Hi Gabriel," she says. "I didn't want to interrupt you two again."

"Thanks," I say, turning my attention back to Gabriel. That's when the questions come all at once. "What's going on? What are you doing here? How did you find me?"

Gabriel laughs and sets me down. "I've been released, Marla. I'm out. Finding you took some work. I can tell you about it if you like."

I start to do the math in my head but there's little point. Instead, I ask, "How long were you in jail? It's only been, what, two years?"

He nods. "I'm happy to explain. Maybe over coffee?"

"Not me," says Helena. "I have to edit our story and get it out in time for the evening news cycle. But I can take care of it, Marla. You should go."

"Oh. Well, that's a lot of work and it wouldn't be fair if I-"

Helena shoots me a look.

"But if you can take care of it, that would be great," I finish.

"It's no problem," she says. She nods to Gabriel, then

makes for our truck.

"Are you hungry?" he asks.

"I know a good place, come on."

—

I spend a lot of time at Leslie's Diner. All the cops eat here, and if I want to ask around about a case, this is a good place to start. Gabriel orders a western omelet with a side of corned beef hash. I get chocolate chip waffles. Both of our meals get cold while we speak.

"My initial sentence was only six years," he explains. "For one thing, there wasn't much in the way of evidence to fuel a prosecution. The whole place burned down. Then there were the women. A few of them — Amber, especially — were able to testify that I never hurt them. I don't know how to thank them."

I had heard that several of the Halloran Twelve, as the media called us, were making inspiring recoveries. Helena had an explanation: "They had a pretty good source of inspiration."

"Marla," Gabriel continues. "I wasn't trying to skirt my penance. But as they caught more and more of Halloran's clients, they came to me to testify against them."

"You could have helped convict them because it was the right thing to do."

"I *did* do it because it was right. But I also wanted to see you again."

In the two years since I watched the police take him away, I haven't gone a day without thinking of Gabriel and how he hurt me that morning. How could I? I've also never gone a day without wanting him back. I may have hated him for leaving me like that, but I can hate somebody and want them at the same time, can't I?

I unzip my jacket and slip it off, revealing the necklace I wear. Gabriel notices it immediately, and smiles.

"I kept it safe, like you asked."

"Thank you. It looks really nice on you."

"Thanks."

Gabriel sighs. "Look, I'll understand if you're not ready to be with anyone — especially me — but I want you to know that I still love you. Whatever you decide-"

"Gabriel, stop," I interrupt. "What you did killed me, but after a while I understood it. You did what you felt was right. I couldn't stay mad at you for that. I just wish you'd have told me."

"You're right," he says. "I'm sorry. I should have."

I catch the waitress's attention and motion for the check. "Let's go back to my place, okay?"

He looks at me with a smile that says his fears and doubts are retreating into the night. He takes my hand, and we kiss.

———

There was a time when I was abducted by evil men and locked away in a tiny cell. Despite having little chance of escape, I told myself I would survive. I'd be free one day, and I would have the life I always dreamed of.

I didn't just believe this life would happen. I had to fight for it.

I'll never forget the monsters who tried to steal my dream, but they lost. I won. The prize was the life I wanted.

And now I can finally live it.

GET A FREE BONUS CHAPTER BY
SANSA RAYNE!

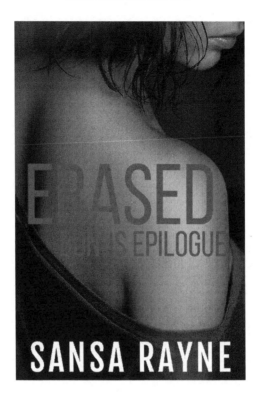

If you liked this book, sign up for Sansa Rayne's mailing list!
You'll receive a free copy of "Erased: Bonus Epilogue," a
chapter that will not be available anywhere else! You'll also
receive announcements about future books by Sansa Rayne.
To sign up, visit http://eepurl.com/ckbVoX

FOR FURTHER READING: "GOOD SICK"

If you enjoyed "Erased," check out Sansa Rayne's first novel,
"Good Sick: A Dark Psychological Romance" — now
available!

ABOUT THE AUTHOR

Sansa Rayne, who also goes by the name Sasha Rich, is a writer from upstate New York aiming to achieve a lifelong dream of being a professional novelist. Sansa likes writing, reading, film — and BDSM. Most importantly, Sansa has a lot of fun ideas and hopes to share many more of them in the future.

For fun, Sansa enjoys cooking, good movies and stepping inside a warm apartment after a chilly walk in the snow.

For updates on all new Sansa Rayne books, sign up for her mailing list at http://eepurl.com/ckbVoX

ACKNOLWEDGMENTS

Thank you for reading this novel! I couldn't have done this without the support of my family and friends — my Squad pals especially — and so many others who freely and patiently dispensed advice. I also want to thank my local police department for giving me a few minutes of their time for research into procedure.

Special thank you so much to Deepti, for everything! You're the best!

And of course, thank you to the readers who have supported me, and who are helping me make my dream into a career! If you liked this story, reviews help us authors out more than you can possibly know! It's really moving to see that somebody read a book you wrote, and felt strongly enough about it to tell others about it.

Made in the USA
Lexington, KY
07 November 2018